WORSHIPPED by MONSTERS

ANN DENTON
KATIE MAY

EXPRESSO PUBLISHING

For all the readers who love tentacles and group scenes full of fighting monsters who have trouble sharing...this one's for you.

THE GROTESQUE

Raw torment.

There's nothing inside my head beyond lashing agony.

The infernati grasping me from behind glides his flaming hands from my torso up to my face, and the scent of my mask melting fills my nostrils. But even the stench of melted clay and paper is not enough to overpower my own natural smell as I burn, fire licking at my skin like a thousand tongues.

Heat blazes a trail through me, encasing me as my entire body fractures. Like a cracked watermelon, I can feel myself oozing, the pain seeping into visual form as fissures appear on my arms, showcasing jagged rivers of liquid rock, molten lava. My stomach melts all at once, and I emanate a glow. The dank walls of the office-lined hallway in Jennison's Meat Factory light up in an eerie orange and cast a hideous gleam across my enemy's face as she gloats.

Though several of her tentacles have been severed, Mishika stands in front of me as her fire-monster lackey attacks me.

An ugly smile settles on her face as she awaits my final moment.

So do I.

As pain slashes hard and deep, so deep that I'm certain it rends my very soul from my body, I prepare to die.

I think of my reason for being here—the tiny, beautiful human who has captured me, heart, body, and soul—and I wish her face would be the last thing I see. I try to envision it even now, but pain steals the memory from me, tugging at it like a breeze blowing away dandelion fluff.

A blink.

A breath.

Another blink.

Though I should extinguish in a furl of smoke, though my body should char and then scatter to the wind...it doesn't.

I remain.

I remain...engulfed by sleek, slithering, burning trails of red-hot magma that stretch my battered soul to its limits, but just to its limits and not past them.

Because rock cannot be destroyed...only reformed.

I realize, with a start, that I'm not dying.

Which means I can't give up.

Aliana.

If this doesn't kill me, then I have to get to my precious mate, save my sweet human from the terrible nightmares my kind want to bestow upon her. Her face is finally able to penetrate the fog surrounding my mind and flashes like a picture from a View-Master in the before times. Plush lips, long dark hair streaked with white, those eyes that make me feel like I'm tripping over my own feet.

The fatalism weighing me down only moments ago morphs into vicious, trembling fury. I glide forward down the hallway on my viscous legs, ignoring the bastard clinging to my back as I surge right into Mishika with a bellow. The pink bitch gasps after I graze her side with a hand that's a dripping, seething molten mass. Vengeful pride swells inside my chest when I see her skin start to blister and bubble, one of her four tits melting into a charred black blob as the air fills with a scent like barbecued chicken.

I smile as I drag my tongue across my teeth. "You smell… delicious."

With a shriek, the female monster turns around, flees into one of the abandoned offices lining the hallway, and disappears from my sight. That's just fine by me because I'll enjoy this particular hunt. I'm going to take Mishika's intestines and spell out a warning with them, a gruesome message on the ground for the other Eights and Nines.

They think they can attack the four Terrors?

After they lay eyes on Mishika's mutilated form, no one will dare threaten us or our mate.

But first, I need to take care of the bastard on my back.

I raise the liquid mass that's now my arm and reach behind my head, letting my molten limb pour down onto the monster behind me. He may be a fire being...but let's see if he can burn hotter than an oven. Does his heat have limits? Because my body clearly doesn't. It has magnified the heat he poured into me ten times over.

Can he absorb the heat of the core of the earth? Can he deal with the volcanic force churning through me?

I slink my hand down over his shoulder and then sink into it. Somehow, even though I'm liquifying and my body is crackling with pain, I still have the ability to determine sensation. My gelatinous lava fingers send up impressions of skin, then muscle, then bone as they seep through the layers of the other monster's body.

It's more than fascinating. It's strangely satisfying in a way violence hasn't been for me in quite a long time.

When the infernati rips himself away from me with a screech, I rotate around, my body bobbing on legs of magma that don't turn with me. My torso twists, but my legs simply ooze and reform in the opposite direction. The backs of my knees jut forward and resettle as kneecaps, and my feet flow through my ankle from one side to the other.

Even though pain screams in every nerve ending, the fury whipping my chest into a cyclone drowns discomfort out. I am vengeance, and death flows freely through me.

Smiling at the panicked monster when his eyes balloon in shock, I lift my arm. A second later, his mouth pops open when I gouge a steaming hole right through his stomach. He sucks in a trembling breath, and when I pull my hand back, his pulsing heart clutched in my fist, he collapses to the ground, his bulging gaze flat and unseeing.

I shake strands of his guts from my fingertips as I slide right over him, not bothering to walk around. His last conscious moments should be terrible, mortifying, and full of anguish. It's what he deserves for being part of this uprising.

Not bothering to chase Mishika yet, because I want her cowering in fear, doubling back on her trail, nervousness driving her mad, I decide to return to the others.

I'm going to prioritize my sweet mate, the only woman to ever kiss me without fear, to ever love me without reservation, to ever want me for who I am.

Moving back down the hall to the main room, I go in search of Dev and Creep. They need to know that Aliana's a target after all, and it will be easier for us to do a sweep of the building together—if only so we don't have to waste precious time fighting monsters one-on-one. If we work together—a feat we've hardly ever managed because Empty or Dev are typically taking opposing approaches, each one utterly convinced they're right—then I believe we can blast through the bastards around us quite easily.

Determination emanates from me, rolling off in waves nearly as opaque as the rippling vapor in the air around me as I march forward. Slosh forward, more like. Though I've killed the infernati, the heat inside of me still rages on, perhaps fueled by my own anger and anxious need to lay eyes on Aliana again. I remain molten.

I have no idea how long it's been since we rushed into this place at dawn, but my intuition is telling me that my separation from my mate is dangerous. Anxiety gnaws at my esophagus. Another monster could be eating Aliana right this second, his mouth consuming her—

2

ALIANA

FROM HIS PRONE spot on the ground, Chase surges forward, recapturing my mouth as I kneel over him. His lips are warm against my own.

Soft. Tentative. A mockery of a true kiss.

It's one of those fleeting touches that's over almost as soon as it begins, yet it sends my mind into a tailspin. Explosions detonate all throughout my body, though I'm not quite sure if they're the good or bad kind.

Because Chase…the Empty Man…the monster who once tried to kill me…

He just kissed me.

The heat of his breath teases my lips yet again a second before his mouth slants over mine. A part of me wants to open myself to him, to prod at the seam of his warm lips with my tongue, but I hold myself perfectly still. My heart thunders like a war drum in my chest, and though one of my arms automatically reaches out to cradle his head because he's injured, I don't know what to think.

The tears smearing my vision at the shock of finding him alive clear as I blink dazedly down at him.

"Aliana…" His voice sounds like Chase's, though it's devoid of the usual cocky arrogance I've come to expect from my rival. He pulls away just enough to stare up into my eyes.

Who exactly am I looking at?

I take in his greasy blond hair, hanging limp around his chiseled face and caked with blood, and the myriad of bruises and scars decorating his skin. Pain etches across his features, though he tries to hide it. However, there's no denying that his once tall and imposing figure is one gust of wind away from crumbling down.

"Chase? Em?" I whisper.

"Yes." His succinct reply has my brain spinning.

Yes to being Chase? Or yes to being Em?

His warm hand comes up to cup my cheek, the calluses on his fingertips reminding me of sandpaper. Except…he's missing a finger. The stark reality of that makes bile spiral up inside my throat, though I swallow it down. That pain is probably the least of what he's had to endure down here.

"I was always told the best things in life hurt the most," the Chase/Em monster whispers almost reverently. "But isn't that the best type of happily ever after? One that is paved in agony?"

I shake my head once in an attempt to disperse the cobwebs infesting it. I need to focus on the mission at hand—-and that means getting the hell out of here. We're underground in a room with a tiny barred window a cat could hardly squish through and only one exit that I'm aware of—a strategic disaster for escape if I've ever heard of one.

Above us, a turquoise spider monster with the head of a deer twitches in its death throes as it bleeds out from the leg I ripped off.

That blood is going to attract hungry teeth.

"We need to leave. Now." I wrap my free hand around Chase/Em's wrist, but he doesn't allow me to tug it away from my face.

He simply…stares at me. Without that cantankerous, argumentative glint in his eyes, he almost looks like a completely different person.

"You came for me," he whispers as he continues to stroke my cheek. "After everything we've done, you came for me. For us."

The smile carved into his luscious mouth is grim, the crack in his personality vulnerable and deep, fathomless darkness swimming in his eyes. When have I ever seen a smile on either of their faces that wasn't full of malice and mockery?

"Em…Chase…whoever the fuck you are… We need to leave." I tug on his hand yet again, and Chase/Em heaves out a weary breath.

"Sometimes I wonder if this is what I deserve. If my fate is destined to end locked away, tortured, forgotten…"

"Really? Now is the time you pick to be all philosophical?" I arch an eyebrow at him incredulously, even as I scan my surroundings for potential threats.

Anxiety claws at my insides.

We need to get out of here. Now.

3

THE CREEPER

My hands move on autopilot, though my head's in an utter daze. But instead of dizzy stars winking around my forehead, there are black specks, which just remind me of all my childhood beatings and how my vision would flicker.

I don't feel the hits of the monsters attacking me, hardly see them as they rush forward, don't acknowledge their pained screams as I slam them into shadowy portals and then zipper shut the openings with a pinch of my fingers—usually when their bodies are halfway through. The spray of blood and squelch of guts squeezed until they're severed serves as a backdrop sound because the percussive force of my heartbeat is so much stronger.

Staring past the slides and rusting machinery set up in this giant meat-packing plant long ago, my eyes lock onto a door with a small, inset window on the far side of the massive room. There, watching the fight, gazing with a brutal smugness out at the carnage he's orchestrated, is my father, his golden dragon tail swishing behind him.

Hatred so strong and putrid that my throat closes and my vision narrows—my senses overloaded by visceral loathing—rains down from head to toe, soaking me.

Of course he's behind this. How could I have failed to realize that?

The Eights and Nines have only ever battled us on an individual level before. Melding together for a cause isn't the way of monsters; it's the way of men. Humans are weak, and individually, they can accomplish almost nothing.

But, banded together, they banished monsters for centuries.

Relegating us to the realm of fairy tales, so that even small children failed to believe in us.

My father always hated that. How before monsters rose up and the Ebony Kingdom was created, monsters were dwindling, waning, scrapping for existence. He'd been a huge supporter of the uprising, of monsters uniting—even if he knew it was a temporary reprieve and schemed to murder all his co-conspirators.

Didn't expect his son to murder him though.

Fail at murdering.

Goddammit.

A rush of self-loathing engulfs me, and I swallow the taste of acid—though along with it is a fatty little bit of gristle from the last monster I just finished off.

I bet my father's loving this little reunion. I glance at him again and note a white-haired monster standing sentinel just behind him, guarding him.

He's such a fucking coward. Always getting other monsters to do his dirty work for him.

Back from the dead—I still can't believe it.

Fuck.

I should have ripped him into tiny pieces and fed him to the Empty Man's menagerie.

I glare into the tiny manager's office he's holed up in. Light fills every corner of the space, beaming out of the narrow window, glinting off his golden hair, his horns, his scaled tail as it curls into a question mark.

I'm certain he's left no shadows in that space so that there's nowhere for me to creep in. Bastard.

My claws curl into a fist and dig into my palm until I draw blood, hungry violence welling inside me.

Anger coils and urges me to spring forward. But that's exactly what he wants. He wants me driven by anger. Fueled by fury. He wants me to make a mistake.

Instead, with every bit of willpower I've got, I uncurl my scarred claws and raise my blue hand until I waggle my fingers at him.

"Hey, Dad!" I call out in my most cheery, 1950s human television show voice. "So glad you could make it!"

To my right, Dev howls as he tackles a potato-shaped Seven. With his fangs, he peels strips of skin off the bastard.

A fake smile plastered to my face, as if this is all just a fun little game, I turn and charge at an orange blob Eight.

But as I run, the ground beneath my feet trembles. The metal machinery above me starts to shake, tiny gears inside of it clanging. Eyes widen all around when a ridge appears in the floor.

Alarm bursts inside of me—me and every other monster still alive. In unison, as if this has been fucking choreographed, we turn toward the slides and start to climb.

The earth rumbles.

My heart pounds painfully as my blood blasts through my veins, sizzlingly hot. My claws scraping at the metal, piercing it, I scramble upward frantically.

Faster.

Hurry.

Higher.

A layer of frost forms on some of the machinery, and around me, several monsters start to slip, sliding down and crashing back to the ground with terrified screams. Only my claws save me, helping me dig into my perch.

The middle of the floor erupts, chunks of cement and dirt spraying everywhere as a sandworm emerges, mouth gaping open, eighteen rows of teeth gleaming. Three monsters fall into its gullet along with a bit of floor and a metal slide that it crunches like a hard candy.

Then the sightless beast flops over, and its mouth starts suctioning up the bodies on the ground like a vacuum cleaner.

Fuck.

At least its priorities seem to be easy food first today.

I search the room to find the Devourer clinging to a giant guillotine device. His red eyes glow, and he's staring right at me. Then his eyes dart to the side.

I follow his gaze and realize that the walls are slowly buckling. The bricks have shifted and are no longer neatly stacked.

This entire place is about to come tumbling down.

I could portal out, but we don't know where our mate is. And I can't leave her.

4

ALIANA

THE GROUND BEGINS to shake underneath me, and I throw my arm out for balance, dropping Chase's hand and scraping my palm against the rough poured concrete on the ground as my knees threaten to buckle.

"Sandworm," Chase/Em growls as he attempts to stand. He almost immediately collapses back onto his ass, a pained moan escaping him in the process.

Fuck.

If he's not even strong enough to walk, then how the hell am I going to get him out of here?

Bits of cement begin to shower down around me as the earth trembles yet again. I curse, knowing that Chase—it's easier to just refer to him as that instead of continuing to alternate between Chase and the Empty Man—is right and that a sandworm is crawling beneath the earth as we speak.

Sandworms are brainless monsters who live beneath the ground and only come up for air when they need to feed.

And these fuckers feed on just about anything—monsters, humans, animals, trash, buildings…

I shudder.

They're the worst of all the teeth. And they're enormous too. Most of them are easily the size of two, maybe three school buses from the before times. I've had the displeasure of coming face to face with this particular type of creature, and I noticed that its skin was pink and bulbous, and it had a circular row of serrated, razor-sharp teeth in the middle of its face.

If one of them is in the factory as we speak…

"We need to fucking move," I snap, though my ire isn't aimed at Chase but at the situation.

Fuck, how could everything have gone to hell so quickly? What happened to Tesq, Creep, and Dev? Are they okay? Worry for the three of them threatens to barrel me over, but I force myself to remember who, exactly, they are.

Three of the Four Terrors, the most feared and revered group of monsters in existence. They probably already killed every monster in this building and are just waiting for me to catch up with them.

That thought bolsters my confidence and courage.

Yes, they're waiting for me…

So I need to hurry the hell up before they send out a search team.

"Come on." This time, I work to gentle my voice as I lower myself beside Chase before slinging his bloody arm over my shoulder.

For some reason, it feels as if I'm attempting to coax a snarling, rabid dog to come with me. I'm afraid if I say something wrong or move too quickly, this monster wearing Chase's face will snap at mine and bite my skin until I bleed.

I should hate him, and I think a part of me does, but at the same time, my body yearns for his in a way that defies all reasoning and logic. He tried to kill me in a misguided attempt to "protect" me, so for all intents and purposes, I should leave him here to rot.

So why did I enlist the help of the other Terrors to break him out of this prison?

Because some deep-seated part of me thinks Chase doesn't deserve to suffer? Maybe. A little. I also owe the annoying human for protecting me when we were captured, for trying to sacrifice himself for me.

Empty's getting a pass because of the human body he's inhabiting.

That's what I tell myself, though I know it's a lie.

Why does fear for him compound with my already present fear for the other three, creating an acerbic, noxious mixture that I can't escape from? Some toxic addiction that I don't want to evade?

Why am I staggering under his immense weight, allowing him to lean on me instead of leaving him behind to die?

I know the answer to those questions, even if I don't want to admit it to myself.

Mate.

That one word flits through my mind like a sparrow flying from tree branch to tree branch. It eviscerates my defenses in a matter of seconds, sending them crumbling to the ground in a pile of ash.

Mate.

Mate.

Mate.

A term that I've been struggling to reconcile since I met the Terrors. I know the truth of their claim that I'm their mate deep in my bones.

Fuck!

Chase moans as I attempt to stand, his features pinched tightly in pain and his body rigid beneath my own. I place one of my hands on the center of his chest in an attempt to steady him, and he hisses in pain. Sliding my grip over, I search for an uninjured bit of skin, but there isn't much, and I have to settle for a green-tinged section that looks like a healing bruise.

"When did you get so fucking heavy?" I grumble half-heartedly, trying to lighten the mood as I maneuver him out of the prison, stepping very carefully over the monster I murdered. "Is the Empty Man fattening you up to eat you?"

Chase stares at me strangely out of the corner of his eyes. His features are so incredibly bruised and distorted, I can barely see the blue of his irises peeking through the swollen mass of flesh. He opens his mouth to respond, his chapped, bloody lips parting, when more plaster and debris rain down on us.

Instinctively, I lower my head to avoid the onslaught of falling ceiling, and Chase uses the opportunity to curl himself over me, protecting me the best he can.

"What the fuck? Chase, stop it!" I snap, pushing him off of me —but gently, keenly aware of the myriad of bruises and lacerations marring his golden skin. "You're already hurt. We don't want you to get even more…hurt."

Ever the articulate one, Aliana.

Once again, Chase's eyes narrow, and I wonder if it's because I referred to him as Chase and not the Empty Man. I expect him to correct me, but he remains silent, though the blue of his eyes seems to find mine unerringly, even through the constant fall of plaster, homing in like two heat-seeking missiles.

"We'll protect you no matter what, mistress," Chase murmurs in a low, raspy voice that spirals heat through my stomach. The longing in his voice is tempered by steadfast deter-mination.

Wait…

Mistress?

We?

What the fuck?

My heart skips like a smooth stone over tranquil waters.

"I don't need your protection." I begin to lead him forward once more, stumbling under his weight. "If you remember correctly, I'm the one who rescued *you*, not the other way around. So I suppose you're the damsel in distress while I'm the knight in shining armor."

I'm sure Chase—the real Chase, not this creature wearing his face—would *love* that. He always had an alpha, "I'm better than everyone" personality. He would be humiliated to know he got rescued by the likes of me.

21

The thought brings a fleeting, tentative smile to my lips. I try to squash it, but Chase sees it. I wonder if he's watching my face as intently as I'm studying our surroundings. I swear I can feel his eyes penetrating my flesh in a way that's almost physical.

"No one will hurt you again, Aliana." His voice is low—a gentle caress that peppers my skin and elicits a fresh round of goose bumps. "Not even me."

He seems to be trying to tell me something, something important, but now isn't the time for heartfelt declarations or whispered promises. Not when the ground around us is rumbling like thunder, though we're far underground.

We need to get out of here. Fast.

So even though it feels like an invasion of tiny drummers has taken over my head, I shove his words aside and focus on the matter at hand.

"Yup. Cool. Awesome," I say half-heartedly as I continue to drag him along. "But we can discuss all of this after we make it to safety, okay?" And then, under my breath, I add, "Since when did you become so talkative? Goddamn. I miss Tesq's grumpiness sometimes."

Once again, Chase opens his mouth as if to speak but immediately snaps it closed. Terror floods his eyes, and the emotion is reciprocated in the tiny spikes that seem to be piercing my very soul.

Around us, the walls and floor shake, and I struggle to remain upright, to orient myself to my rapidly shifting surroundings. I wobble precariously to the side and lose my grip around Chase's shoulder. He falls to the ground beside me with an audible thump. I lunge for him, but before my fingers can make contact with his, something breaks through the floor in front of me like a flower bursting from the ground.

Only this flower has pink, slimy skin, fathomless black eyes, and a mouthful of teeth, each one the size of my head.

A thousand blades become lodged in my throat as I scramble backwards, crab walking away as fast as I physically can.

Then, the sandworm opens its gaping maw, its attention fixed solely on me, and roars.

5

ALIANA

My CHEST IS ready to explode from the panic building inside of it, but after so many years of raids in the city, I use my muscle memory and force myself to think through the chaos, push myself to fight. My hands move for my weapons, and I manage to jab a tiny thought through the surging waves of adrenaline and make myself remember that pouch of jewels.

I just need enough time to reach down, open the pouch, and throw one—

The fucking beast pours its body into the room, smacking into the ceiling with a resounding crack and then denting the floor as it undulates and its rows of teeth snap at me. It's two feet away and then just inches—in seconds.

Shit.

No time. There's no time for anything but blocking my face, and my arms shoot back up on instinct even as my brain screams that the movement will only ensure I get bitten into pieces instead of swallowed whole.

A swirl of furious, panicked anger blasts up from the pit of my stomach and out through my limbs. It's helpless anger, hysteria manifesting through my nerve endings. But—in slow motion, as if it's happening to someone else—the most unbelievable thing happens. Ice shards fly from my palms, rushing outward in a spiral of blue-tinged spikes that pierce the beast's throat again and again.

WHAT?

When my fingers twitch, a second round shoots out like bullets spraying from a machine gun and pepper the giant worm. The second they collide with its skin, cyan veins erupt along the surface, feathering out like the cracks in an icy lake or the filigree edges of a snowflake, spreading outward until they touch. And wherever those blue lines merge, the creature stiffens.

Freezes.

My mind glitches for a second at the chaos, at the craziness of what's happening. It shouldn't be possible.

But I slowly register what I'm seeing as the worm turns a powder blue.

Poised above me like a giant, bald, killer caterpillar, the tooth stops moving completely, its great maw open. A trickle of its saliva hardens as it falls, becoming an icicle that hovers just above my forehead.

In less than three seconds, the sandworm has become an ice sculpture. And I have no fucking clue how.

Too scared to breathe, I slide one foot back slowly, then the other—just in case this temporary insanity stops, just in case there's a monster behind the sandworm freezing it so it can become their own snack…just in case one of the million jumbled thoughts of death flickering through my head comes to pass.

But when I lean around the flabby sandworm to spot my new enemy, there's no one behind him. No ice-wielding fifth Terror. Even if there had been, how could another monster make ice appear from my hands? How could ice even appear from my hands? I'm human! It's not possible…

Unless I'm possessed.

I stop breathing and look down at my body, examining myself to try to determine if there's another entity inside of me.

I don't feel possessed.

But could Empty have flown out of Chase's body and entered my own? Would I have felt it? I'm uncertain, and I furrow my brow. If Empty took control of my limbs, would that have given me a momentary burst of power? Do poltergeists have ice power?

"Empty Man?" I turn and glance at Chase's bruised and battered face, at the lips that are swollen from both my kiss and from any number of beatings before that.

"Yes?" Something flickers in Chase's mossy-green eyes, and his head tilts at an angle I've never seen him use before as I become fully aware that I'm speaking to the Empty Man.

It's an eerie thing to know that Chase isn't Chase. That the pompous ass I grew up with is currently controlled by a ghost.

If Empty Man's there…then he's still stuck in Chase's body, and he can't be possessing me. Not unless…

"Can you extend your possession beyond the body you're in?" I ask softly.

A single shake of his head. "Not now."

Fuck.

I start to cover my mouth in dismay, but I stop short of touching my face, staring at my fingers. I'm not quite sure what they're currently capable of, or why. Or if I'll hurt myself or Chase.

I lower my palms, suddenly viewing them as weapons, even though they look completely normal.

Flicking my gaze back up to stare at the Empty Man, I notice how he rubs Chase's fingers together in a motion the former rebel would never have used.

"Are you the only poltergeist? Or are there other monsters like you?" It has to be possession, what just happened to me. It has to be. The idea that there's another being underneath my skin sends shivers across my shoulders.

"Yes." The Empty Man's response is nearly a hiss, just as horrible a sound as any snake ever makes.

I'm not prepared for his answer because I immediately tense at the thought of another creature inside my brain, wrapping invisible strings around my limbs, toying with me like I'm a puppet. My knees tremble for a millisecond before I lock them stiffly.

I open my mouth to ask how to banish one, but then Empty adds, "I'm the only."

Asshole.

If I didn't hate him before this, I certainly do now. My internal alarm swivels and transforms into outrage. "You could have led with that, fucker."

His eyes widen as if he's shocked that I'd speak to him that way, shocked I'd be angry at the idea of being possessed. Whatever humans he's inhabited before probably thought it was an honor or some bullshit.

I don't. My fingers curl into a fist, and the temptation to punch him rides me hard. Normally, I wouldn't resist, but right now? He's basically just told me that somehow I'm the fucking source of those ice knives, and if I lash out at him and accidentally hurt Chase, I'll have defeated the whole fucking purpose of this rescue mission.

Silence slices through the space, sharp and potent as I glance back up at the monster again. The sandworm no longer has a single inch of fleshy pink skin. A thin crust of ice seems to be forming on him, making him glisten in the tiny shaft of morning light coming in through the barred window in this underground space.

He's the second monster that has succumbed to ice since I entered this damn building. The first time, I thought a jewel dropped from my pouch and activated. This time, I know that's not even a possibility, though I desperately wish it were. Air saws raggedly in and out of my chest as I stare up at this glittering beast that I somehow managed to glaciate.

"What the fuck is happening? I…I…I…" I can't bring myself to finish the thought that's now festering inside my brain, and I stare back down at my palms.

"You help her." A soft mutter comes from Chase's lips, and I glance up to see the wily look in his eyes gone, replaced by human confusion.

"What happened?" Chase's tone changes completely.

How I can tell after just two words, I'm not sure, but I can. There's a gruffness and confusion to it that wasn't there before. His green eyes soften in concern, an emotion I'm pretty sure the Empty Man has never felt before a day in his existence.

My eyes have surely doubled in size as I stare down at my dirty fingertips as if they're going to sprout spikes.

"I...I have a bag of jewels that takes out monsters," I say softly, though I've already ruled the bag out.

There's something else going on here.

Something very different.

Something I'm very sure I'm not going to like.

Something I don't have time to think about.

The universe decides to deprive me of the possibility of a mental breakdown when the walls around us groan, and above us, a metal support beam bends inward. The sandworm must have damaged it.

Fuck.

The building's about to go down.

Shit.

I run toward the door, but the sandworm's mass is blocking it. Only a sliver of space as big as my head is clear at the top of the doorjamb. I shove at the flabby beast, but its icy skin doesn't bend or flex or roll underneath my hands, which just slide along the frozen surface. I can't get the heavy bastard to move a single inch.

Did I escape one terrible death just to exchange it for another?

I want a fucking refund.

The metal I beam in the roof groans again and sinks a little farther toward our heads. I hear a grumbling crack and see a barrage of cement flecks flying from the ceiling along with a puff of dust.

We're about to be buried alive in the rubble.

I turn a panicked look toward Chase, only to find he's moved and is beside me. He's hunched and breathing heavily, a hand cradling his ribs as if he's in pain. But his eyes are sharp and scan the room as he too looks for a way out.

He finds one.

"We have to go down." His tone is steady as he stares at the hole the sandworm chewed through the earth and the cement floor.

Along the beast's ribbed back, there's just enough space for us to try to slither down into its hole, a two-foot gap that would make anyone with the tiniest bit of claustrophobia tense up.

My throat tightens—not because I'm afraid of going under-ground, but the concept of being trapped without a light so far beneath the earth with absolutely zero idea when the tunnel will emerge back up on the surface terrifies me.

What if this tooth has larvae down there waiting to be fed?

But a crashing, crushing noise descends over us, smashes into my ears, shaking my eardrums painfully, and Chase shoves me at the hole.

I quickly jump down into it, stomach first, landing with a plop on the frozen slime of the oversized earthworm. I push myself down with my arms, and I'm forced to hug its body as I slide, trying to move as quickly as I can so Chase can follow.

The clangor above us is so loud that I can feel it in my jawbone, and it rattles my teeth.

His feet soon appear mere inches from my face, and the scent of his unwashed body and the smell of sandworm combine with the freshly churned earth to fill my nostrils.

Down. Ten feet. Twelve. Fifteen.

Dust and dirt cloud around us, and I cough as I finally slide past the tail of the sandworm and drop into a tunnel. I skitter back a few feet so Chase can drop down beside me.

He groans when he lands, cursing under his breath. The walls of the passage shake, and we run forward as Jennison's Meat Factory collapses above us, sending rubble down into the shaft. Within seconds, our way back is blocked along with every beam of light.

We're left fifteen feet below the earth, and our only hope of getting out is stumbling forward through the darkness together.

6

ALIANA

CAUTION ONLY LASTS SO LONG—FIGHT or flight is like a rainstorm pouring down hard at first. But internal clouds can only contain so much dark and foreboding feelings, and eventually, adrenaline sputters and fades to a trickle before evaporating.

Our caution in the tunnel lasted for a solid thirty minutes of stumbling through the dark, anticipating monsters or a collapse. But after a while, the panic receded and was replaced by the overpowering stench of wet dirt coated in monster slime.

Though I try to force my limbs to stay on high alert, utter blindness and silence muffle two of my senses and gradually lull me into a softer and stupider headspace. And instead of focusing on next steps after the attack, I start to wonder why it occurred. As if motivation for this entire fucked-up scenario matters at all. When there's a fight for survival, *why* doesn't matter. Only living does.

But the silence has started to taste like cotton in my mouth, begun to stuff my ears full, and so the question pours out despite its uselessness. "Did they say why they took you?"

"Ebony Kingdom. Why else?" The answer comes out in a hiss of breath that sends a shiver coasting over my shoulders because I'm still not used to the way the Empty Man uses Chase's voice.

The answer isn't unexpected, though it's definitely not what I hoped and makes my sore shoulders sag a bit. Part of me wanted this to turn out to magically be a vendetta against him personally. If Empty Man was the problem, then Tesq and Creep and even the Devourer would be in less danger.

Of course, the fact that whoever took Chase cut off his finger and lured the other Terrors here did clue me in to the fact that this wasn't an isolated event…

So again, my question was a waste of breath down here in this tunnel where oxygen is limited, and there doesn't seem to be a rise toward the surface anytime soon. I can't help but wonder if that's all we're doing down here. Wasting breaths. Are we going to die in this darkness? A slow death now instead of the instantaneous death of crushing as we would have had if we'd stayed in the meat factory?

But I can't let myself think back to that building. I can't imagine the walls falling in without my stomach churning with worry for the other Terrors.

What a fucking turn my brain has taken to start caring about monsters. Not just caring but aching for Tesq, longing for Creep's light-hearted quips as he slings an arm over my shoulders. Nostalgic for Fluffy's purrs and a Christmas-light-strewn room.

They better be okay. They have to be okay, because I'm the one who forced them to come. Otherwise…

The dark possibilities twist my mind toward thoughts of revenge. Just in case.

"Know who it is?" I ask the Empty Man.

"Monsters who'll soon join me in the afterlife."

What a typical male response. Though, on this occasion, I don't disagree with his proclamation. Whoever did this deserves to have their skin shaved off slowly, inch by inch.

Of course, his answer was one of those non-answers that drive me up the wall. He couldn't have just said a name? Then I remember whose body the Empty Man's stuck in.

"Sounds like Chase is rubbing off on you. That's the sort of bullshit arrogant thing he'd say," I observe.

A low, inhuman growl erupts from his lips. "It's not bullshit."

"Yeah, it is. If you could kill them, you'd have done it already."

"I'm stuck in this body—"

"And whose fault is that?" I retort, rolling my eyes even though the gesture has zero effect in this dank, earthy passage because he can't see it.

"The Grotesque—"

"Nope. Wrong. Yours. *You* tried to kill me."

"To protect you!"

"Claim me, you mean. Keep me from the others."

"I've apologized—"

35

"Oh, wow. Yeah, the word sorry erases everything. Just boom. A rag wiping all that shit away so everything's bright and shiny between us again."

"I've said I'll make it right."

"Heard that before."

"What else do you want from me?" Frustration bleeds through his tone.

"I want you to live in reality, not some fantasy land. I want you to take responsibility and realize that you're not just some badass—"

"You deal with her. I can't," Chase mutters under his breath, and I realize with a shock that the Empty Man is once again handing over the reins to the body and mind he's possessing.

Oh, that boils me. That sears my insides and makes me want to lash out with a fist and slap that Terror. "You stay right fucking there, Empty Man. You don't get to run off because my words are too true for you to handle—"

"Aliana?" The tone of voice shifts from the breathy, sibilant sounds that characterize Empty to the familiar, grating tone of Chase.

"How can you stand him?" I snarl.

"Not much choice," he reminds me, and my lips twist.

I reach out to my side, and my hand smooths over some roots protruding from the curved walls as I slide forward. "Fucking monsters."

"I hear that's what you've been doing," he responds bitterly.

All the reasons Chase has always annoyed me resurface.

"Oh, come off it. You'd do whatever it took to survive too." The defensive words fly from my lips before I can stop them.

Regret hits a second later, but it's too late, and it doesn't last. I'm eternally grateful Tesq and Creep aren't here to listen to my impulsive lie, but I'm also utterly irritated with Chase. It's always been like sandpaper between the two of us, abrasive and painful.

"That's all it is, huh?" His skepticism pokes right at my vulnerabilities.

"I don't need to explain myself to you. You fucked nearly every goddamned woman in the resistance," I snarl, my cheeks heating, getting way too worked up over nothing. I don't care what Chase has done. Yet still my mouth keeps moving. "You plucked pussies the way people pick flowers. Big ole fucking bouquets of them."

"How would you even know that? You spent so much time ignoring me, how would you know how many people I slept with?"

"Ignoring you was better than murdering you."

"You wanted to kill me?"

"Oh please. As if the feeling wasn't mutual."

His long, drawn-out silence is as powerful as a shove, and I stumble. My hand flies over to the side of the arched wall, scraping against bits of gravel. The fact that I nearly fall in utter darkness, blind to what's beneath me, has my heart beating unnaturally quickly. At least, I think it's from the fall.

It has to be.

My fucking life has had too many revelations lately. Too many changes. I can't process any more. Our hatred has to be mutual.

A hand shoots out, and Chase grips my upper arm to help stop me from tumbling onto my face. His solid grip helps me straighten, though as soon as I do, I pull away. A thank-you sits on the tip of my tongue, but I swallow it down. Chase and I don't thank each other. We snipe.

"The tunnel's curving my way. I think we're coming up to a bend," I inform him.

"Let me go first," Chase says immediately.

"No way. You're barely upright. and your breathing sounds like a rusty can opener."

He actually sounds almost fine, but his gait has definitely been less steady than mine, and I know he's sporting a zillion internal injuries. Not that I care, but he'll give away our position with his Frankenstein-style foot-dragging.

"I'm fine." His lie falls flatter than half the buildings in lower Manhattan, flatter than the meat factory behind us.

"Fuck the hell off, you're fine. I'm going first."

"Aliana, why do you always have to argue? Just let me go—"

"Why should you get to lead?"

"I'm not trying to lead—"

"The hell you aren't. You're always trying to lead. Trying to put me in my place—"

"I'm just trying to protect you. If there's something out there, it'll get me." He speaks over me, our words crashing together like cymbals in those radio songs that Tesq likes to listen to, a cacophony of angry sounds.

"Why would you want to protect me, Chase?" My nostrils flare with rage. He's always doing this. Always fucking doing this. "I'm not goddamned incompetent."

"I didn't say that," he responds, his voice lowered to a whisper.

"It's implied." I sneer. "I can protect myself."

I swear we just had this argument in the underground room I found him in. Or was that with Empty? I can't see Chase ever calling me mistress, so it was probably the poltergeist.

Amazing. Now I get to have fights on repeat.

I shove forward, needing space, even though I can't see him. I need to be farther from his footsteps, his breaths, his very fucking essence.

I move so fast that I stagger, but I don't care because I feel the ground beneath me start to rise. I'm not sure if it's a trick of my eyes, struggling to find something to latch onto after so much darkness, but the light around me gets a tiny bit bluer, a smidgen less inky.

Behind me, Chase mutters to himself—or maybe to Empty Man. I'm not sure. I try to close off my ears, but since they're one of the only senses I've got right now, they're unfortunately fine-tuned.

"Yeah, she's always like this."

"And you never told her?"

Told me what? Told me off? He's done that plenty of times… though actually, as I recall memories of Chase, I think I did most of the telling off for his awful sexist jokes or whatever dumb thing he was saying that day. And he deserved it.

He deserved telling off, but not to die, which is why you insisted on saving him. And now, you're leaving him behind to do just that if he falls or this tunnel collapses on him. Way to go, Aliana, I scold myself.

With a sigh, I stop stomping forward and wait for him to catch up.

"Do you feel like the ground is rising?" I ask, as if that's why I waited.

"Maybe?" he says.

We walk a few more feet in dimness, in blessed fucking silence, until I definitely see a shaft of light pouring down ahead of us, a lemon-colored wedge cutting through the black.

"Oh my god. We might actually live through this!" Joy fills my chest like bubbles, light and airy and iridescent.

A giddy elatedness that has my hand reaching to the side and grasping at Chase's for just a moment. A single, solitary moment of unity acknowledging that, against all odds, we've made it out together.

I squeeze his fingers. He squeezes back, and his grip is firm and warm.

Then I drop his hand and dart for the light, calling out over my shoulder, "First one to the surface gets dibs on our next food find."

But Chase doesn't scurry after me. Instead, when I'm fully engulfed by the warm, bright, dust-mote sprinkled light, he strolls up slowly, as if he's okay with losing.

And for a second, I'm unsure again whether I'm looking at Chase or the Empty Man because the man in front of me doesn't look arrogant or cold. Instead, he's wearing a soft, boyish grin.

7

THE DEVOURER

"WHERE IS SHE?!" I roar, pushing away more rubble as I attempt to climb myself out of the collapsed meat factory.

For the first time in my life, I'm grateful I can transform into a seven-foot beast with primordial strength and uncanny healing abilities.

I probably would've been in a *much* worse position if I hadn't been.

Being buried alive can really fuck up a monster.

As it is, my fur is matted and parted awkwardly to reveal the numerous bleeding wounds underneath. I don't dare shift back, not when I know that my semi-humanoid form will be even more bruised, bloodied, and disheveled.

Pain radiates from my arm socket, where I probably dislocated my shoulder, but I shove that agony aside—trapping it inside of an iron box reinforced with steel—and focus on what truly matters.

Aliana.

"She's not here." Creep's curt voice drags my attention off the wreckage and towards my closest friend—if you can call anyone in the monster world a friend.

The blue monster stands on the outskirts of the property, where the rubble has ended and shadows begin, his arms crossed over his chest and his dark hair swaying in the breeze beneath his antlers. The cresting sun hits his back in such a way that he almost seems to glow.

"You don't know that." My voice is more beast than human—anger and desperation weaving themselves together in a potent, toxic mixture.

I never should've allowed my mate to go off on her own. I should've insisted that I follow her, or had Creep follow her, or even the Grotesque…

This is why I wanted to keep her locked up. Safe! They all act like I'm a bastard, but freedom in this fucked-up world is often a death sentence.

With a roar, I grab the nearest object—which happens to be a piece of metal hacked off of one of the destroyed machines—and throw it as hard and as far as I can. It hits the chain-link fence surrounding the property and quite literally cleaves it apart, creating a large hole.

Creep, who has been abnormally silent since this entire shit storm went down, arches a blue brow at me. "Are you done having your temper tantrum?"

Condescension oozes from his voice, ruffling my metaphorical feathers.

How dare he treat me this way when my *mate* is missing? The only saving grace is the knowledge that she's alive and well—my mating bond with her would tell me otherwise.

Anger raises my hackles and prickles my fingers where my claws have extended. I want to scratch them down Creep's face, dig up his antlers like one would a damn flower, skin him alive—

With another growl, I kick at a destroyed chair and then stalk out of the mess of debris and cement.

"Have you noticed that we have a pattern of ending up in demolished buildings together? Maybe that's *our thing*," Creep jokes.

How can he be light-hearted at a time like this?

"Maybe you were lying to me when you claimed Aliana was your mate," I bark scathingly, stopping when I'm directly beside the fucking asshole. He's tall…but I'm taller, coming in at over twelve feet. The bastard is forced to raise his chin to maintain eye contact, and I take a sort of twisted satisfaction in the fact. "If you were really her mate, you wouldn't be so fucking calm."

Not when I feel as if I'm crawling out of my skin.

Not when I feel as if my heart is in a pressure chamber.

Not when I feel a knot of apprehension coiling in my throat at the prospect of anything happening to her while she's out of my sight.

Not when I want to kill every last fucker in the vicinity— friend and foe alike.

Creep's eyes flare with anger. True anger, not the cocky, arrogant irritation he normally wears around me like I'm the butt of some fucked-up joke. I'm not sure I've ever seen such a look of profound and unfettered fury pave its way across his face before.

"Do *not* assume things about me, Dev." His voice is cold, hard, and angry, lacking its usual amusement. "I know my mate better than you think *you* do. I know she's not a child in need of coddling. She's a grown-ass woman who's endured unspeakable challenges over the years yet has come out stronger because of it. Aliana's not weak, and she doesn't need you to go all caveman on her ass. Do I want to know she's safe and secure? Of fucking course. Do I think I need to babysit her twenty-four seven to ensure that happens? Not at all. *My* girl could probably kill you with just her pinkie finger if she wanted to."

The smile he flashes me reminds me of the sharp edge of a blade, as do his words.

They're meant to stab and cut and make me bleed.

Frustration and rage expand the knot in my throat, especially at his word choice.

My girl.

No. Not his girl.

Never his.

I flex my hands by my sides, and I don't know if it's because I want to carve Creep open with my claws or find Aliana and spank her until she can't move for a solid week. I want her ass painted red by my hand for daring to scare me like this.

As soon as I find her, the two of us are going to…

Go where?

My museum home, which was destroyed by the Eights and Nines during their last attack?

Tesq's home in the abandoned subway?

No, she wouldn't choose to remain with the goddamn Grotesque, would she? An unnerving feeling frays my gut.

She. Is. Mine.

The direction of my thoughts drags a dry, humorless laugh from my lips. It's fucking futile.

As if I could possibly claim Aliana. I've tried—trust me, I did —but that damn girl refuses to be owned. She's a beautiful, carnivorous plant—pretty but able to swallow you whole. Perhaps I'll only ever have the illusion of owning her, claiming her, loving her.

The revelation is a dagger to my chest. Only this dagger is on fire, has been tipped with acid, and is stabbing me repeatedly.

"Aliana's smart," Creep continues, his gaze faraway and distant.

I know, then, that he's not just thinking about the woman he claims to love. No, that despondent gleam in his eyes is due to the bastard of a monster who came back from the dead. Who shouldn't exist.

His father.

I want to ask him questions—and not all of them are tactful. Actually, none of them are. Mainly, I want to know how he fucked up so badly and didn't really kill the asshole the first time around—but I hold my tongue.

Aliana would be proud of my restraint.

See? I'm learning.

"She would've made it out of the building, probably with Tesq and Em—if she was able to rescue him. They would know to get out of the area. It's not safe for her here." Creep runs the pad of his finger underneath his chin, where a few jagged scars line the flesh there.

"So you think she's heading back to the Grotesque's hovel?" Possessive jealousy and rage flow through me at the thought, mainly because I can't help but remember the last time we were in that room.

When I was forced to witness two Terrors tag team the love of my existence, unable to do anything but watch.

That was the worst moment of my life. And also the hottest.

Fuck.

I shove all thoughts of her red, sweaty face, hooded eyes, and parted lips to the side. So what if I get hard just thinking about that moment? I only ever want her to orgasm for *me*.

But I'm so fucking weak when it comes to her, after all, and my body doesn't always get the memo my brain has sent out.

"We should start heading in that direction," Creep agrees, oblivious to the direction my thoughts just went.

He turns on his heel and begins to walk down the street, and all I can think about is how easy it would be to slice his head straight from his body. One problem would be taken care of.

Yet I know Aliana will never forgive me.

Hell, I'll never forgive myself.

Since when do monsters give a damn about being selfish?

Why does this have to be such a clusterfuck?

I've just taken a step after Creep when a low moan drags my attention back to the rubble. A frown takes over my face as I freeze, straining my ears.

Another moan.

"Dev?" Creep asks curiously, standing directly beside one of the numerous shadows lining the sidewalk. No doubt, he plans to portal us directly to Tesq's home.

I stalk towards where I heard the noise, grab the huge piece of machinery sitting there, and fling it to the side like it's nothing but cardboard.

An unfamiliar monster with neon-green skin, yellow, cat-like eyes, and two vampiric teeth extended, lies broken and bleeding on the ground. Pain splays across his face as he whimpers, blood cascading from a wound on his head.

I sniff the air and quickly determine that he's a Four—not the lowest of monsters in regards to power but definitely not one of the ringleaders of this fiasco.

Still…

A cold, conniving smile twists up my lips as I stare at the beast before me.

"What do we have here?" I purr.

The monster whimpers in terror.

As he should.

8

ALIANA

THE TWO OF us—three of us? Fuck, I don't even know anymore—stick to the shadows as we traverse the unfamiliar streets in the direction of the subway line. I know that's where I need to go if I have any hope of reconnecting with my mates. I can't simply wait around for them to rescue me.

Besides, they're not the "knight in shining armor" type of monsters. More like the "rip the guts from your enemies' bodies and eat them while you watch and try not to vomit" type.

"Where, exactly, are we going?" Empty and Chase have been mostly silent this entire walk, though I swear I hear garbled muttering more times than I care to admit.

Empty Man. Empty. Em. I decide to shorten his moniker since I'm flip-flopping between the two men so much.

I don't answer as I stealthily duck around the corner of what once was a gas station and ensure the streets are empty. Only when no monsters come scurrying out of the gloom do I gesture Em forward—and it *is* Em. That sarcastic, accented drawl could never be confused with Chase's deep, silky, baritone voice.

"Somewhere safe," I respond at last, hurrying across the street and towards one of the staircases that lead to the subway system.

If I had to hazard a guess, I'd say we're on the opposite end of the city from where Tesq lives.

Great. That will be a trek. And after our long sojourn through darkness just ended too. Still, it'll probably be safer for the two of us to walk underground than remain out in the open where anyone can see us.

"You know, I'm not sure I appreciate the two-word, cryptic answers," Em continues, not bothering to lower his voice.

Either he's oblivious to the danger we're in or overconfident in his abilities to protect me.

My guess is the latter.

"Welcome to my life," I quip.

A tiny smirk touches the edges of his cut lips. "Touché."

Once, many years ago, when I lived at one of the human camps outside of the city, my parents secured us a television and DVD player. We had limited electricity, but the council in charge agreed that a movie marathon would boost our morale. We all snuggled up on ratty couches and old armchairs, snacking on whatever food we could find as we watched movie after movie.

One was about a mermaid who was desperate to get legs and walk. Another had a tiny green monster with pointed ears and a strange voice, green and red light-up swords, and a villain who had asthma or something. A third was about a girl who went from a black and white world to a colorful one, all while following a yellow brick road and gathering her own menagerie of monsters.

But the last… The last was some apocalyptic movie that was quickly turned off when some of the kids started to cry.

This subway station reminds me of that movie.

It's strange to think how reality superimposed itself over someone's imagination.

Everything is crusted in dirt and covered in graffiti that has already begun to fade. Animal carcasses litter the ground, and I can't help but wonder if *all* of the yellowing bones are animals. Some look a little too big…

An abandoned train sits on the track, the doors open and the windows shattered to reveal an interior covered in spider-webs, trash, and bugs.

On a cracked bench, directly opposite the subway car, is a tiny doll that appears to have been relatively unperturbed, even as the world went to hell around it. Its cherubic face has a single crack running down its right cheek, and its hair is matted and stained brown with dirt. I can't look away from the horrifying sight.

What is the story behind this solitary doll?

Who was its owner?

What happened to him or her?

"Aliana? Are you okay?" Em places a hand on my shoulder, and the heat from his touch steadily drives the cold away.

It takes a solid ten seconds for my fingers and toes to start prickling as they regain sensation and for my joints to unthaw.

I quickly move away from Em as if his touch burned me.

I shouldn't be taking comfort from the likes of *him*. Even though I kissed him/Chase, that was just relief. That was just impulsive foolishness. It was a solitary moment, one that I won't be stupid enough to repeat.

"Yeah. I'm fine. Let's get moving." I jerk my chin towards the long expanse before us, an abyss of nothingness.

I curse myself for losing my light somewhere in the scuffle back at the meat factory, but perhaps one of my gemstones can produce—

"Not all of us like the way it went down." Em's soft, almost raspy voice snaps my head up, stopping my thoughts in mid-sentence.

"Huh?" I swivel my head to look over at him instead of staring down the tunnel and trying to find the shaft of light I know will appear at the next set of subway stairs.

"The way the world ended." Em's bruised and blotchy face turns in my direction before immediately facing away, following the direction of my gaze down the tunnel. "Not all of us agreed that humans should be hunted down and slaughtered."

"No." I curl my upper lip. "You just thought that humans should be slaves for your enjoyment, right?"

Em scrubs a shaky, bloody hand through his golden hair. "Fuck, you really think the worst of me, don't you?"

"You haven't really given me a reason to think the best." I shrug, trying to ignore the erratic pitter-patter of my heart. The more he speaks, the tighter the anxiety in my chest coils until I fear it's going to burst.

"I deserve that." Em nods seriously, his gaze still faraway and distant, glued on something in the periphery that I'm unable to see. "But you have to remember that I was *once* human."

"You don't remember your human life," I counter immediately.

"No. You're right." He scratches absently at the inside of his wrist, his fingernails digging in deeply enough to draw blood. "I don't think I ever had any real attachments when I was human. No family I loved above anyone or anything else. No girlfriend I cared about. No friends. I feel as if I would've remembered them once I died." His gaze slides to me and stays there, stealing all of the oxygen out of the tunnel. "I definitely would've remembered you."

My heart thumps erratically. "So what are you trying to say, Em? That you're not like the other monsters because you were once human? That you value and respect humans? That you think of them as equals?"

The thought is almost laughable.

Em winces. "No. Because that would be a lie. I suppose you could say I've grown…complacent with the way the world is run. Maybe I was horrified when the monsters initially rose to power, but what I once perceived as sickening quickly became the world's new normal. I could either fall in line or be left behind."

"You did far more than fall in line. And left behind? Get fucking real. You're one of the kings of the realm. You embraced everything that the Ebony Kingdom stands for. You've battered and used humans and loved it."

He flicks his gaze away from me once more, as if it pains him to stare at me for too long. "Yes, but then I met you."

"Me?" A knot of apprehension lurches into my throat.

"You," Em agrees. "And even Chase."

He resumes scratching at the inside of his wrist. A nervous habit, I imagine. I half want to slap his hand away and get him to stop, bile scorching my throat at the sight of blood on his pale skin. Yet the other part of me wants him to suffer. To hurt.

"And I began to realize how wrong I've been this entire time."

My heart seems to be squeezed by fiery hands. It takes considerable effort to take in a full breath, and even then, it feels as if I'm inhaling burning razor blades.

"I don't know what to say to that," I confess after a long moment of silence, where all I could do was stare at his painfully handsome face, drawn in misery.

"I don't expect you to say anything." Em shifts slightly, and pain distorts his features at the movement.

A piece of my heart hurts for him; the rest of me remembers the fear I felt when he ran at me with a dagger, intent on ending my life once and for all, and the pity vanishes in a puff of smoke.

"Heaven only knows I don't deserve a response from you."

"Stop saying shit like that!" I snap.

His brows bunch. "Like what?"

"That!" I wave my hand towards him with a scowl. "Confusing, cryptic shit."

Em's body seems to sag as if the weight of the universe is resting on his shoulders. He suddenly looks exhausted, and dark, circular shadows underscore both of his eyes. How did I not notice them before?

"I know I'm not making any sense to you—"

"Damn right."

"—but there are some truths that you're just not ready to hear, mistress." He stares directly at me then, and for the first time that I can remember, his eyes are unguarded. Vulnerable, even. A plethora of emotions emanate from his gaze, but the most prominent one is…

I must be mistaken.

No, I'm definitely imagining things.

There's no way in hell that the Empty Man—or even Chase, for that matter—would stare at me with *love*.

The sheer absurdity of it makes me want to scoff.

"You're right," I settle on at last, an uncomfortable, twisting sensation settling in my gut. "I'm not ready to hear it." I focus on the tunnel that seems to go on and on forever, no end in sight, nothing but an ocean of black, sticky tar that threatens to cling to my skin. "Let's go."

And when I step onto the track, I don't look back.

9

CHASE

Bite your fucking tongue, I chastise Empty as Aliana walks away from us.

Okay, he responds, and then the motherfucker literally clamps my teeth down on my tongue.

A zing of pain blasts through me. *Not literally, dipshit!*

He relaxes my jaw as he gripes, *Well, why did you tell me to do it, then?*

It's a turn of phrase. It means stop talking. Look at her! She's clearly not ready for what we feel for her.

That's what I told her.

You shouldn't have even done that. You put your foot in your mouth, I seethe.

Silence greets my mind for a beat.

That's another stupid human saying, isn't it?

Yup.

I gaze in frustration at Aliana's receding hourglass silhouette as we follow her through the maze of the subway. As if my arguments earlier with her weren't awful enough, now Empty's gone out there and put feelings on the table, making shit awkward before we've even had a shot at redeeming ourselves.

And worse...I'm associated with his fuck-up. My face is all over it.

When we finally are able to separate, is she even going to be able to disassociate her memories of the shit he's done in my body from me? What chance is there of that? Ugh, I'm pretty sure I'm swimming through an entire river of shit, one worse than the trash-filled Hudson River.

I groan and wrest control from Empty so I can run a hand through my hair in a move full of exasperation but also grief. I'd almost rather go back to being tortured because angst and embarrassment are the most toxic combination.

Anxiety is sewing up my chest in an uneven mess of stitches, just like the ones I had to get on my knee after my first raid at the age of seven. The feeling is tight and uncomfortable, painful in an unnatural way. I'm a breath away from rejection, and Aliana's rejection isn't something I'm certain I can survive.

I don't like this emotion, Em says inside my head, then smacks our lips as if he tastes foreboding and the sour coating it leaves on my tongue.

Yeah, being an asshole's easier, I agree.

Why doesn't Aliana like assholes?

Unsure. A lot of women do.

Yes. A lot of monsters too. In fact, most monsters prefer it. The bigger an asshole you are, the greater your chance of survival. Of having shit. Providing. It's basic alphanomics. Em sounds smug as shit.

I honestly didn't think we'd ever make it to this point and be able to have this conversation.

You? I was certain we'd die in this weak body.

Aw, thanks, dickhead. But same.

We walk past a group of squealing rats, and my stomach grumbles, reminding me that I haven't eaten in days. I hope wherever Aliana's taking us has food. I know she won first dibs and all, but I'm literally starving.

Part of me is side-eyeing the rats scurrying along the tunnel edges and wondering if we have enough time to slow down and set a trap for them. I dive down the rabbit hole—no pun intended—thinking about how I could stew them up, how good they'd taste with some water and a can of tomato paste. I'm so hungry that I can practically imagine their taste.

I've moved on from our prior conversation until Empty asks, in a whisper of thought that's soft and small, *How do we get her to love us? Can we? Without mate bonds? Is love even real for humans?*

Way to start an existential crisis.

Stop it with the stupid human sayings, or the second I leave this body, I'm going to roast your testicles with rosemary potatoes.

My body is most definitely sidetracked by the mention of rosemary potatoes, barely registering the threat at all. My mouth starts watering, and I nearly miss a tooth that springs out of a stairwell that descends from the street above. The figure has what looks like live wires that give off sparks as he arches through the air toward Aliana with a screech.

She doesn't flinch. Doesn't hesitate. Just reaches out and snags the monster by the hair before quickly snapping its neck.

That's fucking hot, Empty groans as he yanks control away from me and reaches down to palm my dick through my ripped pants.

Of course, that's the very second Aliana glances back. Her eyes roll as she picks up the monster corpse and slings it over her shoulder.

"Too busy beating off to beat up teeth, huh? Typical, Chase. Typical."

"I was beating off to the sight of your murder, mistress," Empty calls out in my voice before I can stop him.

NO! I yell, but only inside my head because Empty's taken control of my limbs and is striding after her.

"Classy," she grumbles before she turns and stomps ahead quickly, putting distance between us. "Next time, you get to do the killing, and I'll play with myself."

"Deal." He floods our system with pride and anticipation.

That was sarcasm, fuckwad, I tell Empty. *She doesn't mean it.*

What? Why not?

Aliana doesn't think murder's hot.

His reaction is pure disbelief, a fog filled with hazy dismissals.

It's true. She thinks it's necessary but not hot. If we want her, we have to be good.

Good? What the fuck is good?

I don't have a quick answer for that question, which makes me wonder which of us is actually the monster.

Dammit. Human courtship is frustrating, Empty grumbles, handing me back the reins and retreating so that I hardly feel him for the next hour.

My chest is aching and my foot drags noticeably as we wind through three more bends. I'm pretty certain each one of my ribs has turned into a dagger that's slowly severing my innards. Bleary pain is melting my vision to a point that I hardly notice when Aliana shoves open a metal door and gestures with a smile to an underground room that's somehow lit. The buzz of a generator answers my question about how as I drag my sore bones into the room.

The room is small, with a tiny kitchenette that bleeds into a "bedroom"—though it's nothing but a bed flanked by a night-stand. The entire area is decorated with brightly colored Christmas lights that flash intermittently, following the tune of an unheard song. Whoever lives here must be obsessed with the human world. I spot postcards of various cities taped to the walls, old records, and so many other memora-bilia from the before time that I feel as if I've just walked into a museum.

A strange pang throbs in my chest at the sight of a world I'll never get to live in. A world that Aliana will never get to live in.

Fuck.

Aliana enters behind me and shuts the door, dropping the body of the tooth she killed on the floor right next to it. Immediately, she sprints across the tiny space, and a squeal of delight leaves her lips as she crashes face-first into a dark blue blob in the corner of the room. She emerges from the shadows with her arm wrapped around the world's largest fucking blue tiger.

I swear my balls jump up into my throat when the beast spots me.

"Fluffy, meet Chase and Em," Aliana introduces us before turning her head to nuzzle the beast.

She has her own menagerie, Em says thoughtfully.

Not like yours, I counter.

Mmm. His response is blasé, and if he were in control of my limbs, I can tell that he'd wave a hand to bat away my words.

A little ball of frustration forms deep inside of me, or at least inside the bit of me that I still control, the rear part of my brain.

"Where is everybody?" Aliana asks the tiger as if it can respond.

Shit, for all I know, maybe it can. Is it a tongue?

But Fluffy (world's most inaccurately named beast) just gives a growl that makes me slide toward a shadowy set of shelves full of knick-knacks, reaching for anything that could be a weapon—

POP!

Something smashes into my spine and shoves me face-first into the concrete. Heavy weight crushes my lungs, and the oxygen leaks from them in a gust.

"Aliana!" a joyful voice sounds above my head as the weight leaves my back.

I'm left panting shallowly, trying to refill my lungs and get my blood to flow again as the Creeper, who appeared out of nowhere, hurtles across the room toward Aliana and wraps her up in a hug.

"Creep!" is her bright response as I wearily drag myself to my knees.

Every part of my body reminds me just how fragile it is, how close to breaking. But I can't let Aliana see that sort of weakness, can't let the Terrors. I force my aching limbs to stand up once more, though I do end up leaning against the wall.

A growl sounds beside me, and I glance over to see Dev standing there, red eyes glaring at the picture that Creep and Aliana make as the horned monster picks her up and swings her in a circle, causing her to nearly brain Fluffy and then kick a cup off the countertop.

I have to do a double-take when I spot the neon-green monster slung over the huge beast's shoulders in a fireman carry.

What the fuck?

Please don't tell me that's another one of Aliana's lovers, Em laments, his voice bordering on a pathetic whine. *I can't deal with any more competition for my mistress's heart.*

Ummm... I doubt it. Do you not see the blood? The bruises?

65

Some people like it rough, Em says simply.

Dev, as if sensing the direction of my thoughts, tosses the monster unceremoniously on the ground, not caring when his skull ricochets off a table with a deafening crack.

Definitely not a lover, then, Em muses.

Still could be, I murmur, having heard of the Devourer's possessive tendencies, especially where they concern Aliana.

"I knew you'd be okay. I knew it. You're such a fucking badass little warrior," Creep praises, drawing my attention back to him and Aliana.

Her smile is vibrantly beautiful, so sweet I forget to breathe. But when Creep tilts his head to kiss her, it feels like my veins have been injected with poison. Jealousy blackens the edges of my vision as despair makes my heart stutter.

I want what he has so badly, but I have no goddamned clue how to get it.

Next to me, the Devourer's claws clench so tightly that his nails cut into his palms. If he were still holding the smaller monster, I imagine he would be in ribbons right about now.

He wants her too. Everyone fucking wants her, which is why this will never work. Em's annoyance rattles inside my skull.

His dark proclamation rings true because I can't imagine how the hell the Terrors might share, much less share with me. Somewhere inside my stomach, a shovel starts digging, and a trench appears, then a pit, then an entire canyon.

Happiness is impossible. My happiness, at least.

"Where's Tesq?" Aliana asks.

"I'm sure he'll show any second. I'll even go looking for him if you want. I just need a kiss so that I know how much you missed me." Creep waggles his eyebrows suggestively, mischief twitching up the corners of his lips.

She rolls her eyes, but then she does something I've never seen her do. Aliana blushes. Actual pink colors her cheekbones, and her eyelashes flutter down in a way I've only ever seen in my imagination. Even when she leaned down over my body in that torture chamber, her face flooded with concern, it didn't look like this.

Holy shit.

The feeling that I've slid into an alternate reality doesn't end there. Aliana brushes back a strand of her white-streaked hair before she kisses the Creeper with a wild sort of abandon I've never seen her possess. Her hands cup his cheeks, and her mouth is a very active participant as her lips repeatedly brush his. I even see a hint of tongue—forked tongue. That must be Creep's.

With a feral growl rumbling through his throat, Dev stomps forward and plucks Creep up by an antler until the blue monster is dangling with his feet in the air.

I twist my mouth up in dark amusement at the sight.

I hope he throws him brain first into the wall, Em states flatly.

I can't say I disagree, which just proves to me yet again that I'm not worthy of her. Which makes me hate myself and Creep all the more.

"Dev, if you want a welcome-back kiss, you'll put him down this fucking second." Aliana's tone brooks no argument, as if she's used to ordering Terrors around.

Wait. WHAT?

She's offering up kisses?

The Devourer hesitates, and Creep kicks him in the chest, sending the werebeast back a step. The wolf drops the other monster's antlers, and Creep darts for the shadows and disappears as he gives Aliana a little salute and a wink.

Immediately, the giant werewolf wraps his massive arms around Aliana's waist, pulling her tightly up against him. His snout descends toward her face.

How can he kiss her without human lips?

Just watch, Empty responds, and my dick gets half hard while an image of Dev's monster palming Aliana's ass as they make out floats into my brain.

Fucking stop that! I scold Em.

What? You telling me you don't like to watch?

Didn't you learn your lesson in the fucking subway? She didn't want us beating off to her.

Aliana turns her head, and whatever kiss the Devourer was aiming for becomes a dog-like lick up her cheek.

"You didn't put him down." Aliana's tone is firm and cold. "So you don't get a kiss."

"I'm your fucking mate. And I'll get a kiss when I want a kiss." Dev turns with her in his arms and pushes her up against the wall, stepping between her legs so that they're spread wide around him. His black tail swishes back and forth behind him as he looms over her.

Shit.

I take a step forward to stop this, but Em makes my legs jerk to a stop, and my body wavers in place, off balance for a second.

No. I want to watch.

This! This right here is why we're assholes who deserved to be beheaded. It's about what she wants, not what we want. The words spilling from my head are a revelation, but as soon as I've had the thought, I know it's true.

Fuck! he grumbles. My cock throbs once, pressing against my ripped pants before Em reluctantly hands over the reins. *Fine. But what the hell are you going to do in this weak-ass body? There's no chance you'll stop the Devourer.*

I have to try.

"Put her down!" I call out.

I've barely gotten two steps closer when the door to my side bursts open and heat fills the room, so much blistering, blazing heat that my eyeballs dry out and my lips shrivel.

A huge gargoyle-like monster with red veins like lava running up and down his forearms ducks into the room. His horns are short, pointed white stubs, nothing as elaborate as the Creeper's, but his torso is as wide as two of me, and his bulk fills the room until I can hardly take a breath. Or maybe that's because of the heat emanating from him. A shock of recognition rolls through me because, though he didn't have lava lining his limbs last time, I recognize the monster who forced a curse onto Em and myself—binding us together.

"Aliana?" His low baritone is a grumbling sound that resembles rocks rubbing together.

"Tesq!" Breathy. I never knew her voice could get so breathy.

In two seconds, I've seen more soft emotions from Aliana than I have in all the years we grew up together.

Aliana whacks Dev on the side of the head. "Put me down," she commands the werewolf.

But he and Tesq both growl, "No!" at the same moment.

I think Tesq's response startles the other monster a bit, because he swivels his head around to look at the gargoyle.

"I'll burn you," Tesq explains, lifting his arms and showcasing the tiny lines of lava between the dark-gray striated stone of his body. "Fire monster fight. Lava still."

The blue tiger in the corner whines, and Aliana's expression shifts into worry. "How long will you…?"

"Don't know. Never happened." Tesq's reply is accompanied by a shrug, and the movement sends a drip of lava splattering to the floor.

I jump back as the drip melts a quarter-sized hole into the concrete.

That's when Tesq swivels his gaze over to me. His face is a disastrous mess of melted materials, but those black pits for eyes and that ape-like rounded muzzle are apparent as he takes me in. His appearance alone is horrifying, but his expression is half disgust and half a threat—a promise to end me as he shows me his teeth.

Something about him is more potent than the other Terrors.

It is not! Empty rattles inside my head, but his thoughts are weaker than the panicked response of my body.

Already on the verge of collapse, my heart rate speeds up, and my breathing grows shallow as my lungs forget how to move under the Grotesque's stare.

I feel my feet sliding out from under me.

"Shit. He's fainting!" Aliana calls out as she bats at the Devourer, who still holds her pinned.

All I know is no one is there to catch me when I fall, and my head hits the concrete with a sickening crack.

ALIANA

I MANAGE to shove the Devourer's stubborn ass away from me long enough to get Chase set up on the twin bed that I've now dubbed the invalid cot. Dev grumbles about me wasting energy on a human and a Terror stupid enough to get trapped in a weakling body, which makes me shoot a glare at the werewolf as I arrange the sheets over Chase's limp form.

His pulse is weak but steady. I'll need to make him soup or something when he wakes up. Maybe with that tooth carcass. The thought of soup makes my stomach rumble. It gives a growl that could rival Fluffy.

"Food," Tesq instantly utters, moving toward the countertop.

"I'll get it," I tell him.

Not only because he's a bad chef, but because right now he has a good chance of eviscerating the stockpile with his lava-lined hands. Chase and I are going to need those cans of Chef Boyardee if we're going to make it through this.

I grab the can opener and go about my business, deciding to focus only on physical needs right now. My emotions are still live wires coming down from the adrenaline rush of our rescue mission, and the strange euphoric rush of seeing all my mates safe.

Creep better get back soon. He has to have realized by now that Tesq's here.

I try not to dwell on just how much my heart wants them all tucked into this tiny little space with me, sharing the same air. No, I'm pretty certain my hunger to see all the Terrors at once is just a loopy side effect that comes with the aftermath of trauma. Of thinking a building was going to crush me and then wandering through the darkness for hours on end, certain I'd die without seeing the sun again.

Or them, my mind contributes unhelpfully.

I peel the lid off my can of deliciousness in an attempt to give my head something else to think about. When I finally have my turbulent emotions under control—or under as much control as I'm capable of—I jerk my chin towards the neon-green body on the floor.

"Is anyone going to explain what our new...*friend* is doing here?" My tone drips with sarcasm and disdain.

Dev's smile is more of a baring of teeth as he replies, "Found him. Was feeling cute. Thought a little torture would be fun. I dunno."

He shrugs his broad shoulders as I choke on my own tongue, laughter bubbling up my throat.

Did Dev just make a joke?

No, I must've heard him wrong. Or maybe I hit my head in the explosion.

Yup. I must've hit my head. Dev doesn't make jokes.

Silence settles between all of us, but I wouldn't be able to tell you if it's the comfortable or uncomfortable kind. Something potent and heady hangs in the air, saturating it.

I've just licked a droplet of sauce off my fingertip when the Devourer tells Tesq, "Go outside. You're turning this room into a sauna. And bring our new friend with you."

Strange.

I pause eating and glance over at my gargoyle. Even though I see the lines of lava on Tesq's forearms and watched him burn a hole in the floor, I don't feel any heat. Dev's probably just angling to lock him outside.

I've just downed my third ravioli when I nearly choke on a revelation.

"Shit!" I sputter.

My two conscious mates and Fluffy swivel their heads in my direction. Their gazes are full of questions and concerns.

"Is bad?" Tesq asks, pointing at the can.

"No. Is it really hot in here?" I ask Dev.

The bastard merely uses his claw to wipe a line of sweat from his furry forehead and shakes it off onto the floor. His motion is all the answer I need, and exactly the answer I don't want.

It only creates another question.

I shake my head and lick sauce from my lips as I try to decide how to word the query that's suddenly emerged in my head. Part of me wishes it was only Tesq in the room because then I'd feel comfortable asking him anything without hesitation.

The other mate of mine tends to fly off the handle and over-react. But then I feel guilty for that thought and want to kick myself because who knows? Dev may actually have some answers. He does go out amongst monsters more than Tesq.

A deep breath, and then, "Is it possible for a monster to…I don't know…give me their magic?"

I try to recall if I fought any ice monsters as I moved through the offices in the back of the meat-packing plant, but I honestly have no clue. It felt like there were dozens of them, and adrenaline made the whole thing a bit of a blur.

"Give?" Tesq tilts his head thoughtfully.

But the Devourer gives a dismissive snort before trans-forming to his more human form. I suppose he got tired of stooping in this low-ceilinged room. Not that he isn't tall as a semi-human. He still towers over me, making me feel small and dainty.

His red eyes glow as he fixes them on me. "No. Magic transfer isn't possible. If it were, monsters would kill each other even more often than they do. As it is, we can increase our own power level after killing monsters, but we don't absorb or transfer powers."

His explanation cleaves the little hope I had in half, and it sags inside my chest. "Oh."

"Why would you think that?"

"What did you see?" Tesq adds on.

"It's not so much what I saw. It's what I did," I say in a whisper, glancing down at my can of stale pasta, far less interested in it than I was a minute ago.

They wait patiently. Well, the Devourer's tail swishes back and forth, and I'm certain he's curling those fists as he always does because true composure is anathema to that monster. If he could choke the answer out of me, I'm sure he would.

I'd almost rather he choke me because my own thoughts are doing a damn fine job of it right now.

I do manage to shove out words one by one, as if I'm spitting out sunflower seeds. "When I was going through the offices, I accidentally encased a monster in a snow-globe thing. I thought it was the jewels we had. They, um, are like weapons. Or spells. Something?"

I set down my fork, grab the thin pouch out of my pocket, and set it on the counter, staring at it. Nothing happens.

"Yes?" Tesq prompts me gently.

But his softness plucks at something inside of me that I can't handle. I rip my gaze from his and turn my eyes to Dev's demanding red glare.

"Where the hell did the ice come from?" he barks the second I lock stares with him, as if he were just waiting for me to give him my attention.

Rudeness. Rudeness is easier to handle than warmth right now.

"That's what I want to know. I thought it was these fuckers." I glare at the tiny drawstring bag as if it has personally offended me. Irritation keeps me talking. "But then, my palms shot icicles at this sandworm in the basement…"

I lift the hand holding my fork and examine my palm. Nothing unusual there. No blue lines or ice crystals. Just chipped nails, dirt, and substances I don't want to question because fighting monsters is slimy work.

It takes me a moment to realize that Dev's tail is no longer swishing and that complete silence fills Tesq's hideout. Surprised, I glance at the two monsters only to find them staring at each other rather than me.

Dev's eyes are wide, and Tesq has the shadow of a smile on his face, though I can't tell what emotion he's feeling. The melted mask mars his expression, making it impossible to decipher if he's got a pitying smile on or a happy one.

"What?" I ask, unnerved, needing answers.

"Show me." Dev is finally the one to speak. His gaze turns back to me as he commands, "Ice over your fork."

"You think I have control of this shit?" I immediately burst out. "It's happened twice. When I've panicked!" The sense of foreboding in my stomach mingles with agitation, fizzing and bubbling. "I'm not trained in how to use magic—"

"Magic is a protective instinct. Not a skill. Not usually, anyway," Dev interrupts me, because of course he would.

Arrogant jerk.

I toss him a glare for pulling the rug out from under me. Immaturely, I want to toss him the bird too, but that's only because his words process, and I realize he thinks I can just do magic "like that." As if it's a snap of the fingers, a flip of a switch. Panic swells up at the thought of repeating that ice shit so easily.

"You're missing the point. I don't have magic! I shouldn't fucking have magic. So how the hell did it get here?" I toss my arms out in frustration, and some of my pasta sauce flies out, a red dollop landing on the floor.

But if there was one rule that was hammered into me as a child, it was don't waste food. So I set down my can and fork on the counter on my left side. That way, I can continue my freak-out in peace, without guilt piling on top of it.

The Devourer starts to open his mouth to answer, but Tesq holds up a glowing arm. "Me."

For once, the arrogant werebeast listens to someone else. Perhaps he senses the gravity of this moment, the fragility of my mental state. Or maybe it's the fact that Tesq literally steps so close to him that I can scent burnt hair.

In any case, he takes a few steps away from me as the gargoyle shifts front and center, tilting his neck. Where Tesq's veins should be, there are only glowing lines of lava that make the room swim in soft, pulsing orange light.

We share a long, drawn-out silence, my breath caught in my lungs, unable to escape.

"Aliana." Tesq's soft rumble of my name is so reverent that butterflies flutter in my stomach, but they can't make it up past my swollen lungs, my closed throat, the fear that's gripping me.

"Why do I have magic, Tesq?" I whimper in a tone I'd normally scorn, one that's soft and weak. One that outwardly showcases my worry.

His lips rub together as he considers what to say. Finally, he settles on, "Do you feel the mate bonds?"

His question throws me for a loop, crashes into me out of nowhere, smacks me with violent force as I realize the implications of the question.

My head starts to shake from side to side, my body trying to deny it even as my mind is stitching together a quilt of memories—moments I've been drawn to these monsters even against my will, felt the need for them despite their cruelty, despite my disgust for their actions, despite my own moral code.

It can't be.

Memories of my parents surface, their laughing faces. My father's soft expression when he tucked me in at night. My mother humming when she washed our clothes in the stream. The bright, forest-green light of my memories, those precious treasures locked inside my chest, dims and dulls. A sepia tone invades them, turns them monochromatic, strips the love away.

All those memories occurred under false pretenses: I thought I was human. I thought I was theirs. His. I thought I belonged. And now, the agony of loneliness invades each of my veins, poisons the stream of my blood, leaches into my heart. I'm not who I thought I was. Did they know?

No.

Is my entire life a lie?

My eyelashes flutter, and I find them wet.

Everything's wet. Tesq and Dev's faces smear as a flood erupts inside of me. A surge of water appearing from nowhere, a powerful gush with enough force to knock out my knees.

"Humans and monsters have mated before," Tesq says softly, as if the ugly truth has to be spoken aloud.

"She's half?" Dev states the obvious.

I take a step backward and bump into the counter. A cup falls over on the surface behind me and rolls across the countertop. I don't shoot out my arm to stop it.

I watch it reach the edge and fall off the surface, plunging to the floor, then shattering into a million glittering specks.

Broken.

Ruined.

Just like me.

Everything I thought I was…is a lie.

ALIANA

I CAN'T DEAL with this right now.

I don't *want* to deal with this.

Because "dealing with this" would be the equivalent of shoving a ticking time bomb down my pants and praying it doesn't explode.

My parents are a lie.

My past is a lie.

My fucking *species* is a lie.

It's too much, too soon. My head threatens to detonate into a thousand tiny shards.

I ignore Dev and Tesq's stares—one bemused, while the other is almost pitying—and walk directly towards the neon-green monster.

What better way is there to deal with your shit than beating the daylights out of your enemies? I certainly haven't found one.

I crouch down until I'm beside the unconscious monster and then give him a slow, unimpressed once-over. Not bothering to peel my gaze away, I say to the others, "Help me sit him up."

"Aliana…" Dev sounds as if he wants to argue with me, but now is not the time to test me or my fraying patience.

I'm a grenade whose pin has just been pulled, and if they don't run and take cover, they'll explode with me.

My breaths come out in stuttering exhales, and I curl my hands into tight fists, my nails digging into my palms.

Breathe. Just breathe, Aliana.

Tesq releases a heavy sigh but does as I instructed. Without any fanfare, he grabs the smaller monster by the back of his neck and flings him into the nearest chair. He doesn't bother to tie the fucker up—there'll be no escaping any of us.

My rage burns white-hot in my chest, scalding and fizzing, and I allow it to travel through my veins and into my arm, which has already lifted of its own accord. Then, without second-guessing my actions, I punch the monster in the face.

Hard.

Cat-like eyes blink up at me, the golden color tinged with red from some popped blood vessels. The wariness and trepidation on his face instantly transforms into horror as his gaze slides over my shoulder and focuses on the two Terrors at my back.

But that only amplifies my already shitty mood.

Come the fuck on. I *know* I'm not the scariest person in the room, but does this bastard have to make it so damn obvious? I want him to fear *me*, dammit, not the two monsters standing as silent sentries behind me.

This rage is completely irrational, as is the jealousy that spirals through my chest, but both of these emotions, compounded with the fear from my most recent revelation…

Yeah. They're not a good combination.

"Don't look at them. Look at *me*," I growl as I curl my hand into a fist once more.

I can't punch him again—not if I want to keep my knuckle bones intact—but that doesn't mean I can't make him hurt.

As if he heard the direction of my thoughts, Dev steps forward, opens my clenched fist, and places a hunting knife in my palm. I'm honestly surprised it's the Devourer who understands the me, who understands the violence lurking beneath my skin needs an outlet.

But then I realize…

Maybe the two of us are more alike than I would want to believe. We both crave blood and death, even if I don't want to admit it. Both of our souls are tarnished and painted red from all of the monsters and people we killed over the years.

Fuck.

When did I ever think I'd relate to *Dev*?

The green fucker volleys his gaze between the blade, my face, and the monsters at my back. A mocking glimmer enters his eyes as a smile tugs up his lips.

"What is this?" He directs his next question at Dev and Tesq, pissing me off even further. "Are you guys allowing your pet to have a little bit of fun?"

He chuckles darkly, as if the thought of me hurting him is absolutely preposterous. I don't know if this monster has balls made of steel or if he's oblivious to the fury permeating the room.

Because he then does the stupidest thing known to mankind. Or monsterkind, as the case may be.

He stands and takes a step towards me, that cocky leer never leaving his face.

Maybe he believes that this is a test of some sort from the Terrors—to see if he'll cower when face-to-face with a tiny human woman.

But if this is a test, he just failed. Miserably.

Before he can move even another step closer, I stab him in the arm, directly between his shoulder and elbow. Green blood oozes out of the wound as he cries out in surprise and pain.

My rage continues to swirl inside of me like a tsunami, and I swear—I fucking swear—ice pricks the tips of my fingers. Then I blink, and only smooth, unblemished skin remains.

Fuck. Fuck. Fuck.

Am I losing my mind? Seeing things? Or did my hand actually frost over?

With another roar, I tear the knife out of the fucker's arm and then move to his stomach, jamming it into his flesh. I want him to hurt, to suffer, to feel even an ounce of the fear that Chase no doubt did—

"Aliana!"

Dev. I would recognize that bark anywhere.

He grabs my shoulder and yanks me back roughly. I'm not surprised. Out of all my mates, Dev's the only one who doesn't treat me with kid gloves. Yes, he's a protective, possessive bastard, but he knows what I'm capable of, even if he doesn't want to admit it. He's rough with me...and a twisted part of me likes it.

I blink at him, confused, and then blink again. I feel as if I'm waking up from a long nap. Everything's groggy and blurry, and my head spins wildly.

"Wh-what?" I ask as I attempt to come back to myself.

"We can't ask that fucker any questions if he's dead," Dev reminds me harshly. His hands tighten on my shoulders as he bends down to ensnare my gaze with his own. He searches my eyes, but I have no idea what he's looking for. Whatever he sees makes him straighten and jerk his chin at Tesq. "Grotesque, take over the interrogation."

Some of the cotton balls in my head disintegrate at his words, but my rage isn't appeased. It still flares white-hot inside of me—the type of burn you receive when you touch a block of ice.

"What the hell are you doing?" I growl as I push up on my tiptoes in an attempt to look taller.

His red eyes flare, almost the exact same shade as the Christmas lights directly behind him. "You're not thinking with your head, mate. And that's fucking dangerous, especially when you're facing another monster."

What the...?

"Are you kidding me right now?" I ball my hands into fists and feel something cold sweep over me.

"You're freaking the fuck out right now," Dev growls. "And if you keep acting like a dense bitch, you'll kill one of our only leads."

"Don't call me a bitch, Dev!"

"Then stop acting like one and get your shit together!" he barks.

I know he's right—that I'm acting irrationally—but I can't seem to think clearly. All I know is that my entire world has been turned on its axis, and I feel adrift and untethered. Confused and scared.

And more than any of that, I'm angry. So fucking angry.

Did my parents know? Did they keep this a secret from me? Were either of them even related to me? And if they were, which one of them fucked a goddamn monster?

Dev's voice takes on a raspy, soft quality I've never heard from him before—almost as if he's trying to soothe me and sound gentle but isn't quite sure how to go about doing it. The result is an eerie sound that makes me think he's either about to tear my head off, give me a hug, or take a shit. "You just need to take a breath and calm down—"

"Don't tell me to calm down, Dev. Don't you fucking dare!" I jab a finger at his chest, surprised to see that it shakes erratically.

Adrenaline, I realize belatedly. Too much adrenaline.

Dark specks begin to dance across my vision, but sheer willpower keeps me on my feet.

I know he's right. I'm acting fucking crazy.

But I can't seem to stop myself.

I need…something. Something to anchor me to the here and now. Something to make the earth stop shaking under my feet. Something to slow down the rampant pounding of my heart.

My gaze drifts to Dev's lips and the slightly larger than normal canines. *Everything* about Dev is larger than average, including his cock.

I take a step closer as if pulled by some unseen rope…

When Tesq's voice breaks through the strange tension in the air. "Problem. Big problem."

I spin around, confused, only to see that the green monster is now sprawled on the floor, dead. White foam covers the corners of his mouth, and his eyes are wide and vacant, fixed on the ceiling.

"Motherfucker!" Dev roars.

"Must've had a pill on him," Tesq deadpans, kicking at the body with his bare foot, a tiny bit of lava sprinkling down on the monster's side and burning his flesh.

The monster just committed *suicide* to keep from talking to us? What the hell?

For the first time in my existence, I find myself agreeing with Dev one hundred percent. "MOTHERFUCKER!"

THE EMPTY MAN

IS THERE anything sexier than my woman standing toe-to-toe with the Devourer, defiance in her hooded gaze and her cheeks flushed?

God, would it be weird if I stroked one out? I swear this is better than any porn I could've watched.

Yes. That would be really weird, Chase responds lazily.

Get out of my head, fucker.

You're technically in my *head,* the bastard retorts.

And I don't even have a response to that because…it's kind of true.

Okay, *a lot* true.

Semantics.

The Grotesque, the Devourer, and my sweet mistress are unaware that I'm awake, which is perfect and all for my benefit. It allows me to watch my little mate completely unencumbered.

The way her white hair shines in the artificial, twinkling lights…

The way her chest heaves beneath the skin-tight shirt she wears…

The way red paints her cheeks in response to her agitation…

If I were a broody artist like Dev, I might've been tempted to paint her right in this moment. As it is, the only thing I'm good at is…well…collecting. Coveting.

And Aliana already made it painstakingly clear that she'll never be just another object in my collection.

Not that I want her to be.

Maybe at first, that was where my mind went, but after I've gotten to know her, taste her, feel her…

I will my cock to deharden—*think flaccid thoughts, Em*—and focus on the conversation at hand.

Namely, their discussion over what to do with the dead monster.

I was too preoccupied watching Aliana's confrontation with Dev to notice the green fuck reaching for his suicide pill. Tesq must've been too.

Now, our only lead is dead.

It's not like he would've had anything to tell us anyway, Chase says.

How do you know that?

Because he's low on the totem pole, so to speak. No one would trust him with any important information.

Totem pole? I indolently stretch on the bed, making sure that my shirt rises up just enough to show a hint of my golden abs. *Is that a human term?*

Yeah. It's a— What the fuck are you doing?

Someone *has to redeem us from your fainting mishap and remind our mistress that we're in for the win.*

Honestly, it's like I'm speaking to a child.

And your method of doing that is showing off my abs? I don't know if Chase sounds impressed or horrified.

Our *abs, brother. Our abs,* I correct.

He scoffs. *We won't have abs for long if you keep eating all of those damn sweets.*

You try being incorporeal, I snap back, my stomach already gurgling at the thought of said sweets.

So I have an itty-bitty sweet tooth when I'm in a human body. Sue me.

I yawn exaggeratedly and stretch my arms above my head yet again...but Aliana doesn't even seem to notice. She's still hurling daggers with her eyes at Dev.

"...not my fault!" She folds her arms over her chest and glares at him.

"Maybe if you stopped being so emotional—"

"Oh...you didn't just say that."

Tesq cringes and then takes a step away, as if he's physically trying to distance himself from the bickering duo.

"Fuck you, Dev!"

Goddammit.

She's not even looking over here.

I casually begin to gyrate my hips as if this is just how I *always* wake up in the morning. Yup. Nothing to see here. Just a little air grinding.

I pretend to be completely unaware of Aliana's existence as I stretch yet again, this time pushing my shirt to ride up my toned stomach. I peek at my mistress out of the corner of my eyes…

Nada.

Not even a glance.

Chase's snickers trickle down our bond, and I throw him the mental bird as I sit up in bed. Nobody even turns their heads. It's like I'm just as invisible as always. Fucking annoying.

What good is this human body if it can't fight and can't attract my mate's attention?

It's practically useless, Chase agrees. *You really should leave it behind.*

Will do as soon as I can, I reply.

Directly beside the tiny cot is a nightstand, and on it rests a plethora of magazines. I haul them onto my lap and then begin flicking through them. What else is there to do? All of my sexual prowess is going to waste on my oblivious mate—

Sexual prowess? Really? Chase barks out a laugh. *No wonder she hates your guts. You have no game.* Then, as if a horrible thought just occurred to him, he adds, *I don't sound like you, do I? Oh god. Am I a stereotypical douchebag?*

Probably, I respond as I toss aside the first magazine—the glossy pages full of nothing but tractors—and then begin sifting through the next. *Why don't we both just accept the truth —we're both raging douches? Our goal is to make Aliana fall in love with us, douchebag tendencies and all.*

You're a horrible person.

I'm a horrible monster, I correct. *There's a difference.*

I pause at the page I currently landed on, my gaze scanning over the headline.

"Ten Ways to Win Back Your Lover."

Well…well…well…

What do we have here?

Em, I'm not sure this is the best idea. Chase sounds wary— which is honestly ridiculous. He acts as if I've never won over a girl before.

Shush. The grownups are speaking here.

You're talking to yourself.

I said shush.

"Step one…remind her that you're thinking of her often. Step two…buy her chocolates and flowers. Step three…gift her with something cute. Step four…" I allow my words to taper off as I continue scanning the article.

Genius.

Absolutely genius.

Em… Chase sounds almost desperate.

"I'm not a damn child!" Aliana bellows at Dev, dark-red splotches erupting on her cheekbones. "Stop treating me like one!"

"Obviously, I *don't* think you're a fucking child," he spits back. Then a cold, predatory smirk takes over his features. "If I did, would I have fucked you on every available—"

She throws her hands up in the air. "Of all the idiotic things—"

"Hey!" I holler, cutting Aliana off in mid-shout.

All three of them turn to stare at me, Aliana appearing confused, Dev annoyed, and Tesq as impassive as always.

Please don't do this, Chase pleads in my head.

The magazine told me to.

For the love of all that's holy, please don't.

I grin brightly at my mistress, ignoring the other two Terrors as if they're not even in the room. "I'm thinking of you." Then I wink, just as the article instructs me to do.

Chase mentally face-palms.

Aliana just stares at me, her eyes bugging out of her head. "Um…"

Step one. Completed.

Now on to step two…

ALIANA

"Is this hell? Am I dead?" I ask dazedly under my breath.

I must be. Either I'm dead or I'm in the middle of a fever dream. But this feels more like my personal hell than a hallucination, so I'm going with dead.

The Empty Man is...winking at me? After interrupting what was turning into a fucking verbal war zone between me and Dev? God, this monster has no sense. Neither of them does. If I am dead, I'm stuck in the afterlife with a bunch of idiots.

"Not dead, love," Tesq reassures me. "Would never let that happen."

"Fuck off. I'd be the one to save her," Dev snarls, still bound and determined to argue about something.

Once he latches onto his anger, he's like a damn dog with a bone—he won't let go.

Where the hell is Creep? Someone needs to make a sarcastic comment and make me laugh at the absurdity of this moment so I don't start punching Terrors far above my power level.

Shit.

I probably have a power level. I'm not sure I want to know what it is.

Shaking my head in disbelief, and trying to ignore the queasy feeling in my gut about my newly discovered identity, I watch as Empty tosses aside some magazines and stands. He stretches in a ludicrously uncomfortable-looking way that makes his shirt pull up to show Chase's abs. His back pops. I try not to grimace, but it sounds painful.

With a smug twist of his lips, Empty finishes his back bend and gives me a sultry look before he tries to saunter around the bed. But he forgets that Chase was limping in the subway on the walk here. He stumbles a bit and has to grab onto the bed frame.

I try to swallow my laughter, reminding myself he's probably dehydrated and starving and a tad bit delusional right now from all the torture. That, or Empty hardly ever used a human body before this. Perhaps it's a combination of both. I use that to excuse the wink as well.

He still looks far too arrogant as he steps over the dead monster on the ground and beelines for my abandoned ravioli. He pours the can's contents straight into his mouth until his cheeks are protruding like a squirrel's stuffed full of nuts. Yup. Starving.

The tiniest glimmer of pity sparks in my chest.

"We aren't done fighting," Dev reminds me, and when I turn back to him, I can see a gleam in his eyes that's definitely sexual.

The brutish, controlling beast in him thinks of disagreement as foreplay. Yelling is a caress, throwing objects equates to heavy petting, the sort of sick and twisted mentality that...that I don't want to admit works for me on some level. The most basic one.

Fuck, maybe it's my monster side that likes it.

Now I'm questioning every goddamned part of myself when I don't want to be. What I want to do is more of the stabbing shit that I started but didn't get to finish. Fucking monster and his death pill.

I turn away and force myself to forget about how tight my lower belly feels from Dev's sizzling gaze. Since murder is currently off the table, and sex with that asshole is definitely out of the question, I focus on fixing the one tiny problem in the room I can actually address. Hunger.

I grab an apple from a pile in the corner of the countertop and give it to Empty, saying, "Here. I'll look for some meat."

His crunch becomes the soundtrack in the room for a minute before Fluffy decides to make a snack out of one of the dead monster's arms. A disgusting pop and crunch, followed by a ripping noise, fill my ears before I hear her start to chew.

For me, it's the bone crunching that does it. The clink of her tiger teeth against shards of bone. That little sound parade makes my shoulders scrunch in disgust, and a horrified tickle runs down my spine as if it's happening to me. Ridiculous, I know, but some sounds are just like some flavors— disgusting.

I try to shake off the sensation as I open the fridge and lean in so that the view is blocked from me, though the scent of monster blood wafts through the air. I deliberately don't turn around when I hear Tesq scold her before someone hauls up the body of the two dead tooths.

Staring at the minimal contents of the fridge, I realize there's no good meat to be found in there right now. Not unless moldy chicken is on the menu. We're going to have to eat that tooth I killed and brought back.

"Tesq, can you strip the skin from—" I cut off my sentence as the smell of roasting meat fills the room.

I turn to see the two monsters slung over Tesq's broad shoulders cooking, just because of his magma-hot touch.

Well, that's efficient.

A slight charcoal dusting appears on the skin of one of them.

"Shit. Put them down! You'll burn them!" I say as I run forward.

Without thinking, I reach for one of the bodies as Tesq is setting it down, and my fingertips brush Tesq's arm, right over one of those neon-orange lava veins.

He jerks back, eyes wide and worried.

I give a tiny gasp and stare at my fingertips. But they don't blacken like the dead monsters did. I wiggle them, surprised to find them healthy and whole. Untouched.

I shoot my gaze over to Tesq, and my jaw drops like it did the first time I tasted maple syrup. Shock and delight roll over me. Because there are tiny blue lines ghosting over Tesq's arm, dimming the glow of his lava veins.

"I can touch you," I whisper, and then I look to the floor.

I'm strangely shy and giddy about it. I can touch Tesq even when no one else can.

It feels like the one good thing to come out of this disastrous series of revelations. This beautiful little diamond in a mine full of blackness and coal dust.

I glance at him from under my lashes, uncertain what he thinks of this discovery. He's so damn quiet it's hard to tell.

Tesq's brow is furrowed as he stares at his huge forearm and the striated stone skin there. We watch in silence as the blue tone fades, and so does the orange, his body restored to his former glory. But then he peeks over and gives me his signature shy grin.

"Hug?" he asks in a whisper.

Inside, I twinkle as much as the Christmas lights flickering in the room. Mate bond or not, monster or not, Tesq is the most selfless, caring person I've ever come across.

I launch myself at him and wrap my legs around his torso, arms twining around his neck. His own massive arms curl around me, his palms grazing over my clothes and encasing me. Making me feel safe.

I've never known a person who was both so hard and so gentle. I'm certainly not. My thighs are attempting to squeeze the life out of him, but they're not making much headway. Not that I mind. I don't want to hurt him. I've just got a fierce case of cute aggression when it comes to Tesq. My gentle giant.

Behind me, Dev growls, and Empty curses, both complaining.

I tune them out and nuzzle into Tesq's neck. But what should be an adorable moment ends up with my face covered in ashy grime.

Ew.

I pull back and glance at Tesq and then over at the other two. Dev's hair is matted from sweat, and his body is covered in green blood that I assume is from the monsters he killed rather than his own. Empty, in Chase's body… Well… Let's just say that our slithering trip down a slimy sandworm and through a dirt tunnel didn't do him any favors. I probably look pretty disastrous since I did the exact same thing.

In short, we're all disgusting.

"We need a bath," I declare.

On the word bath, Creep materializes in the corner of the room. "Can't find— Oh, you're here," he states, spotting Tesq in my embrace. "Are we cuddling?"

Without missing a beat, he switches gears and heads over, pushing past Dev and opening his blue arms. Creep's bark-like skin rubs against my shirt as he engulfs both Tesq and me in a massive hug.

But then he pulls back, and his nose scrunches. "All right, no offense, you two. But you reek."

"Agreed," I tell him. "Know anywhere we can go wash off?"

"All of us?"

"Yup."

My monster from the closet thinks for a second before his features light up. Then he waggles his eyebrows playfully. "Oh, I know exactly where we can go. I'll have to portal you there one by one though." He turns and looks at my sullen, pouting mates. "And if our dicks happen to swap during portal time, I call dibs on using yours!"

The other monsters are still gaping at him as he laughs maniacally, yanks me from Tesq's arms, pulls me toward a shadow, and makes the world around us disappear.

ALIANA

WE MATERIALIZE INSIDE A DARK TUNNEL, and for a second, I want to curse Creep for taking me somewhere that feels as claustrophobic as all the other places I've been for the past day. If I never see another underground burrow, it will still be too soon.

I was picturing a stream to wash in, something relaxing and peaceful like we used when I lived in the forest with the human resistance. A tiny ribbon of silver water flowing over the rocks and surrounded by trees. I wanted serenity.

Of course, that's not what I'm getting. This is the monster version of a bath, after all.

Creep disappears again without a word, portalling back to fetch the other Terrors.

As I glance around, I realize that the shadows are shifting all around me. Flickering and wavering. Like water. Strange. I walk toward the edge of the tunnel and lift my hand. A window, a giant arched slab of curved glass, stretches overhead. Water wavers on the other side of the pane, around and above me.

What is this place?

I don't have time to examine further before Tesq appears in midair next to me and drops with a thump that makes the floor shake.

"Boo! We didn't swap dicks this time." Creep pouts. "Well, fingers crossed for the next one. BRB."

He disappears.

Tesq turns toward me. I'm not sure how I know, since I can't see much of anything right now, but I do.

"Wish we had some light," I mutter.

Suddenly, Tesq's palm glows with a little pool of lava in the middle. "Light?"

It's not much, but he's able to extend his hand and reveal what's on the other side of the windowed archway we're under.

In addition to water, just past the glass wall, there's the strangest sort of brush I've ever seen. It's like an underwater hillside full of…plants…or rocks? I'm not certain what they are, never having seen anything like them before.

Leaning close, nose nearly pressed to the glass, I examine them. Bright-yellow tubes, stones that resemble brains, brown branches like bare bushes, spiny balls that may be giant sweet gum tree seeds swollen to the size of my fist. There's an entire world of rainbow colors in that water, and I spot a few bright fish darting back and forth too.

Of course, scattered amongst the beautiful alien-strange world, there are stark-white bones, human skeletons covered in mussel shells, and skeletons that look like they belong to teeth—massive, strangely shaped creatures with rib cages that look large enough for me to walk through.

"What is this place?" I ask, awed but also a little scared.

I've never seen anything like this before.

"Aquarium," Tesq replies.

I don't have time to ask what that word means before Dev's delivered in werewolf form with a snarl and Creep is muttering about how the portal is cheating him.

"Fucking gave me a werewolf ear instead of the dick I asked for. This is bullshit, Universe. Bullshit!" Creep strokes a fur-covered black triangle on the side of his head, which I can only see after Tesq lifts his lava-coated hand to light the blue monster's handsome face. "Actually, that's pretty soft," Creep murmurs, his expression softening as he pets the ear a second time. "Relaxing."

"Stop that," Dev orders, looking a little comical with a smooth pointed blue ear that's a stark mismatch to the rest of him.

But instead of acknowledging Dev, Creep simply says, "Back in a minute!" and poof!

With Dev here, the glass tunnel suddenly feels cramped, which is funny, because he and Tesq are both equally giant in their own ways. Tesq's personality just doesn't extend outward, probably because he's not trying to project macho-asshole vibes every second of the day.

I glare at the Devourer, and he matches my expression with a scowl of his own.

Speaking of macho-asshole vibes, Chase and Em arrive with one arm slung over Creep's shoulder. Looking dazed and about to puke from the thrilling experience of portal travel—which I can empathize with—Chase wobbles when Creep releases him and steps back.

Is Creep concerned about his cargo? Not at all. He's too busy pulling his pants open, checking down the front and saying, "Sonofabitch!"

"Is his dick too small?" Dev jabs, eyes narrowed on the sole human.

"No. Didn't swap. Again! Ugh." Creep's foot stomp is a bit amusing.

"I want my ear back."

"Yeah. Yeah. After. Let's go swimming first! Everybody, get naked." Creep strips in under a second before he claps his hands together and does a jaunty little spin, one that makes his vine-covered horns nearly scrape the glass ceiling.

I try not to stare at his ass as I shuck my own boots, pants, and shirt. I leave on my undergarments, though.

Why?

I guess it's a false sense of modesty since everyone but Chase has seen me naked, but still. When I glance over at the human in question, his shirt is stuck halfway off, caught on his arrogant head. I'm not sure if it's stuck because he was gawking at me or because of pain.

"Do you know what the word *off* means, or do you need me to explain it to you?" I ask, opting for sarcasm because that's my go-to with that man.

"Yeah, well, you've still got a few things on. Maybe I just like my shirt like this," he retorts, though with the way his elbow is propped up above his skull, there's no chance.

I sigh. He must be hurting and not want to admit it.

Typical man.

Walking over to him, I reach up and grab onto the shirt, yanking it off. But when I reach for Chase's ripped pants, Dev growls.

"I'll do that. You follow Creep."

Does he think he's being subtle? 'Cause he's not.

"Don't you get anywhere near Chase's dick," Em hisses, taking control of Chase and making his green eyes appear so bright they almost glow with fury.

"Then get your own damn pants off," Dev retorts, brandishing his claws.

Em grunts and swallows a stiff gasp of pain, but the pants come off, leaving Chase in only boxer shorts. My eyes can't help but notice his abs this time, which are amazing and defined despite the bruises scattered across them.

"Enough ogling. Let's ogle as we splish-splash!" Creep calls out impatiently. "Follow me. Tesq, light the way."

My gargoyle lumbers after the monster in the closet, and I'm not far behind. Tesq ends up letting both his hands become our lava lamps as we follow after Creep, a motley little parade.

I'm about to ask what an aquarium is when a huge shadow flies overhead, and I duck, whisper-shouting, "Teeth!"

Creep stops walking and glances up, eyes tracking a shadow that coils and turns in the waves above us. "Oh no. That's not a tooth," he states. "It's a shark. We're going swimming in their tank."

Curiosity coats my stomach as we go through a doorway and trudge up a flight of industrial-looking stairs. Creep always finds wild and whimsical things to do, but he's also a monster. His idea of fun and mine…

"Is this dangerous?" I ask.

"Nah." He flicks a dismissive hand. "They're too slow to do any damage."

"They aren't teeth?"

"Nope. Just animals. In the before times, people were scared of them, so they'd catch them and toss them in this tank, then walk underneath. Mocking the sharks, I think. One of those 'come and get me' type of things, I think. Not sure. Didn't really visit this place back then, just heard about it from kids I scared."

I try to imagine the before times and people coming here to mock some huge animal, but the whole concept is so far-fetched that I have a hard time with it. Why would people want to lord over animals?

But then I recall the way that kids taunted birds in the resistance, tossing rocks or sticks at them. I wonder if people came to the aquarium and threw things at the sharks. Humans transform into mean bastards when we think we have a bit of an advantage.

We emerge at the top of this massive glass bowl, filing out into a giant, humid room in single file. We stand on a narrow platform that can't be more than three feet wide, encircling the entire pool. From this vantage point, looking down at the water and the plants and sharks, everything resembles a bowl of blue soup left to settle, all the ingredients sinking to the bottom of the dish.

Above us, a few leaf-coated skylights let in solitary rays of light here and there, which dapple the water. The overall effect is not quite as enchanting as the forest stream I'd been hoping for, but it is pretty.

"How are the sharks still here after all these years?" I wonder.

"Oh, these guys are part of Em's menagerie," Creep informs me, and I glance over at Empty, who shrugs carelessly as he gazes out across the water.

"They're useful."

"Yup. He breeds them. Because this is his garbage bin when he's done with a body. He feeds them to his babies here."

"The fuck?!" That outburst comes from Chase's mouth, and all of our heads swivel to watch the human reaction burst out, when just a moment before, Empty clearly had the reins.

I'm assuming that Chase isn't too happy about this revelation.

"Look, that's not going to happen to you." It's strange how a tiny tilt of the head can tell me exactly who's talking.

"Damn straight it's not."

"Not until we're separated, at least," Empty mutters.

"Maybe I'll just take that fucking potion until I die."

Chase's face screws up into an expression of fury so intense it's comical—both beings are clearly battling for control. It makes me wonder if some sort of internal argument is occurring too. If they're in the same body, do they share thoughts?

Creep chuckles at the sight, his blue claws clutching at his belly. He only adds fuel to the fire when he teases, "Bet you want to punch that fucker right in the face, huh?"

The rest of us, even Dev, burst into laughter that echoes across the massive room, ricocheting from the metal walls and returning to us as tinny, musical notes.

The waves on the water seem to grow bigger in response to our amusement. Near Creep's place on the platform, the water begins frothing and churning. A second later, a huge gray shark surges to the surface and opens its mouth, displaying row after row of dagger-like teeth.

Adrenaline and fear shoot through me like bullets. Holes appear in my stomach, and all the amusement leaks out as if it's blood.

Holy shit, that fucker has to be forty feet long.

I take a step back, but Creep turns toward me, a challenge in his eyes. "Scared?"

Of course I can't back down after he's asked me that. I may be a little intimidated by the size of that thing's teeth, but I just froze a fucking sandworm.

You can do this shit, Aliana.

Sharks are nothing.

Because you're a goddamned monster.

It's fucking strange to think that, but also slightly empowering.

I move forward on the cement platform and square off against my blue mate. "Not even a little. How are we doing this?"

"We dive in. We're going to play tag. If the sharks try to play, just hit them on the nose."

"Are you fucking kidding me?" Chase's panic reverberates off the glassy room. "That thing can swallow us whole!"

Chase's body jerks, and his head tilts again, a creepy smile coming over his face. "Not whole. Two bites. Much messier. More fun."

Before they can fall into a long argument, Creep yells, "Dev, you're it!" and he swan dives off the platform next to me.

A second later, Dev cannonballs in werewolf form. They both swim circles around the sharks. I watch, not hesitating, but getting a feel for their movements, for the sharks and how they whip their tails. I set one foot in front of the other, preparing to launch myself off the platform.

"Aliana!" Chase's voice rings out with concern.

I turn to gaze into his emerald eyes, which are full of both fear and reprimand.

"You don't know how to swim."

I shrug. "Doesn't look that hard."

"I'll help," Tesq offers, and his lava hand clasps mine, going dark and cooling at my touch.

Together, hand in hand, we jump off the platform into the water.

And then we sink like fucking stones.

I had no idea water could be so heavy. That if enough of it piled on top of you, it could weigh as much as a brick.

As Tesq and I slide down, down, down, I start to panic. I glance over at my gentle giant, and as if he can read my mind, he pulls me into his body. I think he's going for a hug, but his hands move down to my legs and find my feet. His palms slide under my feet and then he shoves me upward.

I shoot through the water like a rocket: up, up, up.

Bursting past the surface, I fly up into the air and arch above the water. For a second, I feel like a seagull, a bird coasting above the waves. But gravity does its thing, and I'm yanked back toward the water, smacking into it face-first.

Ouch!

If it weren't for Dev's arm shooting out and grabbing me, I may have sunk right back to the bottom like Tesq, who is glowing slightly orange sixty feet beneath me. But Dev's furry forearm contracts around my chest and holds me aloft so that I'm bobbing on the surface, inhaling the scent of salt-water and wet dog.

I cough out the liquid I've inhaled as Dev murmurs, in a voice softer than he's ever used before, "Don't worry. I've got you."

In any other circumstance, I might fight the overgrown beast. I might rage or snark at him and his controlling nature. But my lungs are still aching from the pressure of deep water, my breathing is shallow, and, in this moment, his overprotectiveness is exactly what I need. So I cling to him.

His furry claws rub gently over my spine. Up and down.

After I've cleared the water from my lungs and conquered my out-of-control heartbeat, I find the ability to speak.

"Tesq?" I query, wondering if the other Terror needs a rescue from the awful pressure of that water.

"He's stone. He doesn't have to breathe all the time. He's fine," Creep calls out.

I'm glad it's the elf-like monster who answers me because I trust him and take his word for it.

I also glance down and see my gargoyle walking slowly along the bottom of this giant tank, bending and touching the various plants with a very Tesq-like curiosity. My anxiety retreats, and I look into Dev's glowing red eyes.

Instead of the usual fire banked in them, right now they resemble gently glowing embers. There's something more tranquil there, and I'm not certain if it's this space or the water or what exactly is soothing the dominant Terror. But I'll take it.

So I let myself float aloft in his arms as he maneuvers us both so we're doing belly-up backstrokes around the pool. It's peaceful, so much so that my eyes start to close.

But then I see a gray triangle shape emerge from the water, heading toward us. I stare at it, trying to understand what it is, tapping Dev on the chest and pointing.

"Get behind me, mate." He issues the order, but he's already moving me so that I'm piggy-backing and his body is between me and the threat.

The shark shoots toward us with a speed I wasn't expecting after Creep's claim that they're slow.

Lie.

That fucker's so quick my eyes can hardly take him in. My pulse blasts through my veins, recognizing a threat when it sees one.

Immediately, I wonder when Em last fed his pets.

The fish opens its mouth to reveal jagged sets of teeth, and suddenly, regret pools in my stomach.

I should have stayed onshore like Chase, who's been dipping in one leg at a time to wash, splashing himself with water, sticking to the platform.

Fuck me.

The shark pushes forward a swell of water that crashes over us as it surfaces at a blistering pace.

Luckily, unbelievably, Dev's faster than the fish.

His claw shoots out and scrapes four jagged red lines across the shark's nose, and the force of his hit sends the shark reeling sideways, off course. I clamp my arms down harder across Dev's furry chest, though I can't even begin to describe the relief coursing through me when he bats away a bastard that's as long as a multistory building is tall.

If the shark were a dog, I'd imagine it would whimper. Its big black eyes look like shiny marbles as it glances back at us repentantly before it retreats.

"See. Slow?" Creep calls out.

I chuckle, but the sound is hollow because my adrenaline is still racing.

"Guess what, Aliana!" Creep taunts as he swims. "Dev touched you. He was it. That means you're it now." The blue bastard sticks his tongue out at me before he dives under the waves.

I frown, wishing I could yell after him that I'm not playing, but he won't be able to hear under the water.

Dev pulls me toward his side so he can turn his head and see me. His ruby eyes snag mine, and he whispers, "Ride on my back, and I'll help you get him."

There's an urgent playfulness to his tone that I've never heard before. Of course, the arch of his furred brow is still as cocky as ever, even though the blue ear takes his entire scary alpha persona down a peg. But this impish side of the Devourer is new to me, and it's a facet I want to explore.

I give him a wide grin as I nod, and a genuine smile spreads across his face as he helps me "saddle up" on his back and lock my ankles around his waist.

"Let's go take the blue fucker down," he mutters.

My response: "Yippee ki yay!"

ALIANA

Dev and I cut a sharp line through the water, chasing Creep, who decides to mimic the sharks by swimming around with only his horns peeking above the waves.

Jerk.

"Get me close enough to kick him," I command.

For once, Dev doesn't argue with my orders, just chuckles as he lowers his chest into the water and begins to propel his arms in wide sweeping motions, moving us forward.

Creep is a surprisingly good swimmer, which makes no sense to me because I can't think of any scenario in which he'd ever have needed to swim. He can portal wherever he wants. But his legs are circling like eggbeaters behind him, and he's cruising through the water, punching those sharks whenever they get too close.

Dev taps my thigh and points down, whispering, "Hold your breath."

I do just before he dives three feet beneath the surface. Unlike when I sank with Tesq, at this level, the water isn't terrible. It stings my eyes a bit, but there's no squeezing pressure inside my rib cage, just the strangeness of water flowing continuously over my face as Dev propels us toward Creep.

I let go of Dev's furry chest to extend one of my hands toward that bark-like blue leg of Creep's, past the bubbles he's leaving behind as he churns up waves. Almost there. Almost—

The fucker portals.

"Goddam—" My mouth floods with water as I start to curse, and Dev quickly shoots us up to the surface, where my anger is interspersed with a hacking coughing fit.

"Aren't you even going to try?" Creep calls out as he lazily lies on the surface and backstrokes across the far side of the pool.

"Dickwad," I grouse under my breath while I secretly wonder if I could just make this whole fricking tank into a popsicle to freeze the cocky bastard in place.

I won't test it because of Tesq, who's still wandering around the bottom, but I definitely fantasize about it.

"Don't worry, kitten. We'll get him. Get those claws ready."

It's the first time that Dev's used that nickname and it hasn't annoyed the crap out of me. Right now, we're both on the exact same page. "Let's do it."

He signals with his claws, and I hold my breath before we dive a second time, this time going deeper.

That strategy doesn't help because one of the sharks notices us. The massive torpedo-shaped creature turns in a slow circle that sends prickles up my arms. He swims deftly towards us, and Creep portals right into the shadow underneath the beast's belly. My bastard monster grins at us from the shadows, sticking his thumbs in his mismatched ears and wiggling his fingers before portalling right back out and leaving us to deal with a charging shark.

Motherfucker!

Instead of letting Dev take care of this one, I brace my legs against him and lean out as far as I can. I imagine those ice spears that I shot at the sandworm, hoping against logic that magic really is as easy and instinctive as my mates claimed.

A javelin of ice flies from my palm right into the beast's mouth. While I don't see a streak of blood or any damage, the spear goes right into its gullet. Either the cold or the internal injury stops the shark on the spot. Its body shudders and shakes as if it wants to vomit.

I'm not sure if fish can vomit, but Dev doesn't wait around to find out. He kicks hard and propels us up to the surface. As soon as we've caught our breaths, he pulls me in front of him so that I cling like a koala. Reaching over his shoulder, he collects one of my hands and threads my fingers together with his massive claws. He stares down at our interlinked digits for a moment before looking back up at me.

"That was…hot," he confesses.

Is the Devourer actually admitting he likes that I can stand up for myself? That I can fight and use magic?

"Actually, I'm pretty sure it was cold." I deliberately misunderstand Dev's words, and he rolls his red eyes before scanning the surface of the water for our target.

Creep is popping from spot to spot, cheating like the magnificently underhanded bastard he is.

"We're never going to catch him normally," I murmur, wondering whether I should leave our hands linked or not.

"We just have to get close enough to clock that idiot—" Dev starts to disagree.

"Or we have to tempt him to get close enough to us," I say.

"How the hell are we—" Dev stops talking when I lean up, pushing my face closer to his. Untangling our fingers and looping my arms back around his neck, I enjoy my moment of superiority as I stare confidently up into those ruby eyes. "Like this."

And then I yank on his neck and pull his werewolf face down to mine for a kiss. Our mouths connect, and something feral bursts open inside of me, like an animal that's been caged for years finally escaping its confines and running free. A reeling, unsteady and unstable sort of ecstasy fills me, as if I'm about to stumble but rushing forward so quickly that momentum alone is keeping me upright.

Shit.

The kiss was supposed to be a strategy. Just a silly, stupid move to drag Creep's ass back to us out of jealousy. But when Dev's tongue sweeps out from between his fangs and tangles with mine, I find myself lost. A bit loopy.

My eyelids start to flutter closed, as if this kiss is real. My heart beats faster, particularly when his warm claws cup my ass, the heat of him seeping right through my underwear. All our arguments, his ridiculous, possessive, controlling nature, the ongoing anger and resentment I should be feeling… It all fades.

A low rumble emerges from his chest, something that almost resembles a purr, and the sound calls to me like nothing ever has before. It sinks deep into my bones and rattles the marrow there, churning it until lust seeps from the very core of me. Matches alight. Christmas lights flicker one by one, as if they're strung along my skin, starting at my center and pulsing all the way down to my toes.

I think he can sense it, that my response is different than it's ever been before.

Before, we were hatred and anger and desperation even as our bodies came together. Today, I invited the kiss.

How foolish of me.

Might as well have invited a vampire inside, like in the old human stories. Now, my very blood is abandoning its duties, forsaking my veins, and rushing to any spot that's connected to Dev's body.

My nipples harden through the thin bra where they brush against his chest. My stomach prickles and heats against his fur-covered torso. My legs slide lasciviously up and down over his back, feeling the swish of his tail in the water. The hairs on my arms stand at attention, and goose bumps born of anticipation prickle along my neck when his palms press me more firmly against him so that I can feel him lengthening against me, hardening.

Dev moves his kiss to my jaw and then glides his warm tongue down my neck, creating an entire tidal wave's worth of emotions. I feel simultaneously vulnerable and treasured as his tongue sails over my pulse, those knife-sharp teeth hovering just above my skin. The warm puff of his breath against my clavicle and the shallow nature of his breathing tell me I'm not the only one affected.

It's tempting to forget that there's even anyone else here. But we're not alone.

Glancing up through half-lidded eyes, I spot Empty watching from the platform, boxers shoved down his thighs, cock in hand, stroking. I can tell it's him based merely on his expression and the way he's double-fisting his cock.

For some reason, the fact that he's watching turns me on further—maybe because I've acknowledged he is my mate, realized that I'm at least part monster, and finally admitted that there's a darker side to myself. A side that goes beyond vengeance and revels in violence for its own sake.

A wake bursts across Dev's back, and I see Creep bobbing behind his shoulder. The kiss worked exactly as intended, luring him over. Only now, I'm not certain I want the kiss to stop, not when the Devourer's lifting my torso from the water and shoving down the cup of my bra, his muzzle lowering toward my nipple.

His warm mouth closes over the stiff tip, and the experience is different than anything I've ever felt before. A human mouth can round itself and suckle, but his muzzle is made for lapping, so the long, flat strokes across my areola are a new sensation.

He pulls back just long enough to promise, "I'm going to wreck you, but only in all the right ways."

"Holy fuck, yes," Creep breathes, the voyeur in him taking over as those eyes of his grow wide and sparkle as bright as stars.

My stomach clenches as my fingers thread through Dev's mane. He glances up from where he's lapping at my breast, and my stomach coils, heat welling up inside my center.

Dev gives me a smirk as his lapping grows faster and faster. He cups my ass harder and slowly starts to slide me up and down against his length, which has swollen until it's massive, a size that's intimidatingly unthinkable to take, but feels so fucking good as it rubs against my opening.

"Are we playing a different game now?" Creep asks naughtily.

Barely able to crack open my eyes, my answer is throaty and full of desperation. "I think so. And Dev is definitely *it*."

16

ALIANA

My werewolf smirks, revealing his fangs as he looms over me. In his massive arms, I feel small and delicate. But—unlike prior times when I've resented that feeling—right now, staring up at his broad, dark chest, I absolutely adore it.

Instead of his strength restraining me, it feels like it's seeping into me. Entranced, my teeth digging into my lower lip, our gazes lock for a moment as we bob on the surface of the pool, his black fur matted by the water and my own white streaked locks plastered against my head.

Reflections dance off the water and his eyes, making them sparkle. Or maybe they're sparkling because of my last words.

"Gonna tag me?" I tease.

"More than once," he responds, his tone husky.

And then Dev tilts his head, lifting me at the same time, a motion that drags me against the underside of his stiff cock. If the gusset of my panties wasn't already soaked from our swim, it would be now. Water sluices down my sides and the air prickles my arms as everything above my thighs rises out of the water.

In a daze, I do little more than patiently open my mouth for him when he gives me another kiss, tongue striking out. My lips tingle at the contact, at the way his body demands a response from mine.

Fingers twisting into the black hair at the back of his head, I do my best to return his dominant overtures, though my tongue is tiny in comparison. Realizing my fight is mild at best when he's full beast size, I decide that adding teeth to the battle is fair game, and I bite down on Dev's tongue first until it retreats. Then I chase him with my mouth and roughly snap down on his lower lip.

He likes that. A groan erupts from him, and my brutal mate pulses his claws against my ass, just enough to mark but not enough to hurt me.

His hips jut up against me, and the throb of his hot cock distracts me for a moment, ribbons of pleasure weaving through my brain and tying up my thoughts. My limbs somehow melt but also become desperately needy, which is an utter contradiction, but it doesn't matter because I'm beginning to taste the edge of euphoria. I want to swallow it whole.

I wrap my legs tighter, cinching around him, and though I feel his body against nearly every bit of mine, somehow it's not quite enough. I need more. I graze my palms over his broad back, trying to touch every muscle, unable to reach across the vast expanse and reveling in that fact.

Frustrated with my inability to win the battle of kisses, I move my mouth down to his neck and sink my teeth in there. His pulse throbs hot beneath his skin, and the pressure against my mouth is satisfying in a way that it's never been before. A wicked surge of pleasure rolls over me at feeling his life force against my tongue, vulnerable to my teeth. I bite down harder, determined to mark him.

"Aliana," Dev moans, and the sound kicks off a compulsion to swivel my hips against him.

Fixated on the burning-hot head of his dick pressed against my most sensitive spot through the thin fabric of my panties, I decide to use him to seek my own pleasure.

Up and down, I slide along his length, which is lubricated by warm precum that drips from his tip and clings to his skin. Faster. Faster. A pulsing thrill builds inside, and I chase it higher.

My furious movement nearly unsettles his ability to keep us afloat. We sink down into the water, the temperature change making me gasp, the cold water flooding in and drenching the fire I've been stoking. Apparently, my body isn't immune to the chill even though I have ice powers now; it's merely immune to too much heat.

Dammit. Half of my hips and ass end up beneath the surface, and I pause, my short breaths puffing against his chest as I look up at him in askance.

"Can't handle me?" I taunt, though my heart rate is telling me I may be the one unable to handle this encounter.

"Don't you dare stop," Dev growls, one of his claws shoving my ass, forcing it to move as his legs resume the circles they've been churning to keep us aloft, and I rise out of the water once more.

Creep swims sideways through the water, his long arms cutting expertly as he circles around the Devourer to get closer to me, a hungry look in his eyes as he watches me ride the other Terror.

Dev swivels me so that Creep is behind his back once more, blocked from the werewolf's view and also blocked from watching me.

"Keep rubbing yourself against my cock, kitten."

Creep tries again, swimming closer, and Dev continues to spin me, ignoring the other Terror with such intensity that I get a sense of sibling-level rivalry. Like one brother batting away the other.

It's both distracting and annoying because he's ruining my tempo—disrupting the moment and reminding me how selfish he truly is.

Slowing my pace, I deliberately slide softly down the ridge of his cock this time, decreasing that friction we both crave. "What's wrong with sharing, Dev?"

"No!" His snarl ripples like its own wave across my skin.

It feels like a challenge.

"But don't you want to feel how tight I'll get if you're in my pussy while Creep takes my ass?" My query starts as a jest, intended to rib him, but by the end, I'm picturing that very scenario with such intensity that there's nothing remotely funny about it.

Two at once. I've had Creep take me in both holes before, but Tesq only held me. He didn't actually fuck me. What would it feel like to be sandwiched between two monsters, both wild and bucking, driven mad by the feel of my body? What would it feel like to have both of them lose control and come inside of me?

Under my panties, my pussy starts to flutter against Dev's cock, but I slow my motions even further, dulling the sensation because I don't just want to come now. I want *that*. That experience of watching Dev and Creep both give in to their base instincts, both claiming me but submitting to my desire. Letting me have them both at once, not because they want it that way, but because I do.

The power rush of such a vision makes me nearly giddy. My body purrs in expectation. I lick my lips as I stare up at the Devourer's muscular form, water droplets dripping down his black pelt and massive pecs.

"I'm your mate, Dev."

A thrum of approval starts to rumble through his chest but cuts off when I add, "That means you're going to do what *I* want. You're going to fuck me together. And then you're going to admit how much you like it."

Dev's eyes glow like coals stolen from the depths of hell. Immediately, I know I've crossed a line.

"No." His tone is low and sharp.

A tiny fringe of fear shreds the edges of the lust that's been weaving lacy patterns across my skin as Dev stops circling. The game of keep-away ends when he starts determinedly kicking, putting distance between us and Creep.

I glance over Dev's massive, furry shoulder to see the antlered blue monster bobbing behind us, staying in place and shaking his head at me. Clearly, he's more aware of the line than I am.

Do I care that I've angered Dev?

Not really. Last time, anger pushed us into the best, most intense sex I could imagine. This time, I'm going to use that anger to push him so far past the edge that he's blind with lust.

And then...once he's there, I'm going to get my way.

I try to silently communicate this to Creep with a look. I think he gets it because the corner of his mouth ticks up in a naughty half grin.

"I didn't tell you to stop grinding on my cock. If you stop again, I'm going to have to punish you. And you're already going to get it for that little proposal. So move those hips." Dev's threat slinks down and tightens my nipples.

Yes, my fire-breathing fuck buddy. Get all worked up and angry.

I bite my lip to hide my smile as I pretend to comply with his orders, let him think he's in charge.

"I was just swimming close to tell you that there's a shallow area off to the left," Creep calls out behind us, one hand cupped to his mouth, the other pointing helpfully even though Dev can't see it. "One where you could lay our mate down and pleasure her as the water laps at her toes."

"SHUT UP!" Dev's order rings through the room, and even Chase startles at the sound from his perch on the far side of the pool.

Unable to swim, he merely watches.

My werewolf glares back down at me, where I've frozen. His expression is nothing short of unhinged as he cups my ass tighter with his palm. Tighter, but not roughly. No, he gently and deliberately resumes movement on my behalf, lifting and lowering my entire body along the length of his shaft, jostling my soaked panties until they slide down just enough to bare my clit.

"Mine, Aliana. Mine."

"Yours."

His cock pulses when I say that word, and a new bead of precum slides down to drip warmly over my clit. My eyes start to flutter at that sensation. I can't resist poking the beast as we get closer to the cement beach that rises gently out of the pool.

"But you're mine too, you know," I add. "Which means you are going to give me what I want."

"I'm going to make you choke on my cock for—"

"Yes. Yes, make me choke on it. Pull my hair and fuck my face. But don't you dare come down my throat. You save it for my pussy." My nipples are stiff, poking through the thin fabric of my bra, and I rub them across his chest. His hair teases my sensitive skin, making my breasts feel more swollen and heavy than ever before. God, I ache for that massive tongue of his to lick them.

"You don't get to decide—"

"Yes, I do." I smirk when Dev's cock pulses despite his angry words.

His tone may argue that he's in charge, but his dick can't lie.

I grind against him, bringing my lips as close to the shell of his ear as I can get, considering he's twelve feet tall in this form. "You're going to stay in this form and let me take all of that giant dick. You're going to make me take it, and you're going to muffle my screams with your hand."

I paint a picture that he can't resist. The illusion of force. Of control.

With a roar, Dev's hands reach up and lift me. His claw curls underneath the leg openings of my panties, slicing roughly through them and leaving the wispy thing floating away behind me on the surface of the water.

Then his mouth opens in a wild howl that bares his teeth as he slams me down on his cock. The fact that we're in the water dulls the impact, and we both groan in frustration, because even though the stretch is epic, it doesn't come with the friction or bone-pounding sensation we're both craving.

He wants to be cruel, and right now, I'm salivating to feel that roughness. The madness. I want us both frenzied.

Despite his clear anger at Creep, Dev proceeds to the exact spot the blue monster suggested, probably because it's the only space in the entire room where we'll have enough room to lie down and fuck as angrily as we both need. He swims the remainder of the way one-handed, still pumping me up and down on his dick with the other. His thrusts are brisk and shallow, just enough of a promise of more to come to keep me edging closer to the promise of an orgasm.

Over his shoulder, I spot Creep swimming for my panties. My blue monster gathers them up and makes a show of deliberately licking right up the gusset as his shoulder pumps up and down, hand obviously wrapped around his cock beneath the water. He strokes off to my taste, lewdly and unashamed.

The sight makes me hot and even more determined to get what I want.

The heat of Dev's cock and the gentle friction between us in the water make my eyes roll back in my head. It's a drawn-out tease of sensation that goes on just long enough to leave me on the brink of madness.

The scent of him or of the saltwater, or the combination of the two, messes with my head, adding somehow to the experience. I keep drawing in deep breaths even though I swear my lungs are shrinking because I can't seem to get enough air. By the time we reach the cement bank at the edge of the water and Dev starts to wade up with me in his arms, I'm panting.

Lightheaded and clinging to him, I stare up at his muzzle. I nearly forget my diabolical plan as the unrelenting need to be fucked hard manifests in small, soft sounds. Not quite begging, but close. Needy moans.

God, I need to be held down and fucked within an inch of my life.

To my surprise, he sits down in the shallows, where water is still lapping around our ankles. He doesn't go up onto the completely dry bit of floor above. My legs are still wrapped around his waist, locked into place after being in one position for so long, and he ends up reaching out to gently unwind them. His soft palms slide up the outside of my calves, over my kneecaps, and then gently up my inner thighs.

Expectation sends a whimper up my throat, and my mind zooms ahead of his motions, already imagining what it's going to feel like when he cups me.

Massive palms that nearly match my thighs in width spread me wide before pushing me backward off his lap, off his dick.

No!

I land with a thump on the platform, the water breaking what otherwise might have been an uncomfortable fall.

But…but…

"You've been bad, Aliana." Dev is on his hands and knees, looming over me as dangerous and deadly as a nightmare.

Fuck. That shouldn't be hot. I should argue.

But my tongue gets tangled when his claw reaches down and swipes at my bra, severing it so that the cups fall open and display my breasts for him. My nipples are little ruby peaks and strain toward his mouth, my back arching without any conscious thought telling it to do so.

I blink up at him.

That tongue has never looked so tempting. I want it on me. In me. Now.

Instead, Dev reaches down with his index finger and uses his long, sharp claw to scratch a solid line from my chest down to my belly button, going just deep enough to draw blood.

The tiny bit of pain is nothing compared to the desire sparking in his eyes or the way he leans down and laps at the tiny beads of red. Fuck. That hot, wet tongue is perfect.

My entire body squeezes tight as I lean back on my elbows and let him lick my torso. Once. Twice. Even though his tongue isn't touching the spots I want, there's an echoing pulse from my body, a phantom sensation as he laps at me.

Eyelashes fluttering closed, I'm shocked when the air moves around me, and suddenly, I'm flying, spinning, flipped over. My stomach crashes into the saltwater, and that ragged red line up my stomach becomes a biting sting as Dev's palm presses down on my back and forces my torso into the inch of shallow water.

Smack! His other hand collides with my bare ass in a harsh spanking that makes me gulp.

Asshole.

"You will remember your place, kitten." Dev's tone is smug as he lands blow after blow, making my ass flare with pain.

I grit my teeth and swallow the words that I want to spit at him. I focus on planting my hands and pushing myself out of the water, eliminating this saltwater sting. He pins me down, chuckling when I squirm uselessly in his grip.

I'm going to kill him. Forget fucking. I'm going to murder—

Just as I start to snarl, his clawed hand reaches between my legs, and his fingers drag over the edges of my slit, teasing me just enough to silence me. The writhing pit of red anger in my stomach is tinted pink with lust, and I realize he's trying to do nearly the same thing to me that I planned to do to him. Make me lose control. Drive me to angry, lust-filled madness.

Well, I won't. I refuse.

He's not going to win.

I sneak one of my hands closer to my body and twist my palm. Hoping that instinct will help me keep my magic subtle, I imagine freezing the droplets of blood lining my scratch, forming a protective barrier from this saltwater punishment. An ice-cold line slowly snakes down my breasts and over my stomach, stopping just above the crackling heat of my pussy, where Dev's fingers are expertly fanning the flames.

I debate reaching back and trying to touch his dick, which brushes heavily against my thigh every few seconds, almost as if he can't resist, but I decide that pretending he has control means that I should orgasm for him, making him think I'm soft and compliant afterward.

Yes, this is a winning strategy. I'm a genius. Orgasming and then one-upping the werewolf. I'm not sure life gets better.

"Dev." I make my tone breathy, a wispy remnant of what it normally is. It's not a hard thing to do, considering how his huge claws are dragging up and down the entire length of my slit.

His fingers amp up the sensation and circle my clit, and the smugness in his tone is apparent as he says, "You have something to say, little kitten?"

"I— I—"

He pinches my clit lightly, rubbing it between his fingers, his claws so near to my delicate skin that they add an exquisite edge of danger to his motions.

"You want to apologize?" He amps up his teasing by bringing his precum-covered cock between my legs from behind and pumping it deliciously along my inner thighs.

My breasts swell, and even without being touched, a tingling sensation runs from my nipples down my stomach to join with the roiling heat in my pussy.

"Dev! Yes!" I add the *yes* to let him think I'm responding to his question, when I'm really just responding to his motions, to the way he's started to tug my clit in a tiny little circle.

Lustrous streaks start to glimmer in my vision, and my entire body fills with heat, buzzing and beaming.

The one word must be enough for now because the Devourer indulges me, quickening his pace and letting me fall over the edge. My muscles tighten as my bones melt, and my body is overwhelmed with a delectable blaze of pleasure. Gluttonous, I buck against the Devourer's hand, drawing the sensation out for as long as possible, until my arms are barely able to hold up my trembling body.

Fuck.

Oh god.

It's not until Dev's hot cock has slid into me, stretching me and making me tremble, that I remember my plan.

Shit. He's fucking me from behind, and there's no way Creep can join in this position. I have to get him to switch.

The snap of his hips and the resulting jiggle of my ass and breasts make it hard to think. So much sensation at once. Especially with those balls of his, which are twice as thick in this monster form, wrecking me with each and every thrust.

My knees scrape across the pavement when he starts going faster, and a trickle of blood seeps into the water. I follow it dully, my head short-circuiting because my nerve endings have overloaded it.

That's when I spot a lone gray fin.

"Shark," I murmur dazedly, wondering why the fish is so close to the shallows.

Immediately, Dev pulls out of me and spins.

I nearly fall onto my face into the water but catch myself just in time to look over my shoulder and see my werewolf stomping down the ramp of this platform through the shallows. His stiff cock sways with every step, and his fury at having his fuck interrupted makes the very air vibrate.

With a roar that echoes so loudly that I swear the skylights shake in their frames, Dev reaches down and hooks the nosy fish on his claws. Lifting the shark that's five times as long as he is, he hurls the beast through the air. It flies across the room and smacks into the glass before sliding with a squeak back into the water.

Then, with a dominant rage that seems to pulse around him like an aura, Dev turns back to me. His cock hasn't grown soft from this distraction. If anything, it looks harder, jutting up and bouncing against his toned lower belly as he wades back toward me.

The sight of him makes my pussy flutter, and I nearly orgasm just from the intensity of his gaze.

I don't fight when he scoops me up and stomps to the cement shore. I don't argue when he lays me down on my back and throws both legs over his shoulders. I merely gasp when he drives into me all the way to the hilt with a single thrust. The spread, the pinch, the power of his body ripples through me, and I come, tightening on his dick as he rapidly thrusts faster and faster.

"That's it, mate. Show me you're mine."

I do. Clawing at the cement and ripping my fingernails, turning my head side to side as he pounds hard into me, I clench down on his thick cock over and over until I'm utterly wrung out. I can tell by his moans that he's getting close.

Yes.

Yes.

It's time.

Staring up at him through hooded eyes, I manage a half smile as I reach up to cup his muzzle. "That's it, mate. Show me you're mine," I repeat back to him. And then I add, "Creep."

In a flash, I lift from the cement floor, and a body is wedged underneath mine, appearing right in the shadow cast by my body. Blue arms reach around to cup my tits. A thick cock nudges at my back door as Dev's eyes grow wide.

But before the Devourer can react further, Creep's thrusting home, the burning sensation coursing through my over-wrought nervous system and making me buck. Creep twists my nipples, which have been aching for touch for what feels like ages. And I detonate again, tightening.

So fucking full. Two mates at once.

Dev's powerless then, thrusting mindlessly even as curses spill from his lips. But Creep alternates a rhythm with him, and I can tell the Devourer likes it. I can tell as I lie limply back against Creep's scarred chest because Dev's hips start to jerk. I feel his cum splash hotly inside of me, filling me up.

Then, Dev doesn't pull out when Creep takes his turn using my body. The Devourer leans over me, watching it all, feeling the brush of another man's dick through the walls of my body as my other mate claims me.

His eyes burn red lasers into me. But we both know the truth —I've just claimed him back as much as he's ever claimed me.

And he likes it.

17

BARNABAS

INCOMPETENT, useless monsters.

The whole lot of them.

Why the fuck am I letting them live if they can't do one simple job?

It should be a—how did the humans phrase it?—walk in the park to eliminate my son and the rest of those good-for-nothing Terrors.

Yet, Creep and his friends live on, a quarter of my army is dead, and the Empty Man has been set free.

Anger thrums headily through my veins as I stalk down the hall of the prison I converted years ago. It seems fitting to live in a complex that once housed the worst of the worst humans.

After all, what's more depraved and malevolent than a human murderer? A monstrous one.

The individual cells have been made into barracks for my rapidly growing army, and the warden's office has become my very own throne room.

These foolish, idiotic monsters believe I'm eliminating the power structure once and for all—the system that sees monsters moving up in ranks with every life they take.

But you can't change evolution.

We were *born* to kill and maim and destroy. It's in our blood, chiseled onto our souls, written in the motherfucking stars. It's who we are meant to be.

The Terrors have been in power for far too long, and it's time someone took them—what's that saying?—down a peg. Yes, we need to take them down a peg.

If I would've known what my bastard son would become, I would've murdered him when he was an infant. Alas, father-hood had made me soft and *sentimental.* I allowed the fucker to live, unaware of the formidable creature he would turn into with time.

The Terrors aren't just at the top of the food chain because of the power they procured over the years. I'd bet my life that I killed more monsters and humans than all four of them combined.

What makes them powerful is the mere fact that they're nearly impossible to kill—a revelation that sluices in my stomach like acidic candy, even after all these years.

It was why we kidnapped the Empty Man in the first place. My monsters had one job and one job alone—to figure out how to kill a creature who's already dead.

Honestly, it's such a menial task. All of their complaints that it's "too hard" and "impossible" are bullshit.

Nothing is impossible.

So how do I kill four monsters who are basically immortal?

The Grotesque has skin as hard as stone, making it nearly impenetrable. There are rocks that have been around for millions of years. Apparently, even heat can't damage him. Only a damn meteorite will destroy him.

The Devourer may have fleshy skin, but he's strong and fast and ruthless in a fight. His strength and endurance are staggering. He could be stabbed twelve times and still fight like he hasn't been injured. Annoying pest.

And then there's my *beloved* son. The Creeper.

The bastard is too damn fast and stealthy for me to kill.

Now, if there was a way for me to remove his ability to portal…

"Sir. Mishika is here, as requested." My second-in-command moves to keep pace with me, his back perfectly straight and his attention fixed straight ahead.

Tennious has been with me for years now, having reached out after the Devourer destroyed his home. The monster is tall and broad, with snow-white hair styled away from his aristocratic features and a sharp jawline. His humanoid features are juxtaposed by his sharp, triangular ears, scaled arms, and clawed hands.

"Yes, perfect. Thank you, my old friend." I clap Tennious on the shoulder, but his impassive expression doesn't waver.

He simply nods once and then walks away to grab me the girl.

Ah. I love a monster who knows his place in the world—under my heel, inferior to me. And Tennious is most certainly that monster.

Probably why he's one of the only creatures I consider a friend.

The warden's office is large and spacious, with walls painted eggshell white and varnished floorboards. A huge mahogany desk dominates the center of the room, with a high-backed leather chair behind it. When I initially chose the prison as my new home, my workers offered to completely redecorate the office to make it more…homey.

I refused.

I want to *feel* like a warden of the before times.

Powerful.

Imperious.

Confident.

Cruel.

I clasp my hands behind my back and move towards the window looking down into the yard far below. The grass has begun to wither and die, the color more brown than green, and the trees that once dotted the lawn are now twisted in such a way that they crash through the building's windows. It's chaos and beauty in its simplest form.

Otherwise known as perfection.

Sometimes, I wonder what this place would look like full of prisoners. *My* prisoners.

Crying, screaming, and begging for scraps of food I refuse to give them.

How long can a monster survive without sustenance?

Hmm…

Something to ponder…

"Sir." Tennious waits until I turn around to gesture towards the disheveled monster at his side. "Mishika."

The pink, tentacled monster whimpers under the force of my glare, and I take great satisfaction in that. Briefly, I note the blackened state of half her chest, but her injuries are of little consequence.

Tennious moves to stand at my side, a silent sentry, while I keep my focus on the female before me. She lowers her head subserviently, the way she knows I like, and I step forward to run my hand across her sharp jawline.

"Mishika." I tsk my tongue in disapproval. "How could you have let this happen?"

"Sir." Her voice trembles in a way that sends lust straight to my cock. "It was an ambush by the Terrors. We were unprepared and—"

I backhand her across the face with enough force to send her toppling to the ground. A pained whine escapes her.

"You used all of my least favorite words in one sentence," I comment indolently, rubbing my nails on my jacket. "Ambush. Terrors. Unprepared." I crouch before her, watching in grim satisfaction as she attempts to crawl away, before yanking at her pink hair.

She screams as I tug her backwards until she's flush against my chest.

"You and your crew had one job to do—figure out how to kill the Empty Man."

"Y-you can't kill him. You can't kill any of them!" Her tears fall on my hand, which I've moved to curl around her throat.

Such a delicate, tiny thing…

One snap, and poof. She'll be gone forever. Forgotten.

I tighten my grip, cutting off her airways, and she whimpers.

"No creature is invincible, my dear Mishika, least of all my idiot son and his friends." With my free hand, I begin to stroke her sweaty hair, soothing her the way one would an animal or a pet.

Maybe that's all she is—a pet.

My pet.

"Everyone has a weakness, Mishika," I continue in a deceptively soothing voice. "A vulnerability. We just need to find theirs."

My grip tightens.

"I know their weakness." Her voice is a mere rasp, nearly inaudible, but I hear her words as if she shouted them. They cut through the air like the crack of a whip.

I release her, and she slumps forward, breathing heavily, tears streaming down her face.

"Well, why didn't you lead with that, my dear friend?" I ask jovially, straightening from my crouched position and smoothing out my suit coat.

As I move towards Tennious, I catch a glimpse of my reflection in the mirror.

Blond hair lying neatly combed around two antlers.

Bright golden scales rippling down both of my arms.

A similarly colored dragon tail that swishes when I walk.

This… *This* is what a leader is supposed to look like.

How can anyone even think to follow a monster as disgusting as the Grotesque? As savage as the Devourer? As lackadaisical as the Empty Man?

And as idiotic as the Creeper?

No, the monsters of this world need a *true* leader, one who will finally wipe out the humans once and for all and return our world to its true glory.

A cold smile curls my lips as I move to claim the seat behind my desk. Tennious stands at my side, his eyes never straying from our…ahem…esteemed guest.

"The Terrors… They're all in love with the same girl. A human girl." Mishika rubs at her bruised throat as she stares up at me through glossy eyes.

She doesn't stand, though, which is smart on her end. I can easily forget about her incompetence when she's lying prostrate before me like a grateful servant eagerly awaiting her master's cock.

"A human girl…" I scrub at my jawline as I mull over this information. It isn't the first time one of my sources claimed that the Terrors have found their mate, but I haven't believed it until now.

Who could possibly love those four?

149

And what monster would ever be foolish enough to risk his power for a thing as stupid as love?

"Yes." Mishika shakily climbs to her knees, her head lowering to avoid eye contact. "Her name's Aliana."

18

CHASE

ALIANA IS gorgeous when she falls apart. Don't you agree? The Empty Man moans obscenely in my head.

Even though he tries to sound lighthearted and jesting—as I'm beginning to believe is his MO, especially where feelings are involved—I can hear the undercurrent of longing in his voice that he doesn't even bother to hide. The unbridled *need*, which I'm sure is a replica of my own.

Watching Aliana unravel with two of her Terrors caused a deep-seated ache to rise in my chest. It wasn't jealousy, not really, though a part of me will always want to claim Aliana as solely mine.

It was…grief.

Grief that I'll never get to hold her, kiss her, love her the way they were able to.

Grief that I was such a pompous asshole when it was just the two of us, a fool whose idea of romance was pulling on her pigtails.

Grief that I'll never be her mate.

Grief that I'll never be *hers*.

And while Em is surprisingly optimistic for the future, I've been sinking deeper and deeper into my own pit of despair.

How long will it be until Em no longer needs me?

Until he and the rest of the Terrors send me on my way?

Until Aliana decides she's better off without me?

What can I provide her, after all? I'm only a human—and we're not the predators of this world, but the prey.

I can't even blame her for the way her position has changed. Who wouldn't go from hating monsters to caring for them when you're treated the way she's been? Creep and Tesq adore her, pamper and pleasure her, and Dev will protect her fiercely with every ounce of power he's got.

And now, she seems to have some sort of power too, which just increases the divide between us, expanding it into a canyon that seems nearly impossible to cross.

As soon as we returned to Tesq's hideout, I volunteered Em and myself for guard duty. I didn't think I could stay in that room a second longer, watching some of the scariest monsters known to mankind pleasure the woman I love.

I thought I would be jealous seeing her with the others, Em continues, oblivious to my turmoil. *But that was fucking hot! Can we jack one off? Pretty please? I'm so fucking hard right now, it's ridiculous.*

No. We're not going to masturbate. I grunt and fold my arms over my chest, scowling at nothing in particular.

The subway tunnel is quiet and empty—which is exactly what we want but also makes everything immensely eerie. The dank, moist air pervades my nostrils with each inhale, bringing with it the smell of coppery blood, decaying flesh, and piss.

You're a party pooper.

We're on guard. Now shut up, and...guard.

Em's quiet for a moment. But just a moment. I swear this monster loves to hear himself talk more than any person I've ever met. Errr. Any monster.

Do you think Aliana looked at me while she came? I swore we made sweet, beautiful eye contact...

We're not having this conversation. My scowl deepens.

I still have to finish winning her over. He pushes an image into my head of himself rubbing his chin in deep contemplation— well, my chin. Our chin? I still can't wrap my head around the fact I'm sharing a body with none other than the Empty Man himself.

Yeah, well, good luck with that, I gripe.

Where do you think I can get chocolates? And roses? And jewelry? Women like jewelry, do they not? What about water guns? Yes...I think I'm going to get my little mate water guns.

I've been tuning him out, my attention fixed on the left tunnel, when Em's words penetrate my pity-induced daze.

Water guns?

I read an article that said women like water guns. He speaks so matter-of-factly, I can't decide if he's joking or not.

It's always hard to tell with him since his perpetual state seems to be "sarcastic" with a heaping side of "irreverent."

Why the fuck would you get Aliana water guns?

So we can have a water gun fight, of course. I swear, sometimes you're intentionally daft...

"I don't even have a response to that," I say out loud, scrubbing my hand through my tousled blond hair.

I cleaned myself the best I could, considering the fact I was too chickenshit to actually jump into the shark-infested water, but at least I don't stink anymore.

You have a response by claiming you don't have a response.

Em's logic. I fucking swear...

"You can't reason with stupid."

Don't make me take control of the body, pretty boy.

I snort. "Yeah, right. You love to give me control of my body when we're doing boring shit, like guard duty."

I'm stronger than I was when Em first entered me—god, that sounds so fucking sexual even in my head—but nowhere near powerful enough to stop Em from taking over if he ever felt so inclined. And a part of me is terrified that if I choose to fight back, if I push against the intrusion, Em will make me disappear for good.

I'll never make you disappear. Emotion burns and crackles in his voice like an out-of-control fire. *I can't promise you Aliana or a future free of me or anything like that...but I can promise I won't push you away.*

This is my body, not yours. My anger builds and builds and builds, like a snowball rolling down a hill.

I know.

If anyone should leave, it should be you.

I know.

I don't want to disappear.

I know.

My fear and anger burn like dry tinder, reduced to nothing but ashes that will mix together forever. Once they're gone, though, only one emotion remains.

Resignation.

I'm going to be trapped in this cage for the remainder of my human life, watching Aliana fall in love with four different monsters while I'm pushed to the wayside. It won't be long until she forgets about me. And then, when death claims me and my body fades away and withers to dust, she and her monsters will remain.

A knife wedges in my chest, and it suddenly hurts to breathe past the tightness in my throat.

She won't forget about you, Em says. *I won't let her.*

You hate me.

I'll admit that you're growing on me...like a fungus. Or a tumor. Or mold.

Geez. Thanks.

What I'm trying to say, you overdramatic human, is that I may not hate you that much anymore.

A tiny grin unfurls on my lips. *You can just admit that you like me, Emmy.*

Don't call me that.

You like me. Admit it, Emmy.

You know what? I changed my mind. I hate you, and as soon as I'm separated from your body, I'm going to kill you.

I snort out loud. *Yeah, right. You'd miss me too much.*

I'd miss— Wait. Did you hear that? Em's mental voice turns anxious, and I strain my ears.

There, in the distance, farther down the tunnel, are voices.

And a strange retching sound that makes my blood run cold.

I've only read about this particular sound in books, but there's no mistaking the distinct gurgling, clicking noise that permeates the dark tunnel.

Shit! They have a tracker! Panic laces Em's voice.

Trackers are a type of monster that fall somewhere between being a tooth and being a tongue. They hold animalistic intelligence that far surpasses anything found in most teeth. Their long, angular faces are covered in pink pores, and they have huge antennae poking from the tops of their heads.

And as the name suggests, they're fierce trackers, able to find anyone anywhere at any time.

Not a lot of research has been done on them—considering they're thought to be extinct—but I was once told that the pores on their heads provide electromagnetic sensing that can somehow latch on to a person or monster. The tracker *must* see their target in person, at least once, and then they'll be able to track him or her anywhere in the world.

Fuck. Fuck. Fuck.

They found us. Em's voice is uncharacteristically grim.

I thought trackers were extinct?

From what I gathered, the tongues became terrified that one tooth would gain too much power and not have enough intelligence to handle it. And if another tongue were to get their hands on a tracker? It would be chaos—no one would be safe in the cases of grudges and revenge, which are both common occurrences in the monster world.

Em turns quiet in my head.

Em?

They are extinct. Sort of. He pauses, as if bracing himself for my reaction, before blurting out, *But I had one in my menagerie. Those bastards must've stolen him and then used him to track me.*

My spine tightens, and the hair on the back of my neck stands up. At the same time, depression, dark as molasses, sticks to the inside of my ribs. *So they're going after you? Us, I mean?*

I debate the merits of running away to protect Aliana and the others, but I'm terrified of leaving her. What if something happens to her and the others while we're gone? What if we're wrong, and the tracker is actually after one of the others?

We're not leaving, human, Em snaps vehemently.

But the tracker will continue to come after us, even if we all run.

There's an edge of cold, hard fury in Em's voice when he speaks next, and a chill works its way down my spine. *Then we take the fight to them. And we kill every last monster who dare try to attack the Terrors and their mate.*

ALIANA

I'M HAVING a wonderful dream that features me, a beach, and four extremely sexy monsters doting on me hand and foot. There are margaritas involved—the fancy ones with umbrellas I've seen in old, ripped magazines—and foot massages and orgasms.

Lots and lots of orgasms.

But then my happy, blissful bubble is eviscerated when someone bellows, "Aliana! Get up!"

I jerk upright in bed, frowning.

I've fallen asleep on top of Creep—yes, on top, because the bed is way too small to sleep side by side on—and my blue monster appears just as confused as I do. He blinks rapidly and focuses on the figure in the doorway.

Tesq and Dev are both already up. The former chose to sleep on the couch, while the latter became entranced by a puzzle he found in Tesq's collection. It's adorably nerdy, though I'll never admit that to him out loud.

And the other two…

Well…

Chase's chest heaves as he reaches for a huge carving knife Tesq keeps in his kitchen. "Monsters. Lots of them. And a tracker."

All of us are instantly on alert.

Tesq growls something too low for me to hear and then moves to grab a backpack from a shelf. He begins to throw supplies haphazardly into the bag while Fluffy whines at his feet, her front paws extended as she stretches.

Dev's claw elongates with the force of his fury, and coarse black fur explodes on his arms.

"How far away, and how many?" he growls.

Unlike the others, he doesn't reach for a weapon.

He is a weapon all on his own.

"Their voices are muffled but echoing, thanks to the tunnel. I would say a few minutes away. Maybe longer." Chase inspects the blade beneath the flickering Christmas lights before nodding once—probably in response to something Em said internally—and sliding a blade under his belt. "I heard at least six different voices."

"And you said they have a tracker with them?" Creep asks with concern, quickly throwing his clothes back on.

The two of us didn't bother with them once we returned from the aquarium.

I dress as well, back in all black since it will help me blend in inside the tunnels. Then I move to grab my own backpack. I have a gun, but it's low on ammo, a blunt knife, and a bow and arrow. I also have my collection of magical jewels…and my own ice powers.

"They couldn't possibly have a tracker," Dev barks, staring at Chase as if he has a few screws loose. "Trackers are extinct." His tone eloquently implies "duh."

Chase winces nearly imperceptibly. "Errr. Maybe not as extinct as you thought. Because they definitely have one with them. I heard it."

Tesq, who has finally finished filling up his backpack with food, weapons, and other miscellaneous items, shoves the bag into Creep's arms. "You leave now. With Aliana."

"Fuck no!" I protest instantly, my irritation flaring white-hot and blistering as I glare straight on at my mask-free gargoyle.

His deep black eyes are unrelenting, but I don't back down, crossing my arms.

Overprotective idiot.

Didn't I prove myself at the meat factory when I not only saved the Empty Man but also killed a monster and escaped through its tunnel? I'm not a defenseless human anymore.

In response to my growing agitation, my power flares to life, and frost coats the tips of my fingers.

"If nothing else, we need to take out the tracker so they'll be unable to follow us," Chase muses, and I wonder if he's speaking to us or the Empty Man.

Then his body shakes, his lips curl, and a decidedly indolent expression paves its way across his face.

The Empty Man has come to join us.

"I agree with Chase," he begins in his lilting, unfamiliar accent. "If we take out the tracker—or capture the tracker—they won't be able to find us if we portal away." Em licks his upper lip and focuses on me, his eyes at half-mast. "And I also agree with Aliana. She has proven herself, has she not? She killed the damn worm with just a"—he wiggles his fingers with a salacious grin—"poof of magic."

"It's dangerous," Dev growls, pacing. "We don't know how many monsters we'll need to fight and what we're up against and…" The humongous monster trails off at whatever look he sees on my face. He barks out a laugh—a cold, brittle sound like crackling icicles. "You're not going to let this go, are you, mate?"

"We're a team," I growl, stomping towards him so I can jab a finger into his chest. Tension rises deep within my chest like a wave about to break, cresting and then falling, torn apart as it hits the craggy rocks lining the shoreline. "All of us." I turn to address the others as well.

Dev grabs the finger I have on his chest and holds it reverently between both of his huge hands. A strange feeling arrows through me as I meet his red stare, and our time together from last night plays on a loop in my head.

I care about him so damn much, but I can't be with him if he doesn't trust me to take care of myself. To take care of him and the others.

Indecision wars with his possessive instincts before he finally huffs out a breath. It's a resigned sort of breath, nothing but a hiss of air in tandem with his shoulders deflating.

"You're right." Those two words are nothing but a primal growl. "But I swear to god, Aliana, if anything happens to you—"

"Nothing will happen to me."

"—I'll spank your ass until it's bright red."

Mingled shock and lust root me to the spot, despite the horrendous timing.

I blame my dream.

And the sex from yesterday.

In a husky voice, one I barely recognize, I breathe out, "Is that a threat or a promise?"

His eyes flare.

"As much as I would like to continue this conversation…" Creep sidles his way between us and smiles crookedly. "And I really, really would like to finish this conversation. Trust me, you have no idea how badly I want to finish this conversation. I really, really, really want to finish this conversation—"

"The point?" Tesq grunts, his hands curling into fists by his sides as he stares out the doorway towards the darkened tunnels.

I can't imagine what he's feeling. This place is his *home*. Or at least, one of his homes.

And it's the place I fell in love with him.

Pain reverberates in my chest at the thought of never returning here.

"Ah. Yes. My point!" Creep dramatically lifts a finger in the air. "As much as I would love for you two to finish this conversation, is now the best time?"

Em arches an eyebrow. "*That* was your point? Seriously?" Then, under his breath, he adds, "And you guys call me dramatic."

Before Creep can retort, Tesq stiffens, the rivulets of lava lining his back dilating and contracting in response to his tension.

"They're here," he hisses as ten monsters emerge from the right tunnel, just ten feet from us.

And then all hell breaks loose.

2 0

ALIANA

TESQ CHARGES THROUGH THE DOORWAY, Dev on his heels, and immediately, the underground tunnel fills with the sounds of fighting. Roars of fury, the smash of limb against limb, the buzz of an oversized insect from a flying monster who looks like a box with wings, a snarl from Fluffy.

The rest of us follow in a rush, grabbing whatever is nearest to use as a weapon. In my case, I snatch up two cans of vegetables.

Creep whoops and leaps on top of the box monster who zips toward him. His antlers scrape the ceiling, but he doesn't seem to notice, riding the other bucking tongue like he's a cowboy.

A shimmering, mirror-covered monster stomps in my direction, and I launch one of the cans at his head. It smashes into his cheek with a satisfying crack, and bits of him rain down, revealing a black skull beneath.

His angry roar surges around me, and there's a strange instant in which I somehow know this bastard's power level.

It's almost as if it's a blinking sign hanging in the air over his head, only there's nothing there. This disco bastard is an Eight.

He extends his arms, heading for me, but Tesq reaches out with a lava-coated palm and melts him in less than a second, turning him into a puddle of silvery goo.

I blow my gargoyle a kiss, and he gives a shy smile in return, a little blush forming on his cheeks, which are bared to me now. I absolutely adore it, and a warm, fluttery feeling that has no place in a fight takes up residence inside my rib cage.

Our little moment is rudely interrupted by a bastard with an ax trying to behead me.

Of course, the arrogant tongue doesn't expect me to be quick enough to duck or expect a can of corn to smash right into his unimpressive dick. When he gives a garbled gasp and starts to double over, I freeze him in place, his entire body icing over. He ends up looking like an ice sculpture arch with that ax of his drooping over the other side.

Or maybe...what were those human treats? I've seen pictures. Candy lanes? Canes? Something like that.

In any case, he's done for.

Chase sidles up to me with a grumpy look on his face. "I was just about to stab him for you."

Oops. Not Chase. Em. I've been better about knowing who is who, but I must be a bit tired today because I've been struggling.

"I'll let you kill the next one so you don't feel totally emascu-lated," I retort with heavy sarcasm as I see an entire gaggle of new monsters pouring toward us through the tunnel, drawn in behind the original ten.

"Thank you— Wait—" But Em doesn't get to finish that thought because a tooth with a bull head charges at us, and he's too busy dodging horns attempting to gore him and swiping with his knife to discuss whether I just insulted his fragile male ego.

I turn my head to find a hugely entrancing sight. Tesq and Dev are both double fisting, crushing the necks of some spindly shadow monsters in each hand. Their raw power radiates down the tunnel in pulsing waves that seem to crash right into my pussy, and I find myself taking a step backwards, struggling to find my balance as I watch them toss dead monsters aside like it's nothing.

Fluffy lifts a leg and pees on one of their corpses, eliciting a chuckle from me.

I have no idea what activated my monster side or how, but all of these new feelings are awakening in me, and I can't say that I despise them. It's a shock for me to think that, after I fiercely hated their kind for so long, but my new instincts feel so much stronger than logic.

Aggression and bloodlust surge up through my veins stronger than ever before. Caution always used to draw a careful circle around the other two feelings, and they didn't dare step outside the line. Because then I thought I was human. I thought I was fragile. Little did I know…that's not the case at all.

Now, I unleash a banshee scream, not holding back as I launch myself at these other belluas. I don't care that we're outnumbered, don't carefully take the most strategic position. I let raw rage flow through me as I join the fray.

A green slime blob comes rolling toward me, the body of a decaying cat stuck in its center, and I shoot out icicles at it. The spears fly uselessly right through the bastard, and it starts to pulse as though it's chuckling at me.

That pisses me off. "That funny? You goddamned oversized booger! Well, let's see if this is funny."

Impulsively, I shove my hand right into it and let cold burst from my palm. The slime hardens all around me, turning into a giant green ball of ice. I kick out, and it cracks. A second kick, and it shatters and falls into shards at my feet.

My smirk down at it is short-lived, because even though my Terrors are wreaking havoc on the monsters around me, more feet sound in the distance. Peering into the tunnel, I see an entire horde of new monsters heading for us. What does that make? Thirty? Fifty? I can't even count how many are in this third wave.

Dammit.

"Get the fucking tracker!" Em's voice is wild behind me, and I spin to see him darting left down the tunnel, away from the crowd after something that's nothing more than a blur.

Goddammit. Nobody killed that thing yet? I thought that one of the guys had taken care of it.

Of course, I've never seen anything move that quickly before. Maybe they tried. I've just been able to fight off the bastards that came directly at me so far. I haven't had a free second to be strategic about it.

I start in that direction, but Creep portals ahead of me, skipping from shadow to shadow easily in the darkness of the tunnels. A rat squeaks when he lands on its tail, and the little creature scurries away as soon as my monster disappears again. He appears in a shadow near Chase's body, but the tracker is already pulling ahead. Far ahead.

No.

I lift my hands, ready to fling spears of ice, but Creep is portalling so quickly, disappearing and reappearing, that I don't think he'll be able to hear any warning I give. And I won't hurt him.

Meanwhile, the crowd of new monsters is getting closer, their feet a stampede, the sound deafening in the tunnels as it echoes off the walls.

"Fucking fools," Dev says nearby.

"Move and I'll swamp the ground with lava," Tesq orders, stepping through the crunch and slush of the slime monster's corpse.

He bends and puts his hands to the cement ground. It cracks beneath him, and I blink, awed, as it quickly morphs into cobblestone and then into liquid, a soupy mass of molten orange.

Steam starts to curl through the air in the tunnel as a result, the moist air billowing around us.

"Come on." Dev scoops me off the ground.

I wriggle in his arms, but as I cast a glance around, I realize he's attempting to be tender, not overprotective.

There are no monsters left on our side of the lava moat to fight. The others are trying to cross, shoving their companions into the bubbling orange mass and trying to walk across their backs, but the bodies disintegrate too quickly, burning or melting into nothing but a stench.

He runs in the direction of the tracker, and we quickly catch up with Chase. But Creep is nowhere to be seen. And neither is the tracker.

We head in that general direction, slowly and silently, me in Dev's arms, Tesq leaving little puddles of lava like a checkerboard behind us to slow down whoever might actually breach his lava moat and come after us.

When we reach Empty, he's breathing heavily, and he's stabbed his knife into the wall, grinding the blade uselessly against the cement in his frustration.

"Did Creep catch him?" I ask, wiggling until Dev puts me down.

A shrug is my only answer, and my stomach immediately sinks. An ominous feeling unfolds inside of me, growing bigger with each passing second.

When Creep appears in the shadows in front of us, an angry expression marring his gorgeous face, I know.

The tracker got away, which means the other side will know where we are. And they'll be able to find us wherever we go.

ALIANA

THE MONSTERS HAVE SHOVED a pile of their brethren into the moat behind us and are stomping across the melting, sinking mass of the dying as quickly as they can. Even with the checkerboard obstacle course Tesq left for them, the bastards will be on us all too soon.

As one, we turn and race toward a set of stairs leading to the surface. While being out in broad daylight where we can be spotted isn't ideal, at least a lot of monsters will be sleeping. With any luck—not that we've had a lot of it lately—we'll be able to take cover before we're found.

Though, no matter where we go, we can't stay long. Not until that tracker's dead.

Worry gusts through my stomach as we run because, though I know my Terrors are strong, they aren't invincible. Even monsters tire. Even monsters need to rest. But if this uprising goes on long enough and they're able to suss us out no matter where we hide…eventually…

I shove aside the dread and push myself to run faster. A set of stairs painted in yellow slashes by the sunlight is set just to our right, and we bound up it. Legs burning, I huff and puff as we hurry. It doesn't go unnoticed that my mates, even Empty in Chase's vulnerable human body, surround me. Determined to protect me.

Annoyance and appreciation weave together inside of me, and I have to clamp my lips down to avoid any sassy quip. Now isn't the time.

When we reach the surface, we walk out under a diagonal awning, and I glance up at huge electronic signs posted all around us. All of them are pitch-black squares that wrap around the edges of the moldering skyscrapers. There are oversized posters too, four times as high as I am tall. Now, the words are so sun-bleached that they're unreadable, and many of the posters have been shredded by teeth who like scratching posts.

Those signs stretch along the buildings as far as I can see, stacked up on top of one another, extending over remnants from when humans ruled the world. I can only wonder what important things flashed across those screens. Did news? Did the first emergence of monsters make it up there? If it did, it didn't help.

We skirt around rusted-out taxi cabs left on the street from the final invasion, searching for a spot we can hole up and hide.

When we reach an overhang that has the letters AMC in busted-out plastic on top of it, Creep points at the glass doors. "Let's go in here."

He grabs my hand, and I follow behind him, wondering what kind of building we're heading into. We've just reached a little glass cube set outside the main building when Creep pauses, staring at a neatly printed sheet of paper that looks fresh and clean, unlike nearly everything else on this street.

Creep's blue claws snatch up the paper, and his eyes darken in fury as he reads, his fingers curling and crumpling it. "Do you see this?" His voice trembles with fury, and the light-hearted monster, the teasing brat of a male, is nowhere to be found. They radiate unadulterated fury.

He passes the note to Tesq. My gargoyle stares down at it in silence.

Chase gets it next, standing on Tesq's right side. The note is passed down into his hands, and I can tell the moment that Empty wrests control away from him because his head tilts and his eyes light up, an evil grin spreading across his features.

"What is it?" I ask.

But Dev rips the paper from Empty's fingers, tearing it as he reads. A growl rumbles up his throat, and I can see his entire body tensing—he's getting ready to roar.

"Shut up!" Creep tells him, glancing around the abandoned street. "Let's get inside."

The guys pile ahead, pushing through the glass doors. We enter a huge lobby with rundown patterned carpet, a tall ceiling, and moldy posters on the wall. There's a lingering scent of salt and something else in the air—I'm not quite sure what. It's foul.

A long counter runs along the back wall of this room, and it's covered in spiderwebs and dust. Off to the right, a hallway extends into darkness. Of course, Creep's drawn to the shadows and heads in that direction.

"Hey! What the hell did the note say?" I ask.

My hackles rise when the only answer I get are Dev's claws sinking into the wall and dragging a huge scratch across it. Since the fuckers won't tell me, I reach to swipe at the paper myself, determined to see what has all of their panties in a twist. Dev lifts the paper out of reach.

When I smack him, his eyes turn my way, glowing, his wolflike form primed and ready to fight. Or fight and fuck, as is our tendency together. But I'm not hot and bothered right now. Merely bothered.

I cross my arms and say, "Give me the paper, *mate*."

"It's a lie," Dev snarls.

"No. It's his version of reality," Creep retorts as he yanks open a door into a dark room.

"Whose version of reality?" I ask as all the men follow him into the pitch-black space as if they can see just fine.

Even Chase strides in confidently. My anger grows as I follow behind and am forced to drag my hand along the wall as I walk up a ramp so that I don't trip and fall. Who knows what's in this room?

Tesq's hands light up with tiny veins of lava, letting me see circles of light as Creep leads the way to a long line of chairs. The blue monster sinks into one, and for a second, his features soften in sadness, mouth tipping down at the edges with a pain I haven't seen from him before but immediately recognize as a deep-seated wound. It calls out to something inside of me and propels my feet forward, even though I can hardly see.

I reach out and stroke one of Creep's antlers, my fingers trailing over the tiny bumps of moss and miniature flowers blooming on them. His gaze tilts up to mine, and for a second, I'm lost in his eyes, in the soft glow of them in the magma's light, in the pain swimming in their depths.

"Creep. What is it?" I ask softly.

He pulls me down onto his lap and buries his nose in my neck, inhaling my scent for a moment. I feel the rapid beat of his heart against my side as he holds me close and breathes deeply. Though patience isn't my strong suit, I wait because Creep struggling is not a normal sight.

But when my monster pulls back, there are no tears in his eyes. None of that sadness is left.

There's only violent ferocity as he snarls, "My father has declared himself the new king of Ebony Kingdom."

22

THE EMPTY MAN

KING.

Puh-lease.

As if that golden-tailed, suit-wearing monster could ever hold enough power to rule a land as vast as the Ebony Kingdom. He's just a cum stain with a tiny cock who's desperate for any sort of power—even the kind that comes from trickery and deception.

Barna-ass isn't going to know what hit him when we inevitably attack.

And we *will* attack.

I owe that fucker a few rounds in my own torture chamber. Repay him for the lovely facial reconstruction he gave my boy Chase.

Ha. Ha. Very funny, Chase quips dryly in my head.

I am hilarious, aren't I? I make myself laugh daily.

The two of us have volunteered to secure our venue for the night—what humans once called a "movie theater," at least according to a few brochures I found.

In all honesty, I wanted to take a little bit of time away from the others to finalize my plan. Operation *Win Over Aliana* is well underway.

And I just found the final piece of the puzzle—chocolate. Lots and lots of chocolate.

I eagerly begin throwing the bars into a tub that reads POPCORN on the side in big block letters. I don't even want to know what popcorn is. Is it a mixture of that human drink root beer and the yellow vegetable? I once "borrowed" a human's body who seemed particularly attached to the fizzy drink.

Are you seriously not worried about Creep's dad? Chase asks, sounding annoyed with me.

He's not a threat, I assure my little human tagalong. *Barna-ass is just like every other monster we've ever faced—a coward with little power, who hides behind other monsters. There's a reason we've never fought him head-on before. Now...do you see any flowers?*

Em... Chase growls. *Why aren't you taking this threat seriously?*

Because it's not a threat that needs *to be taken seriously.*

I don't find any flowers, but I *do* find a couple of straws covered in a strange, greenish-brown fur. Those could work for my bouquet, right?

I gather them all up, tie them together with a strip of paper I found, and then happily gather all of my goodies to bring back to my sweet mate.

Nervous anticipation skitters across my skin like a bunch of angry fire ants. I can't say I particularly like this sensation.

When have I ever needed to work to get a girl to like me? Most monster females flock to me, entranced by my power and striking good looks (snort. I'm invisible. For all they know, I have six eyes, a microdick, and giant pores all over my face). Monsters constantly allow me to jump into their bodies and take them for a joyride.

I've been a seven-foot-tall female monster with claws as large as kitchen knives and boobs the size of Chase's head. I've been a tiny green monster that would barely reach Aliana's hip. I've had horns and fangs, pores and gills, striated fins and barbed tails.

I've sucked dicks, licked pussies, fucked asses and vaginas. It honestly doesn't matter to me.

The moral of that story? I didn't have to *try*.

And now, I'm attempting to woo one human female who hates the very ground I walk on. I don't even blame her.

I'm not just doing all of this because she's my mate—though I'll admit, that's what drew me to her in the first place.

I think I would've fallen in love with Aliana even if there wasn't this mating bond between us.

She challenges me in a way I never knew I needed or even wanted. One look into her ice-blue eyes, and I know I need to be a better person, both for her and for myself.

I want to ask her about her day, learn her likes and dislikes, fight her enemies, kiss her goodnight, and cuddle with her in the morning. It's sickeningly disgusting how badly I want her.

I never really thought I would fall in love. I'm a monster without a body, after all. I'm not even sure I technically have a heart. But I know I have a soul, and it yearns for Aliana in a way that surpasses logic or common sense.

She's an angel sent to smite us all and drag us to hell. But if the price of her love means I'll need to prostrate myself before her and pray for forgiveness, then I will.

Yet even loving her feels like the gravest sin of all.

What have I done for her, besides nearly killing her, nearly killing her a second time, and oh yeah, nearly killing her a third time?

Grumbling under my breath, I push all self-deprecating thoughts to the side and hurry back to the room I left Aliana in.

She's sitting where I left her, in a tiny seat beside a sleeping Creeper. I'm not sure I've ever seen the blue monster sleep before. He's always been too wary to let his guard down around me, even before Aliana came into the picture.

But now, his chest rises and falls with slow, even breaths, and his features appear peaceful. The furrow between his brows has smoothed out, and I know we have Aliana to thank for that.

"Where are Grumpikins and Broodilicious?" I ask, noting that the Devourer and the Grotesque are no longer in the room.

Aliana places a finger to her lips, indicating for me to remain silent, and then slowly rises from her seat beside Creep. Almost immediately, the horned monster cries out, though his eyes remain closed.

Aliana places a gentle hand on his bicep, and his thrashing instantly ceases, his breathing steadying.

She waits, ensuring he'll remain asleep, before jerking her head towards the back of the room. I follow like a besotted puppy, not even caring how under her spell I truly am. I'll do just about anything she asks of me.

The next room we enter is significantly smaller than the one we left. There's a tiny window that looks out over the sea of seats—and a sleeping Creep—with a strange camera-contraption pointed in that direction. The room is cluttered with faded posters, tiny boxes that I know to be DVDs, and huge circles of…the thingy that goes inside of the camera thingy.

Film, Chase supplies with a tired sigh. *Those are rolls of film.*

And what is the camera for?

It plays the film on the screen out there.

Huh.

I don't even ask how Chase knows all of this. Some humans, I've come to figure out, know more about the before time than even the monsters who lived through it do. I imagine it serves as a source of nostalgia—to be able to remember a peaceful, happy time before monsters destroyed it for them.

My heart clenches at just the reminder, and I turn my attention to my mate.

My *human* mate.

"Dev and Tesq are discussing battle plans," Aliana explains. "They're in the room next door."

"And?" I arch an eyebrow. "What have they decided?"

She scrubs both of her hands down her face with a tired sigh. "Nothing yet. But enough about that." Her gaze dips to the bucket in my arms. "What's that?"

I grin triumphantly, pleased she noticed.

"It's a gift for you, m'lady." I all but shove the bucket into her arms as I rock back on my heels, waiting with bated breath for her reaction.

Her brows crinkle in a way that shouldn't be as adorable as it is. A tiny frown touches her lips.

Wait…

A frown?

What the fuck?

Aren't women supposed to be happy when given gifts?!

Fear roils in my gut and pricks my fingertips. I suddenly want to grab the bucket back and awkwardly say, "Just kidding! Hehehe!"

What did you expect? Chase sounds amused…and a little annoyed. It's a combination I imagine only Pretty Boy here can pull off, the arrogant prick. *You gave her chocolate bars covered in mold and maggots and a bouquet of fungus straws.*

And that's…bad? I query.

Fuck. Fuck. Fuck.

Chase mentally face-palms himself.

But then Aliana smiles—and it's the most beautiful thing I've ever seen, like the clouds moving away from the sun after days of gray, overcast skies. Her eyes sparkle with something akin to warmth.

"I… Thank you, Em. For the present."

I fucking *preen*. "I read that women love chocolates and flowers." I begin to bounce on the balls of my feet in excitement. "But that's not your only present."

"Oh god. Please, no," she says, her eyes widening.

Obviously, she's pretending to be terrified. I know she secretly loves my gifts. She smiled, didn't she?

"Silly girl. Don't you know I'll give you everything your heart desires?" I stare at her, and this time, I don't bother to hide all of the adoration I feel for her. I want her to see just how much I've come to care for her, crave her, need her. Dare I say, love her. "I meant what I said before. I'm determined to fight for you, Aliana, and prove to you I'm a monster worth caring about." I reach for her hand, and a tiny thrill shoots through me when she doesn't pull away. "Come on. Part… what is it now? Seven? Yes! Part seven of my master plan to win you over is underway."

23

ALIANA

I DIDN'T HAVE the heart to tell the Empty Man that his "gift" makes me want to dry-heave. The pungent stench of decay and mold threatens to overwhelm my senses. He just looked so *happy*, and I couldn't ruin that for him.

So I allow the crazy monster to grip my hand and lead me out of the room.

I know I should probably be cautious, especially considering our sordid past, but I know Em will never hurt me now. He's brash, a little eccentric, and most definitely insane, but I believed him when he said that he changed.

An innate voice in the back of my head repeatedly whispers, *Give him a chance. One chance.*

I shush that voice and remind her that *she* wasn't the one who was almost stabbed by the sexy ghost monster.

Still, I don't pull away as Em guides me to a theater—I've learned that's what each individual room is called—we haven't yet explored. It's smaller than the one we left Creep in and is missing the majority of its seats.

In the center of the room, in front of a huge white screen covered in claw marks, is a collection of pillows, blankets, and unlit candles.

"TA-DA!" Em gestures towards the setup with dramatic jazz hands.

A strange fluttery sensation—reminiscent of hyperactive puppies—explodes in my chest.

"What is all this?" I ask, venturing a tentative step closer.

The blankets appear to be clean, if a little musty, and I don't see any bugs or mold…

"We're having a candlelit picnic," Em declares happily. He drags me towards the blanket and gestures for me to take a seat.

I do so, albeit timidly, and he plops down opposite me.

"Now, I don't have any matches, so the candles will be unlit… but…" He holds up what appears to be a tiny box. I recognize it as something humans would store their money in. "I have a picnic basket-ish."

He looks so fucking pleased with himself that a tiny smile curls up my lips unbidden.

"This is actually really sweet, Em." Heat slithers its way up my cheeks.

Am I actually…blushing?

What the fuck?

"I used some of the food we brought to make dinner," Em continues excitedly. He holds out a bowl of ravioli and another of corn. "We didn't have any bread for me to make a sandwich like a *true* picnic, but…"

With an excited yelp, he rips apart one piece of sticky ravioli. Red sauce stains his fingers like blood. Then, he grabs a tiny bit of corn, shoves it inside the now opened ravioli, and attempts to stick the two halves back together.

"I call it a pasta corn sandwich!" He holds his creation out to me, his eyes glimmering with joy.

"It looks delicious, Em." I take the ravioli piece from him and hesitantly chew off one end, trying not to grimace.

When he just continues to watch me, his eyes expectant, I give him a thumbs-up.

He fucking beams.

All at once, his smile fades, wilting at the edges like a drooping dandelion, and he focuses on his red-stained hands. "I like it when you call me that."

"Call you what?"

He glances up, and his eyes hold a plethora of emotions that are nearly impossible to read. He quickly looks away and focuses on a thread coming free from the blanket we're sitting on. He twines it around his finger almost absently, the green color a startling contrast to his golden skin.

"Em," he says at last, peeking up at me through his lashes. "I like it when you call me Em."

"Oh." I wonder if my cheeks are as bright red as his.

Silence descends between the two of us, but it's not uncomfortable. The Empty Man—Em—continues to create his pasta corn sandwiches, and I continue to eat them. They actually grow on me after a while.

"Is that what Chase calls you? Em?" I ask, licking sauce off my fingers.

Em cocks his head to the side with a decidedly curious expression. "He does?" Those two words somehow come out sounding like a question. "You think about him a lot, don't you? This human whose body I'm inhabiting?" Something wistful and forlorn paves its way across his face. "It was him you wanted to save, not me, wasn't it?"

There's no point denying it. "Yes."

Em nods once, as if he expected as much, and then hands me another ravioli. "And now?" His eyes are guarded.

"And now what?"

"Would you want to save just him?"

"I…" I open my mouth, close it, and then open it again. I don't quite know how to respond to that.

Mainly because the truth terrifies me.

I should hate the Empty Man, even now, but it isn't hate I feel when I stare at him. It's not love, not yet, but something warm and tingly and so freaking confusing that my head begins to pound.

But even if I chose to give in to the strange emotions rampaging through me, we'll never work the way things are now. Em is in Chase's body, and Chase…well… He may not hate me, but I'm certain he doesn't have any romantic feelings for me. I can't even imagine what it must be like for him, being trapped in his own body, watching someone else puppet it.

I can't do that to Chase.

Em leans towards me, his eyes ensnaring my own, and my breath siphons straight from my lungs.

"I really want to kiss you right now, my little mate," Em breathes.

"W-we can't." My voice is just as soft as his, just as breathy, barely audible over the roaring between my ears and the rapid thudding of my heart. "Not while you're still in Chase's body. Not…not when I'm not sure I forgive you."

A look of pure devastation warps his handsome face, and for a moment, I don't believe I'm looking at Em…but at Chase. I don't know how I can tell the difference, especially when they're not speaking, but I swear that for a fraction of a second, Chase wrestles control away from Em.

It's *Chase* who's staring at me as if I plunged my hand into his chest and removed his still-beating heart.

It's *Chase* whose eyes glimmer with pain and betrayal.

It's *Chase* who looks destroyed by my words.

But then the Empty Man returns, and though his smile is sad, it's there all the same.

"Very well, my dear mate." His eyes abruptly begin to shimmer with mischief. "How about you call your huge gargoyle mate in here? We may not be able to have a candlelit picnic, but how about a magma-lit one?"

ALIANA

WHILE EM DARTS over to the other room to recruit Tesq to be our living lava lamp, I recline on the blanket he's laid out and stare up at the ceiling. The poltergeist leaves the door to the hall propped open so that I'm not left in complete darkness, which is strangely thoughtful of him. Just like this picnic. And his gift. Strange but thoughtful.

We're in such an utter mess, I think as I note that a group of bats is sleeping off in one corner of the darkened space.

I sigh as I watch one of them flutter their wings and shift into a more comfortable position, closer to his little friends. Snuggling. If bats snuggle, which I'm not really certain they do. Creepy critters. Maybe. I never thought monsters had a soft side either, but every passing day with my mates is proving me wrong.

The other bats shuffle slightly so their companion can wedge himself between their bodies.

I tilt up the corner of my lips. At our core, we all just want to figure out where we fit.

Of course, the little bat chooses that moment to thrust its ass out and shit where it hangs, the white drop ruining my desire to associate any of my own problems with the little fucker.

Bet it's a male bat.

And with that, my brain has moved on to other things in new directions.

Cracking my neck side to side, I wonder if the Terrors have come up with a plan of attack yet. I know that everyone is furious about the public declaration that their reigns are over. But I'm not sure if they know exactly what to do about it.

Yes, they can attack and maim and kill.

But we've done that a few times in a row now, and I'm not sure it's helping.

I have no idea what the monster version of "politicking" is, but my gut tells me the guys should try something like that. Back in the human resistance, those who wanted to lead a squad made dinner for current leaders, watched their children, even washed their clothes. They worked on sucking up to prove their dedication.

I snort at the very idea of my monsters working. Tesq may cook, but his cooking was just as likely to kill those around him as feed them. Dev and Em would scoff at the idea of doing chores. Creep would be good at the smooth-talking and glad-handing. He could charm every monster in the room, if they let him live long enough to open his mouth. Given the current state of things, that's highly unlikely.

Apparently, we've got no choice but violence.

A little smile bursts across my lips, and I chuckle at how much I grow giddy at the prospect.

Maybe I should be thinking about ways I can get creative with my newfound powers instead of trying to brainstorm non-violent solutions. I wonder if I could freeze someone's tongue and make the ice grow thick enough that they literally choke on it.

Dark daydreams flit through my mind as my monster side takes control.

I'm biting my lip and rubbing my thighs together at the thought of impaling another monster's ass with an icicle when Tesq stomps into the room trailing Em.

"This is not urgent." Tesq's tone is a low rumble that cuts off abruptly when he spots me laid out on the blanket, hair splayed out around me.

While I can't hear how hard he swallows, two lines of lava crack open along his neck and pulse slightly as he does, making me think my gentle giant is a tiny bit affected by the sight. It makes my imagination shift from the idea of razor-sharp icicles to rounded ones. I wonder how my gargoyle would handle me teasing his ass with one of those...

"You sure? Looks like our mate has a pretty urgent need to me." Em's grin is both devious and filled with lust as his eyes trace over my form.

"FUCK!" Creep screams from the other room.

Immediately, I jolt up into a seated position, and Tesq begins to dart sideways, back toward the entrance.

Em, not registering the horror in Creep's tone—or perhaps just immune to it after all the hideous things he's supposedly put his menagerie through—calls out, "Yeah. That's what I'm trying to do. Kindly SHUT THE HELL UP!"

But I'm bolting for the ramp, following after Tesq and avoiding Em's fingers as he tries to grab me.

"Aliana." Em's tone is genuinely hurt and confused, but I don't have time to explain.

My heart's pounding with the intensity of a nail gun. Each thud feels like a sharp spike shot right into my ribs.

"Come on," I urge, waving my arm for him to follow as I sprint up to the swinging door left in Tesq's wake.

"Dammit," Em grumbles behind me as he starts to move.

His shuffling feet make a smudge of sound against the carpet as he hurries after me, but that noise is quickly overpowered by another, stranger sensation. It almost feels as though something's vibrating inside my skull.

I burst out into the wide hallway, Em just steps behind.

That's when I spot the tracker rushing away from me, Creep leaping after him. To my shock and amazement, the pink-faced beast crawls up the wall like a lizard and darts along the ceiling, which rises twenty feet as he makes it into the lobby.

"Goddammit!" Creep's gaze roams over the high ceiling, looking for a shadow he can portal into.

But there's a hole in the corner of the ceiling I didn't notice when we walked in. Whether it's new, I can't say. It does, however, let a terrible beam of light stream across the top half of the room. That beam spreads out into weaker bands around the space, but it does the work of banishing Creep's shadows. There are no dark corners or inky pools of blackness he can emerge from.

The tracker, almost as if the stupid tooth is sentient and knows that shadows are a danger to it, sticks to the brightest areas as it skitters across the ceiling. I crane my neck and grit my teeth as I glare at its smug, angular face soaked in sunlight.

Em grabs a small candy box from behind the long counter at the back of the room and throws it at the creature, but the cardboard is so flimsy and disintegrated that it breaks open as it flies through the air. Circular candies in every shade of the rainbow fall from it, and the box flops to the ground empty, far short of its target.

I launch my arm back, muscles wrenching, and throw ice darts, but the sun softens and melts the tips just enough that they smash into the tracker's spine but don't stab it through like I want.

Motherfucker. I wish I had a crossbow right now.

Tesq tries to hurl a ball of lava, but it sloshes down onto the floor, too heavy. It burns a hole as it sinks through the carpet, and the stench drifts over us, leaving a bad taste on my tongue.

We are all forced to impotently watch as the monster wriggles through the hole in the ceiling and gets away. Gone to give our new location to his master, no doubt.

Fucking hell. Is this our life now? Running constantly?

"What the fuck is this? Are we Terrors or not?" Creep seems to share my frustration.

But his rage doesn't stop the reality of the situation.

In a fight, my mates are fierce. But in a chase after a lone creature…we need to learn to work together. That much is obvious.

We're also going to have to learn how to hide. I'm not sure it's something any of them have had to do for a long time. I know Creep can—clearly he's fond of closets and shadows. But with a tracker tailing us, we are going to have to set a sentry. We're going to have to be on guard at all times. It's a new experience, one that stiffens my spine and sends an uncomfortable prickle across my shoulders.

Even in the resistance, the monsters typically left us to our forests. They didn't come find us every few hours. A dark sort of dread pulses inside my chest because I can already tell this tracker is going to give us no such reprieve.

With a snarl, Creep turns to me, his eyes flashing furiously. "Back into the hallway. We need to portal out of here. Now."

He's obviously come to the same conclusion.

We stride down the wide, darkened hall, past moldy posters and cardboard cutouts. Dev meets us near the end, striding up nonchalantly in his human form, unaware or unashamed of his nudity. He seems to be completely clueless about everything that just went down.

"Where the fuck were you?" Creep lashes out.

"Nowhere." Dev's response is too quick to be honest.

"The goddamned tracker found us." Creep's harsh words are accompanied by a rough grip on my wrist as he pulls me to his side, tucking me under his arm. "We need to portal out of here. Where are we going to go? Any of my spots are out. That bastard who bred me will have eyes near all of them."

Tesq's lips twist into an angry, frustrated expression. "My favorites are gone. The others won't fit all of us."

I glance up at Creep, who's standing next to me, practically vibrating with anger, and reach out to put a soothing hand on his chest. The quick thud of his heartbeat betrays his agitation. "Don't worry. I know a place."

He stares down at me before grabbing onto my hand.

"So...what do I..." My words taper off.

"Just picture where you want to end up, very clearly in your mind," he tells me gently.

I nod. "You might want to—"

But before I've finished my sentence, Creep's sweeping me into his arms, and that uncomfortable squeezing sensation surrounds me. We jolt through space and time, and I keep my eyes firmly closed, not wanting to see the blur, not wanting to end up distracted. I keep our destination front of mind until our feet smack down, and a loud *whack* sounds next to me.

"Dammit!" Creep curses as his antlers smash into the ceiling. "Coulda warned me we were portalling into a space the size of a matchbox."

"Sorry," I mutter, reaching out to my side to find something to brace against.

My stomach sloshes around uneasily after the jolting sensation of traveling through space and time. It takes a few seconds before my eyes adjust to the darkness, and I can take in the stone pillars and low ceiling.

"A cave?" Creep questions, glancing around as he posts his hands on his knees.

Guess I didn't think about how my monsters would fit into this space, only that no one else really knows about it.

"Sybil's Cave. Old human place. My parents took me here once." I shrug.

Creep grunts as he walks toward the entrance with his back hunched over and scanning for threats. "Can see why monsters don't come. It's not much to look at."

It isn't. But the stone cavern is clean and empty, and though it's just a few hollowed-out rooms, it's better than being in the open. At the front of the cave, there's a Gothic arch with a broken wrought-iron gate from the before times. Creep glances around and spots the Hudson River, startling a bit as he stares at the murky brown expanse of water and the city on the other side of it.

"You brought us to Jersey?"

I shrug. "I guess."

He grins. "Good work. I don't think any monsters come this far out unless they've got wings."

"That was kind of the point. Wanna go get the others?"

"Not really." He turns toward me, desire and a little glint of naughtiness lighting up his eyes.

"Creep." I try to sound firm and not at all intrigued by the prospect of an uninterrupted hour of fun.

But that tracker found the other Terrors and the pitter-patter of fear inside my heart won't abate until they're here in front of me safe and sound.

"What will you give me if I bring them to you?" he bargains.

"How about I won't try to rip your dick off?" I counter.

He chuckles and reaches out to ruffle my hair. "Try again. I know you love this dick."

I narrow my eyes, and he just swoops down to nip at my mouth, peppering me with kisses as he says, "Promise me something for being your good little monster, Aliana. Please."

Fuck. It's the please that does it.

"Fine."

"Okay, good. You promise to fuck me when I get back. And I get you all to myself. Okay, bye!" Creep deliberately rolls each word into the next, speaking as quickly as possible as he backs away from me toward the cave, a grin that can only be described as diabolical on his face.

I don't even have a chance to respond because the second that darkness sweeps over his shoulders like a cloak, he's gone.

Standing amongst the scrubby trees growing around the mouth of the cave, I turn and glance over at the ripples running across the river like silver ribbons.

"Guess I have some sex to look forward to," I say aloud to no one.

A few birds twitter in the trees like they're mocking me, but I just flip them off and walk under the canopy, soaking in the fact that for the first time in months, I'm back beneath the leaves.

I inhale the scent of mud and roots and rot and life, all the scents of a forest. All the scents that should fill my heart with a sense of homecoming. But though the air is clean and refreshing, I don't get any such sense.

Not until Tesq emerges from the cave, so hunched that he's practically bent in half. When he straightens, the wind catches hold of his scent—clean rock, heat, a tiny hint of ash. And my heart fills up.

The forest may be the place I used to live. But it's not my home anymore.

ALIANA

NIGHT HAS FALLEN by the time Creep has portalled us all over and Tesq helped me scrounge up something to eat in the forest. We end up circling a small fire in front of the stone arch leading into the cave. It's testing our luck with the tracker, but we're all so hungry that we're past caring. Besides, we're confident that it'll take the monster days, if not weeks, to reach us here.

Crickets sing all around us as the fire snaps and jumps, flames dancing yellow and bright. Juices drip down my chin, warm and delicious, as we feast on a squirrel and two rabbits I speared with ice and a pot full of mash from rinsed and roasted acorns Tesq gathered. Dev's stomach still growls afterwards, and I imagine none of my mates are incredibly full, but none of them complain about it.

Em keeps trying to slide some of his share of the acorns over to me, annoyed when I won't take them.

"Can't I just be nice and give them to you?" he grumbles, his eyebrows furrowed.

"First off, you're a monster. Nice is unnatural. Second, you're in a body that needs food, and I won't let you starve Chase. He's still healing." I cut off the "idiot" I want to add at the end of the sentence, but I think Em gets the insult even though it remains unspoken.

"Always Chase this. Chase that. Did you *even like* my picnic?" He stands up with a huff and stomps off into the trees. Hobbles really, the stubborn fool.

I glare after him, wondering what the hell his problem is.

"He's trying to woo you," Creep whispers unhelpfully, leaning over my left shoulder.

"Yeah. Got that. He sucks at it."

"Of course he does. He's a shit, and you don't need to be his. You're mine." Dev's eyes glimmer like rubies in the firelight from his place across from me.

I throw one of Em's abandoned acorns across the fire at him. "Fuck off. You like sharing me, and you know it."

Dev just narrows his eyes and glares at me for calling him out as he pops the acorn into his mouth. "Making him jealous is just going to make him want to kill Chase once they can separate, you know."

Goddammit.

"It's not like I want Chase," I say, though my stomach tightens at the lie, and Creep backhands my shoulder lightly.

"You need to work on that poker face," he tells me. "Or actually, don't. I'll portal around and rummage up some cards, and we can play strip poker before the hot sex you promised me."

My blue monster gives me a salacious wink that rolls my eyes to the back of my head.

Tesq interrupts the obnoxious direction the conversation is going by speaking up for the first time since we started eating. His joints grind a little as he swivels on a tree stump to face Creep. "You need to portal to find Uni."

Both the other monsters turn to look at him in disbelief.

"I don't want to find that fucker," Creep protests, lip curling.

Dev leans forward closer to the fire, and the flames seem to jump higher in an effort to touch his face. They don't, but their dancing stripes him with color, and his entire face seems to glow eerily. "That asshole was banished. For good reason."

"Wait. Banishment is an option? I thought monsters were all about beheading," I pipe in, glancing curiously between Creep and Dev, who both seem to be vibrating with fury.

"He was banished. Once we divided the kingdom." Tesq's reply is slow. His sentences are broken, but his tone is steady, and when Fluffy emerges from the trees after her own hunt for dinner, he softly lifts his hand and turns his attention to her, as if nothing out of the ordinary is happening.

I glance between my three monsters, waiting for further explanation, but Dev and Creep are busy having a facial expression conversation with one another, and Tesq is busy nuzzling his tiger's blue fur.

"Fuck!" Creep says as he jolts to his feet.

Guess his naughty plans will wait.

I quickly rise off the dead log I dragged over for my dinner seat, but before I can say a word, my monster under the bed is gone. Portalled away.

Turning to Dev, I open my mouth to demand an explanation, but he gestures off into the trees. "Go get Em before he hangs the human boy. He'll want to be here for this."

"Here for what?"

"Hurry. So you don't miss Creep when he gets back."

I narrow my eyes at Dev, who has never let me walk away from him from the second we met. The overcontrolling bastard would prefer that I inhale his every exhale—and yet, he's sending me off into the forest? Suspicious.

He turns his attention to Tesq. Clearly, he has words for the other monster he doesn't want me to hear, which only makes me all the more curious. I don't know if my newfound monster abilities include extra-sensitive hearing, but I send out a wish that they do. And then I stalk off toward a stand of pines, grumbling about shithead asshole monsters under my breath.

It takes me a few minutes to find Em, who has wandered off farther than I expected. He's sitting on a boulder, breaking a twig into tiny pieces when I approach. Though his clothes are a hodgepodge from our brief visit to Tesq's lair, a random T-shirt and some jeans, he looks better than he has in recent days. Except for his expression. That's as downcast and dejected as I've ever seen on a monster.

"Hey," I call out, not wanting to startle him.

He doesn't even glance my way, though he nibbles on his lower lip. He sighs and tosses a bit of twig at the dirt. "What?"

The defensiveness in his tone immediately makes my hackles rise, and the snarky side of myself wants to snap at him. I have to take a deep breath and remind myself that I've not only hurt his ego, but our mate bond is a permanent thing, and something tells me I don't want to damage that.

Instead of simply summoning Em back to the fire, I sigh and lean against the trunk of a nearby tree. My fingers automatically peel at the bark, mimicking Em's destructive little style of contemplation. "Look. I want you to know it's not you."

"It's not you. It's me. Really? You're going to try to use that line?" Em snaps.

"I was going to say *it's Chase*, you invisible asshole," I retort. "I don't think it's fair to him. I mean, would you want someone to invade your body and make you kiss someone you've loathed your entire life?"

To my shock, Em bursts out laughing. "Loathe! You think he loathes you? He's been fucking *pining over you* for years!"

His right fist balls up and socks him right in the jaw after that proclamation. It's hard enough that his head twists sideways, and his eyes gape in shock.

I bite down on an amused grin as Chase goes to war with Em. His hands batting at the air and the growls and grumbling threats streaming from his mouth are fucking hilarious. Somehow, he ends up on the ground, rolling around as the two souls inside one body battle it out for control.

I wait.

Finally, Chase spits out a mouthful of dirt and rises onto an elbow. I can tell it's Chase immediately by the way his eyes narrow as he gazes up at me. We've thrown each other enough loathing looks over the years that I know exactly what that intense stare of his feels like. The way his eyes try to cut right through me.

The stare continues.

He doesn't blink, and neither do I. Slowly, that hot anger flushing my cheeks and neck, an instinctive reaction to his gaze at this point, cools. I swallow hard, wondering why Chase isn't arguing with Em's last statement. Why isn't he thanking me for saving him from experiencing all the unhinged things I'm certain Em wants to do to me?

Because he's a horny guy. That's why.

But those words don't feel true. Chase hasn't been like that since I rescued him. Actually, he hasn't been like that since we were captured and auctioned off.

He's actually been decent.

But there's no way what Em said is true. Pining? For years? Impossible.

"We've always hated each other."

"You always hated *me*." Chase's response is soft, and his emerald gaze is so intense that I can't meet it. "I deserved it. But I never hated you."

I scoff and snort, trying to make light of the situation. "That's still a far cry from pining. Tell Em to get his human emotions straight."

Silence, as loud and unnerving as a thunderclap, fills my ears.

Finally, Chase says, "He's telling—"

"We need to get back! Creep's bringing in some monster that Tesq knows so we can plan." Words gust out of me, a nervous whirl of sound. I spin on my heel, heading back toward the cave and the campfire.

The entire way there, my head is a confused riot of sparks, and my heart thuds wildly.

A monster battle for a kingdom? Four mates? I'm a fucking monster or part monster or who knows the fuck what?

My life doesn't need another complication.

But it seems like I've got one.

THE CREEPER

"*Go get Uni,* they said. *It'll be fine,* they said," I mutter under my breath as the portal deposits me on a rocky beach in a place that was once known as South Carolina.

Or perhaps it was North Carolina.

Fuck knows I've never studied a map of the before times.

Either way, the air here is balmy, and the sun rays seem exceptionally close. My skin immediately begins to overheat, and I suddenly wish I had Aliana's powers to control ice.

"Fucking hell. They soooo owe me for this. I better get a million blowjobs. No, a million and *one* blowjobs."

I narrow my eyes and squint at the water lapping ferociously against the shoreline. I suppose some may say that the scene before me is serene and picturesque, but I know the truth.

I'm keenly aware of the monsters that lurk beneath the ocean's surface.

Grumbling under my breath, I search my surroundings until my gaze dips to a red piece of ribbon tied around an over-turned tree lying on its side. I reach forward to run my fingers over the smooth silk and then begin to move in that direction. After one hundred or so feet, I stumble across another red ribbon.

This continues until I reach a massive cave naturally carved into the cliffside. Unlike the cave I'm staying at with Aliana, it's large enough that I don't have to duck my head in order to venture inside. Mud squishes beneath my shoes as I shove my hands into my pockets and glance around.

There, to the right of me, is another red ribbon.

I hurry in that direction, continuing to follow the trail of ribbons as the tunnel branches into numerous directions over a dozen times. I'd be completely lost by now if I didn't have the red ribbons to guide me.

"Uni!" I holler, cupping my mouth so my voice is amplified. It's never a good idea to sneak up on the large bastard. "It's Creep."

I turn at another fork to see that I've entered a surprisingly large cavern with a pool of water in the very center. High above—nearly two hundred feet—sunlight filters through an opening and illuminates the water like a thousand shimmering diamonds. I hadn't even noticed that I was descending deeper into the cave with every step I took.

"Uni!" I glance around in dismay just as the water begins to shake and tremble, almost as if the earth is being ripped apart by an earthquake.

I brace one hand against the cave wall to keep myself upright as a huge figure emerges from the water.

To say that this monster is ginormous is an understatement if I ever heard one. He's what you would get if you crossbred a kraken with a human. His large, bulbous body is gray and almost silky in appearance. Numerous tentacles explode in all directions from his body. The blob that consists of his face, however, holds distinctively humanoid features. Uni once told me that the more time he spends in the water, the larger he becomes, as if his body *absorbs* the water surrounding him.

A wide, beguiling smile curves up on Uni's face when he sees me.

"Cousin!" he booms, and two of his tentacles come to plop down on the ground surrounding the small pool.

He carries his heavy body out of the water and settles on the cold rock, his tentacles flopping dramatically. He changes and distorts—his body shrinking and becoming thinner, his tentacles retreating inwards until they're only a few feet long instead of a dozen feet, and legs and arms popping out of his gray body like four toothpicks being shoved into a ball of playdough.

Before I can even catch my bearings, Uni—now roughly my size—is lunging at me and pulling me into a tight, exuberant hug. I awkwardly pat his back—because what else am I supposed to do?—as Uni practically squeezes my innards out of my body. I feel like a tube of damn toothpaste.

"Hello, my old friend," I say with a cheeky smile, trying to push him away from me.

But the damn monster just continues to *nuzzle* me. Yeah. Nuzzle.

"Come, come!" Uni finally pulls away, but it's only to grab my arm and lead me towards a tiny room-slash-cave I hadn't noticed earlier, directly behind the large pool of ocean water.

It appears to be a makeshift house, with large crates positioned to resemble a bed, a stump that serves as a chair, and a huge piece of rock that is probably supposed to be a table.

"Let me introduce you to the girls," Uni continues eagerly.

Girls?

I furrow my brows.

Uni happily points to two porcelain dolls sitting at the table. One of them has long blonde hair and glasses, while the second has black hair cut into a short bob. They look to be in immaculate condition, which is strange because most items from the before time are nothing but garbage by now.

Tesq would blow a nut if he could see them.

But then Uni's words register—slowly clicking into place—and I don't know whether to smile, laugh, or cry.

"This is Brittany." Uni points to the blonde doll. "And this is Sherry. Girls, say hello to the Creeper."

Silence.

But Uni begins to laugh as if the dolls just told the most hilarious joke. "Sherry, I'm not going to ask if he's single." He playfully swats at her arms. "That's inappropriate." He pauses again, his head tilted as if he's listening to something I can't hear, and then he says, "No, Brittany. You're not on birth control. We talked about this."

I stare at Uni in horror before forcing my expression to lighten. Turning back to the dolls, I say, "Hello, ladies. It's a pleasure to meet you."

Then I wink for good measure.

Yeah. I wink at two fucking dolls.

What is my life turning into?

Uni wiggles his fingers together like a diabolical mastermind. "Ohhh. I'm sensing fireworks." He claps a hand down on my shoulder and gives it a squeeze. "I just ask that you wear a condom. I don't want any babies running around."

Then he begins to laugh raucously while I just stand there awkwardly, hating my life.

Shaking his hand off of me, I turn towards Uni completely. "Uni, I actually came because I need your help."

He doesn't have any brows, but the gray skin between his eyes begins to furrow. "Do you not know how to put a condom on?"

I take a deep breath as I pray for patience.

This is why we chose not to keep Uni around.

My cousin is a little…odd, even by monsters' standards. But he's so damn powerful that he can obliterate entire streets in mere seconds if he felt the need. His temper tantrums were infamous in the Ebony Kingdom before the other Terrors and I decided to…send him on a prolonged vacation, so to speak.

Even now, standing in front of him, I'm keenly aware that he may be able to kill me in the time it takes me to blink. He wouldn't even have to try. We're in his domain, after all, and he's the only monster I know with complete control over the water and all the creatures in it. His power level even rivals that of me and the other Terrors.

Which is exactly why we need him.

"Would you be willing to head back with me? I can explain it better there." I reach my hand out in silent invitation.

Uni seems a little confused, but that smile of his never fades from his face. After a long moment, he nods and then gestures towards the dolls behind him. "Can I bring the girls?"

"Err…of course."

Uni nods seriously and picks up both of them. When he pushes one at my chest, I hesitantly take it.

"Now, don't be handsy with Brittany there," Uni warns seriously, a hint of that familiar violence seeping into his eyes as he threatens me. "She talks a big game, but she's still a virgin."

Oh my god.

"Um…" I gape at the doll in horror.

"Sherry's the whore of the family," he continues as he strokes the other doll's shiny black hair. He leans forward to whisper conspiratorially, "Don't worry. I always keep the morning-after pill on hand."

For fuck's sake.

Grumbling under my breath, I wait until Uni places his hand in mine before backing into one of the shadows plaguing each corner of the tiny cave.

I just pray that when I portal back to my mate and the others, I don't end up with any plastic body parts.

Fucking Uni.

ALIANA

WHEN THE OTHERS mentioned a monster that has been banned from entering the Ebony Kingdom, I pictured one so terrifying and grotesque that I'll be shaking in my boots.

What I didn't imagine is…Uni.

Uni, who's currently sporting one blue arm thanks to his portal travel with Creep.

Uni, who's stroking the hair of one of his dolls, muttering about "promiscuous sluts" under his breath.

Uni, who doesn't seem to be listening to the stone-faced Devourer as the huge wolf man attempts to tell him his plan while the sun dips down behind the hills.

Creep sits beside me on a fallen tree branch—courtesy of Tesq—and his tentacle circles around my ankle teasingly. Well, technically Uni's tentacle, but it belongs to Creep for the time being. Swapsies and all that.

The gray is a startling contrast to his blue skin, and the appendage is nearly the length of his body. Suction cups rest at the bottom, and he uses them to apply the slightest bit of pressure to my suddenly overheated skin. A flush works its way up my neck instinctively as Creep continues to torture me with that tentacle of his.

I force myself to focus on Uni and the others once more.

"It's simple," Em snaps at the water monster in his lilting accent. A scowl mars his handsome face as he folds his arms over his chest. "We need you to take to the water with your little water friends—"

Uni casts Em a withering glare. "The dolphins are *not* my friends. Prickly little bastards." He mutters that last statement under his breath as he resumes stroking his doll's hair.

Dev attempts to take over the conversation, though his voice is hard and grating, more of a bark than anything soothing. "We need you to spy on Barnabas. Gather information and bring it back here."

"He won't expect you to be back, so he won't be keeping an eye on the water," Creep adds.

The tentacle snakes upward from my ankle, suction cups kissing at my kneecap, tantalizing my thighs, before brushing against my crotch through my pants, and it takes everything I have not to screech and buck my hips. A flood of arousal cascades through me, as inappropriate as the timing is. I have to grit my teeth and pant shallowly through them as I try to maintain focus on the conversation and ignore Creep's naughty, knowing grin.

Uni ignores the others and continues to tenderly alternate his attention between his two dolls.

An idea begins to form.

Clearing my throat, I wait for Uni to turn towards me. "Their names are Brittany and Sherry, right?" I ask, recalling the first thing Uni said to us when he stepped out of the portal with Creep.

"Sherry, Brittany, meet your uncles! No...you cannot call any of them Daddy. Sherry, it's inappropriate to ask the Devourer to 'wreck your porcelain body.' We talked about this. No, Brittany, you can't ask the Grotesque if his tongue is stone too and if he's willing to 'rock' your world, pun intended."

Uni frowns at me, and then that frown turns into a scowl when he turns towards his dolls.

"She doesn't look like a whore, Sherry. Don't be crass. Maybe she's a little slutty, but a whore is too crude of a term." He tsks at the doll disapprovingly as I try not to squirm.

Dev growls threateningly at the water monster, his eyes glowing red, and I know it's because Uni implied I was a slut.

I throw my mates a warning look before turning back to Uni. "We need your help. I don't think you understand what Barnabas will do if he becomes leader." I don't know for certain myself, but I can imagine, at least based on my mates' descriptions of him. I allow myself to laugh—the noise dry and bitter. "Do you really think he'll allow your...girls to live? He's not just a monster but a psychopath. He'll kill Sherry and Brittany just to get *you* under his thumb."

Uni gapes at me in horror before dropping his gaze back to his dolls. His borrowed blue arm reaches out and curves protectively around them, and the tentacles near his face flare in distress. "No…"

"You know it's true. The others told me you used to live in Ebony Kingdom. You must remember Barnabas and his evil ways. Do you really think he'll allow Sherry and Brittany to live? They're not monsters"—at least, I don't think so, but what the hell do I know?—"and they're defenseless. If you help us, I promise you we'll help your girls in return. We'll protect them."

Uni's eyes are impossibly wide in his slimy, gray face.

"You promise me you'll take care of them, even if something happens to me?" he asks seriously, his grip tightening around the dolls nearly imperceptibly.

"Cross my heart and hope not to die," Creep responds, his tentacle once again brushing against my most sensitive area.

I squirm, grateful for the fact that shadows are now draped over all of us and his actions are—hopefully, maybe, probably —hidden from view.

"Now, Dev, Tesq, and Em are more than happy to continue negotiations with you. I have somewhere to be with my pretty, little mate," Creep declares.

Tesq scowls. "Where will you be?"

In answer, Creep jumps up, grabs my waist, and then flings me over his shoulder. I wiggle instinctively, but Creep's tentacle slams down on my ass before I can actually attempt an escape.

Not that I want to.

"Oh, I'm just trying out a new toy I got." I can hear the smile in Creep's voice.

"New toy?" Dev sounds confused.

"You mean the tentacle?" Em asks dryly from his spot on a nearby stump.

But Creep merely laughs and carries me away.

Yes, please.

ALIANA

I'M NOT sure where I thought Creep would take me, to a clearing maybe, or down the road to an abandoned building. I definitely didn't expect him to walk me through the forest to the visitor parking lot.

He stops short for a second, and I pull myself up, twisting to see what he's looking at.

"The tracker," he breathes, and I spot the antennaed bastard who's been following us.

Only, right at this second, he's face down in a puddle. Creep walks over and roughly kicks the monster, rolling him onto his back. The tracker's eyes are glazed with frost, and the front of his shirt is soaked with a combination of water and blood. There's a massive hole in his stomach.

"Dead," I whisper.

"Thank fuck," Creep responds. "You use your powers while I was gone and freeze the son of a bitch?".

I shake my head.

"Well, all's well that ends with my cock in your pussy." He immediately reverts to his cheerful self as he rounds the body and smacks my ass.

He carries me across the visitor parking lot to the other side, where a handful of cars are parked. Then he slams me down from his shoulder onto the hood of a rusted-out green Dodge Challenger.

My ass lands with a bruising thump, and my hands end up braced on the windshield. Pain as bright as the emerging moonlight shoots through my nervous system.

I'm about to bitch Creep out for rough manhandling when he leans forward over me, his eyes practically aglow with lust, and whispers, "I'm going to shove this tentacle inside of you and suction your G-spot from the inside while my mouth sucks that clit. I'm going to wring sounds from your body that you didn't even know you were capable of making."

Well. Fuck.

I press my lips together and swallow my anger because I'm signing right up for that. A black and blue ass seems like a small price to pay for what promises to be the orgasm of the century.

Of course, because it's Creep, I cock a brow and muster all the challenging sarcasm I can manage while my body is practically thrumming with lust. Pressing my hand against his chest, I can feel his racing heartbeat under my palm.

"That's pretty big talk from a monster who can barely get one orgasm out of me."

"One? Oh, we both know that's a lie," he purrs, using his tentacle to stroke down my body over my clothes.

I fight off a shiver as the appendage runs lightly down from my shoulder and over my chest. A suction cup teases my nipple, gripping and pulling lightly through my shirt before sliding farther down, planting what feels like gentle kisses across my abdomen.

Though our words are teasing, and though we're both brimming with lust, there's also an undercurrent of something more as he stares at me. Something that tangles in my stomach and makes me bite my lip as I blink up at him.

Creep leans over me, his antlers lined with silvery moonlight, the tiny blue flowers on them opening up, as if they bloom based on his emotions. I feel the weight of his gaze as if it's a physical thing while his claw slowly taps my boot.

"Undress for me," he breathes.

I'm tempted to ignore him, to shove up straighter and capture his lips with my mouth, take control of the situation until I can command him to do exactly what he just promised.

But I don't.

My mate's earned enough of my trust to also earn something else I almost never give—my compliance.

Eyes locked on his, I reach down and slowly unlace my boot. Energy crackles wildly between us, and the way he licks his lips in anticipation has me hurrying to kick that boot off and rid myself of the other. My socks follow, as do my pants, until I'm in my shirt and panties in the cool night breeze.

Creep brings his claw to my knee and gently pushes on it, the simple touch sending a flare of yearning up to my core. "Open. Spread those legs—"

"Do you want my panties off—"

"Not yet," he whispers, leaning in close enough to capture my lips for the first time.

My mate's kiss is swift but sure. He knows exactly how much to press against my mouth to make my lips part for him, but also maintains enough control not to give in when my tongue swipes against him and asks for more. He pulls back slightly, enough to gaze into my eyes, but I can still feel his words ghost across my skin.

"Spread. I want to stare at you. I'm going to burn this moment into my brain of my mate spread eagled on the hood of a car, waiting for me to do unspeakable things to her."

God. Those words alone tighten my nipples to points so hard they threaten to cut through my shirt.

I lean back onto the windshield and widen my legs across the hood like he asks. The metal is cold and stiff against my back, but I'm nearly feverish with anticipation at this point, so it doesn't bother me. All that matters is the rush of my pulse, which soars like a bird in a wild wind current and brings a flush to my cheeks and to other parts of my body.

Creep steps between my legs, eyes roaming over me. "Aliana."

Just the worshipful way he murmurs my name sends heat spiraling into my lower belly and makes my thighs quiver, wanting to rub together and ease the ache building inside.

I wait and let him look his fill, even though I'm practically trembling as a result.

"Shirt," he finally orders.

I sit up to comply, tossing the shirt over the side of the vehicle and then growling, "Touch me."

I may implode if he doesn't put those hands on me soon.

Creep reaches forward with his claw and gently scoops my breasts out of the cups of my bra, propping the globes up on top of the material so he can stare down at the evidence of my arousal.

It takes all of my self control not to arch my back and beg him to put his mouth on me. They feel so heavy and full and needy, but I resist the urge to ask for what I want. There's something more thrilling about encouraging this budding tension between us, this stolen moment of freedom where I'm trusting my other mates to take care of the world's problems and this mate to take care of me.

Creep has always taken care of me, I realize with a start. The thought tightens my throat.

"I wish I had a camera," Creep murmurs, a lone claw coming up to trace the underside of one of my nipples.

"Cameras still exist?" I ask brokenly, that touch sending me into a floating headspace where the errant emotions that just rose up mingle with the wisps of lust and start to swirl like the clouds just before a storm.

He gives me a one-shoulder shrug, eyes focused on my chest and the panting breaths I start to take when he slowly wraps his tentacle around my ankle. Soft and wet, the texture of his new appendage is more intense as he touches me without clothing. The tentacle itself is rubbery, but the suction cups are like circular tongues, warm and wet and perhaps just the tiniest bit sticky.

Every inch or two of tentacle, there's another sucker, and as Creep slowly trails the long limb up, wrapping my leg as he goes, those suckers lap at my exposed skin in delicious ways. The teasing, suctioning kisses all along the length of my leg makes my toes curl. Then the pointed tip of the tentacle reaches my inner thigh and strokes along the seam of my panties, and my breath shudders and stalls.

I've never been so close to begging.

"Are you wet for me?"

"Dry as the Sahara," I tell him.

Creep's crooked grin shows the sharp fangs of his canines. "Liar."

"Prove me a liar," I retort, though I'm certain that my heaving breasts give me away.

"Hmmm...I think you really want me to touch you to prove it," he murmurs. "But I think there's a better way."

My fingers curl against the hood as I try to hide my agitation that he hasn't already slid that tentacle up another inch. "What's that?"

"Get you to beg for it."

"I don't beg," I scoff, though I'm fairly certain he knows just how close I am.

But if that's what he wants, I'll definitely fight it. My inherent stubbornness won't allow anything less.

My monster leans down and sucks my nipple into his mouth, rolling it against his tongue, nipping with those teeth, before releasing it and blowing on it. When his gaze travels back up to meet mine from where he hovers above my chest, I have to hold my breath in order to avoid showing him how affected I am.

Those suckers pulse again along my leg, and he wiggles the tip of the tentacle closer.

I can't resist. My body automatically twists, seeking friction.

The tentacle tip lifts up, denying me access, and I stare down in outrage as I see the tip grow rounder, blunter, more dick shaped—all of it mocking me.

"Creep," I hiss from between my teeth. "I swear to fuck, I'll call Dev over here and tell him to cock block you for the next decade—"

In a flash, my panties are shredded by Creep's claw, and his hot, thick tentacle is stroking up and down my entrance. I don't have time to gloat over the fact that I didn't end up begging because the feel of him right where I need him is too damned overwhelming.

"You are wet, little warrior," Creep moans before he plants a soft kiss on the thundering pulse of my neck. "I can feel it soaking into me even more than usual."

He lifts the tentacle so we can both see the proof, my wetness glistening in the moonlight.

"I'm wet, but I'm also mad right now. And I'm going to get even more mad if I'm not stuffed with that—"

Creep's tongue shoves into my mouth, silencing me as the tentacle shoves an inch inside of me before pulling back and then pulsing gently in and out, just deep enough to tease me. Warm and hot and growing thicker—it's perfect.

His fingertips reach between us, and he pinches my right nipple, tugging on it lightly and causing fireworks to dance across my chest and send sparks shooting down my spine. Meanwhile, the tentacle presses in a little deeper, spreading my lower lips lewdly as it slides against them. I swivel my hips to increase the tingling charge bolting up my opening as the first suction cup enters me.

Holy shit.

I nearly bite Creep's tongue in surprise as a scandalous sensation ripples through me. The slurping, wet drag of that cup seems to pull at every nerve ending until it's taut and vibrating with a note of pleasure I've never even heard before. It rings inside my ears and makes my eyes flutter closed. If angels exist and make fucking sound—this is it. This is their heavenly chorus.

My fingers wrench up and grasp Creep by the shoulders, fingernails digging into his scarred, bark-like skin, warning him not to stop.

He presses in another inch, and I moan deeply against his mouth as the suction cup finally seats itself over its intended target. It pulses, and I wrench back from Creep with a scream of pleasure as it pulls at my G-spot.

His smug grin doesn't even ruin the moment because I'm too busy seeing stars. An orgasm rumbles through me and leaves me gasping but still greedy for more. It's like a precursor to an earthquake, the early trembling in the ground that signals disaster is imminent.

God, how I want Creep to destroy me. I want him to wreck me so that I tumble down and collapse, shattering into bits.

I travel my fingers up to his beautiful face and cup his sharp cheekbones. "Remind me what you promised you'd do to me," I tell him, not quite managing sass with my breathless tone.

A smart monster, he takes the hint and sinks down my body until his mouth presses against my core. His forked tongue splits apart to lick up each side of my slit repeatedly before those lips of his descend to suck on my swollen, aching clit.

The pull and stretch sends me whirling. Meanwhile, somehow Creep's discovered how to pulse the suction cup inside of me so that he can control the timing and coordinate it with his mouth. Suction inside. Suction out. Inside. Out.

I plant my feet on the hood of the car, and my hips rise of their own accord. My hands were on Creep's face, but they've migrated to his antlers, which span across my belly. Palms clamping down, those horns become my lifeline as I scream out my pleasure again and again.

I don't build up to one more orgasm; I become a giant rolling orgasm as debauched bliss consumes me. The entire world tunnels until all I see are the pinprick stars above, all I feel is the gentle moss and vines on Creep's antlers, and all I know is the sparkling euphoria inside of me.

By the time Creep lets me sink down onto the hood of the car, my legs are cramping and my throat is hoarse.

"'Bout time you finished with her," a deep voice growls. "I need a turn."

I turn my head until my cheek rests against the chilled hood and gaze out at the shadows. Heartbeat fluttering madly, I spot a figure beneath the trees.

But my heart drops when I realize that it's not another one of my mates.

ALIANA

I'VE JUST OPENED my mouth to warn Creep when green blood splatters into the clearing. The bushes part as a headless corpse falls forward through them, smashing into the parking lot and making my eyebrows shoot up.

From the shadows behind the body, Dev emerges. He marches forward, the antennae-laden head of a decapitated monster leaking gore down the length of his arm.

"Fucker saw you naked. He can't live after that." The Devourer tosses the head carelessly to one side as he strides closer, red eyes gleaming in his human face. His expression is a combination of violent fury and potent lust, and it's a heady combination to witness.

I watch him as I return to my boneless state now that the threat is gone. Sinking back against the hood of the car, I moan lightly as Creep's mouth retreats and the tentacle slowly slides out of me, suction cups detaching all along my leg with a series of low pops. The air rushes over my heated skin, and even though I've just had a series of reality-altering orgasms, the flush of pleasure inside of me hasn't quite subsided, and I find myself ready for more.

"You'd better be about to fuck me," I warn Creep as I turn my eyes from Dev back to him.

"You'd better be ready for it because it's not like I'm going to give you a choice," he snarks back.

"Good."

"Good."

Our retorts are lame—addled by lust, we can't maintain our normal repartee—but I don't mind. As long as Creep's dick fucks me into oblivion, I couldn't care less about anything else. Our outside problems have ceased to exist, and the only issues right now are that our bodies aren't close enough and his mouth isn't on mine between whispering dirty words because neither of us knows how to utter sweet ones to each other.

Creep yanks his pants down, not bothering to pull them all the way off before he grabs my legs and slides me down the hood toward his straining, thick cock. The tip of it is swollen, but not nearly as big as I know it can get. I know the tip of his dick can swell to the size of a tennis ball, and right now I'm up for the challenge.

"What the fuck happened to sharing?" Dev's indignation rolls over us as he steps closer.

I shrug, shoulder sliding against the hood as I turn my face toward him. "You want some? Come and get it."

I'm definitely not opposed to taking the both of them at once again. In fact, I'm a little smug at the fact that Dev clearly sought us out after fervently denying how much he liked last time aloud.

I'm not the only liar tonight.

Creep thrusts into me then, the sharp stretch of him forcing me to catch my breath. His claw digs into my hip as he uses the tentacle to slide underneath my lower back and raise my ass to give him a better angle. The head of his cock swells inside of me, brushing against my inner walls deliciously.

I watch with interest as the long appendage stretches and grows until it wraps around us both and dips down between Creep's ass cheeks. The suction cups nudge at my ass until my cheeks part and one little tongue-like protrusion is firmly planted around my rosebud. If I had to guess, another sucker is playing with Creep's too. My blue monster starts to gently thrust into me, and I'm so wet that I can feel my honey-like arousal dripping down my thighs.

My eyelashes flutter in pleasure as Creep builds up a rhythm and starts to coordinate the suction cups the way he did before so that they squeeze each time he retreats. Both of us end up panting out short little sounds of pleasure, our eyes locked, gazes screaming things at each other that our lips would never allow.

Fuck, we'd better survive this shit. All of it. Because one day, I want to be able to tell Creep just what he means to me.

A sheen coats my eyes suddenly, and I blink in surprise at the intensity of my own reaction. I don't cry. Almost ever.

Creep's expression softens in response.

"Goddammit, Aliana! Look at me!" Dev's roar startles me out of the moment, and when my eyes flicker over to my right side, I realize he's naked and next to me.

His bloody claw is already outstretched, reaching for my breast. He swirls a wet, green-blood-stained palm across my nipple before roughly squeezing.

"You're going to use the blood of my enemies to jerk me off, kitten," he orders, completely changing the tone of the moment. Turning it dark, twisted, perverted.

In any other circumstance, I might argue with him. But Creep has perfected his rhythm. His dick is tapping perfectly inside of me, and the suction on my ass is adding a layer of fuzzy-headed sensation that I don't think I've ever experienced before.

And, for some reason, Dev's mention of the blood of his enemies sends a sizzling volt through me, like a power line surging to life with an electric hum. There's something so intriguing, compelling, almost satisfying about that thought. So, I limply extend my hand to give the Devourer what he wants.

"I knew you'd end up liking sharing," I taunt as he palms his dick, coating it in monster blood.

"I don't like sharing. But like hell if I'm going to let him fuck you and just stand here and watch your tits bounce." Dev roughly thrusts his blood-coated cock into my outstretched hand. "You're *mine*."

Even though I clamp down in a way I hope is painful, his only reaction is a dark grin as he reaches forward and palms my chest.

"You're a poet," I critique.

"You know it," he retorts, completely deadpan.

Creep cracks up. "That rhymed!" His laughter makes his rhythm falter for a second, before that tentacle gives us both a solemn squeeze. "Save your jokes for later. I think our mate needs to be coated in our cum."

"I'm going to shoot it all over your face, little kitten, so that I can watch you lick it off," Dev promises, angling his hips so that his dick does point a little more toward my face.

I simply twist my hand in response, curving his cock so that it's away from me. "You're going to put that cum where I let you put that cum."

I'm proud that I don't react at all when Dev roughly tweaks my nipple, though it sends a pain-laced pleasure flowing through me, which is exactly the intensity my body needs after a good orgasm. I've had pleasure. Now, I need pain-laced pleasure to top it.

"Fuck. Aliana. I like when you say the word cum," Creep moans as he slowly resumes his prior speed, his hips snapping against me with every thrust. "Your pussy is so damn wet and hot, and it clamps down on my dick so good."

Dev growls, and the tendons in his neck tighten as jealousy threatens to overwhelm him. I can tell that he's about two seconds away from backhanding Creep and ruining this fucking orgasm building inside of me.

So, I say the only thing I can think of to distract him.

I give him a better offer. "Climb up on the hood and let me taste that dick."

He doesn't have to be told twice. Two seconds later, Dev's straddling my torso, pressing my breasts together on either side of his bloody dick, the tip aimed right for my lips.

I lean up a tiny bit so that I can get a better angle, and when he slides that cock into my mouth, I find myself surprised by how much I like it. But I do like everything about it—from the fact that he's actively sharing me, to the fact that Dev the bossy listened to an order, to the way his cock fills my mouth.

I even like—to my utter shock—the taste of monster blood. It sparks something inside of me, some dark, shadowy craving that I never knew I had. My monster side—that has to be what's turning me wild—driving me to press down harder on Dev's cock, to swallow farther, to attempt to deep-throat his dick. It makes me manic, an appetite like nothing I've ever felt surging through me.

More. I need more of this.

Even Dev seems surprised by the ferocity I use to lap at his dick. His hands soften against my breasts as I try to quench this vicious need coursing through me, only to find myself frustrated when his dick is licked clean.

"More blood!" I demand, and my mate swipes his palms over his forearm, gathering up the remaining blood there.

My pussy tightens just at the sight, and Creep groans from behind Dev's back.

I pant roughly when Dev slides his dick from between my lips and slowly lubes it up for a second time, barely clamping down on the desire to snarl at him to hurry.

When he feeds it back to me, slowly and deliberately, our eyes stay locked. Both of us breathe shallowly, on the cusp of deranged pleasure. Our dark words seem to have evaporated in the face of my newly discovered darker craving, and I can see by the look in Dev's eyes that he's thoroughly enjoying this depraved side of me.

"My black-hearted little kitten," he murmurs, his bloody fingers gliding over my nipples before roughly twisting them. "I'm going to make every blood-soaked desire going through your mind come true."

His delicious dick reaches the back of my throat just as Creep's cock taps against my G-spot, and I moan. Both of my mates are spurred on by the sound, and the car beneath us creaks as two monsters speed up their thrusts. I writhe beneath them, animalistic pleasure unraveling my thoughts until there's nothing more than their touches, their masculine scents, the coppery smell of blood mixing with the scent of my own arousal.

There's a quick jolt of friction against my clit—Creep's finger swipes over it.

That's all it takes.

Two monsters roughly fucking me so hard that the hood of this car threatens to buckle, a blood-soaked cock in my mouth, and a quick flick of my clit. My muscles seize up in a hot wash of pleasure that soaks into my very bones, leaving them weakened and soft. I slump back, and Dev slips himself from between my lips, tugging himself roughly until I feel the hot splatter of his seed against my neck, my chin, my lips.

With a groan, he rolls off me and splays on the hood beside me as Creep digs his claw farther into my hip and intensifies his thrusts. Quick, sharp snaps, and suddenly he yanks himself free, the bulbous head of his dick dragging against me and popping out all at once. I watch through hooded eyes as the tentacle encasing us both seems to pulse and kiss my puckered hole, and Creep's dick erupts like a fountain along my belly.

Just like they promised, my mates have covered me in their cum.

Unlike before, I don't mind a bit. I lick my lips and taste Dev's satisfaction with a tiny smirk playing across my lips.

When my blue monster crawls up onto my other side, collapsing with a sigh, the sports car beneath us gives a groan of protest. But we all ignore it, staring up at the stars and enjoying this stolen moment of bliss. This tiny bit of calm before the shit storm.

THE GROTESQUE

I STARE across the water as Uni slides beneath the muddy waves of the Hudson River, off to spy on our behalf.

On either side of me are his precious dolls, whom I've sworn to guard with my life. I glance over and exchange a long-suffering look with Fluffy because, while I do enjoy human-made curiosities, the pressure of keeping these two dolls feels like a weight on my shoulders.

It also leaves me tethered here in the clearing where we met with Uni while Dev goes off to search for our mate. I don't dare pick up these dolls. What if the lava in my hands suddenly activates? I'm still learning to control it.

As if my tiger can sense my unease, she comes over and shoves her head underneath my palm.

That gesture alone, so common between us, sets off alarm bells, and I quickly retract my palm and check it for glowing orange lines before settling it back onto her head and giving her a pet.

"Thanks, girl," I tell her solemnly.

"How did you get Aliana to fall in love with you?" Em calls out from his spot on the other side of the clearing.

I turn to see his face, half painted blue with moonlight and half in shadow. His lips are twisted, as if he may already regret asking the question, but his green eyes are steady as they stare at me.

His question is as startling as it is baffling. "I…don't know."

Frustration fills the air when he steps forward and glares at me. "That's not an answer."

It's not. I know it's not.

At my hip, Fluffy growls, showing her teeth to him, but I gently rub her ears and whisper, "It's okay, girl."

"I read a human magazine about courtship, but clearly it's full of shit and not working because Aliana is part monster." Em tilts his head, and his eyes burn with a desperation I recognize, a desperation I felt inside my own chest for years, the ache of wanting.

Wanting to be worthy. Wanting to be lucky. Wanting to be someone else.

I try to keep pity from my expression as I turn my gaze to my stone feet. "I was…nice?"

It ends up sounding like a question because I'm not sure it's the right answer or even the reason she cares for me.

I am certain she cares though, which is as strange and wonderful in an utterly beguiling way because I don't understand it at all. Kind of like the human circus. Who would want to jump through a hoop of fire for fun? Why is that entertainment?

There are things in the world that I don't understand. Her emotions are one of them. It's why I can't do anything more than offer a shrug to Em when he stares at me expectantly.

"I told you!" Em mutters under his breath as he half turns away from me.

Oh, wait, that's not Em. It's now Chase controlling the body in front of me. He stands differently, a little more hunched. Less…strutty. Honestly, though, it's confusing to know who's in charge. They should carry a stick. Red side up for Em talking, blue side for Chase.

I sigh.

"I don't know how love works." I search for the right words, though I'm pretty certain I'm terrible at this. "I just know I will do anything for her."

Chase runs a hand through his blond hair, and I marvel at the irony that a man as attractive, even beautiful, as he is should struggle with love. I always blamed my hideous appearance, always assumed that I was too frightening for anyone to love. Aliana has shown me love is more than skin deep, however. It's a feeling that soaks right into your bones and transforms you from the inside out.

"She won't let me do anything for her, though," he grouses in frustration. "She thinks anything I do to help her is an attempt to hold her back. I've tried to help her escape when we were captured. She mocked me for being stupid. She wouldn't even let me walk in front of her when she rescued me from that building." He shakes his head in despair.

"But she insisted on rescuing you," I remind him. "She argued with all of us. Insisted on going. Insisted on separating. And she was the one who found you."

"So?" I can tell Em's taking control of the body again when he throws his arms wide, pacing in his frustration.

"So…I'm not good at words. What if she's not good either?"

"What the hell does that mean?"

"She did whatever it took. To protect you." My words are halting, sentences incomplete as I try to slowly walk Em through my thought process. "Maybe she just needs time."

"Time for what?"

"To realize she loves you."

Em laughs up at the stars, a harsh and bitter sound that fills the entire clearing. "We don't have fucking time. Our kingdom's under attack. God-fucking-dammit. You're useless. I just want to get fucking laid before I die in this shit body. Is that too much to ask?"

He storms off into the trees, and I share a startled look with Fluffy.

This was all about sex?

I sigh. This is exactly why I've avoided monsterkind for years. Solitude is easier than reading between the lines. And Em's a rude asshole. But he's right. I am useless on the subject of sex. It's been decades since I've slept with a monster because I never really believed that someone could want me that way. And humans? Never.

That's why when Creep swapped dicks with me and was so eager to use it on Aliana, I let him. Why not? It was the closest

I'd ever come to touching her, to touching anyone. And I was so worried about breaking her when I thought she was human.

But she's not human.

She's not breakable.

And Em is right.

Our kingdom's under siege, we're about to have the fight of our lives, and who knows if we'll come out on the other side of it?

I swallow hard and sink down onto a tree stump, my hand still stroking Fluffy's head.

After I realized Aliana cared for me, that someone could love me despite myself, I didn't think I could ever want anything more.

But that painful, desperate ache is back inside my chest, throbbing like an open wound.

I want to be with Aliana so badly it hurts.

The problem is, I have no idea how to be with a woman. And I have no idea how to ask.

I sink into that painful knowledge and cease to hear the crickets chirping or the stars gliding overhead. I don't notice the changing shadows or when Fluffy stalks off to hunt her dinner. I don't feel the wind blowing a few stray leaves onto my lap.

I'm as still and silent as stone as I stew on the realization that I once again am the monster who is different from the others. What comes so easily and naturally to Creep and Dev is a struggle for me. Em appears to be in the same boat, but that realization doesn't make me feel any better.

Aliana may love me, but does she want me that way? And if she does, there's an entirely new and terrifying set of possibilities. Scenarios in which we could be together, and I could disappoint her.

Bile rises in my throat, and a cinching sensation straps my ribs, pressing them inward until they feel like they're stabbing me.

"Grotesque."

The sound of my name rouses me from my daze, and I glance up to realize that the sky is beginning to turn pink and Uni's standing in front of me, shrinking as rivulets of water sluice down his gray features.

His eyes dart to his girls, who haven't moved all night, before glancing back at me and giving a nod of approval.

I simply stare at him, blinking, still coming back to myself and the present moment.

"I have seen many things, but Barnabas is a disgrace to monsters. Did you know that his minions are killing monster babies in order to quickly level up?"

That revelation jolts me, sizzling under my skin and igniting the lava that still churns somewhere deep inside of me. The veins along my arms and legs start to glow orange. "What?"

Uni nods, his tentacles whipping around his body. "It's true."

My lip curls, and I open my mouth to express my disgust, but Dev's voice calls out from the trees. "He WHAT?"

Dev, Creep, and Aliana emerge from the forest, and the scent of sex is heavy on all three of them, filling my nostrils and setting off that painful ache—though right now, that ache throbs dully underneath the thick layer of disgust I have for Barnabas.

I knew the bastard abused his son, but wholesale treating monster children as expendable? As simple tools for leveling up?

"That explains the ridiculous number of Eights and Nines at your place," Creep tells Dev. "And at the meat factory."

He doesn't look surprised to find out what a sick fuck his father is, just repulsed.

Aliana reaches for his claw and squeezes it.

Uni lifts the blue arm he swapped with Creep and points at the tentacle attached to the Terror's side. "I'll be wanting that back. My girls don't like pointy fingers. They prefer tentacles on their tits."

He scoops his two dolls up with one of his tentacles and pulls them close.

"Of course," Creep responds, a slight scratch in his tone that betrays how much this information upsets him.

"Did you figure out their location?" Dev asks.

Uni looks offended. "Isn't that why you sent me?" He turns to one of his dolls and shakes his head at her as if he can't believe the question. Then he faces me again, as if I'm in charge, which is ridiculous. "Barnabas and his main crew are holed up in the space that the humans used to call the Empire State Building."

ALIANA

Tomorrow's the day.

The day we'll fight for our lives.

The day we'll fight for our love.

The day we'll fight for a world that isn't ruled by a malevolent tyrant.

Nerves tangle together in my belly, and I can't decide if the skittering sensation on my skin is from fear or adrenaline. Whatever it is makes sleep impossible.

All I can do is pace.

Dev, surprisingly, was the first of my monsters to fall asleep. I thought he would stubbornly remain awake, guarding us while we slept, but Creep told me Dev needed time to recharge before the fight tomorrow.

Creep collapsed next. I think the prospect of seeing his father tomorrow—and hopefully ending his miserable life—is taking its toll on my snarky, silly mate.

Uni disappeared shortly after we finalized our plan for battle, and Chase and Em walked off an hour or so ago. They didn't tell me why, but I suspect it's because Em wants to learn how to fight in Chase's body. But of course, they won't confess that out loud. They don't want to be perceived as weak by me or the other Terrors.

Soon, the only people left in the clearing are me and Tesq.

My gargoyle watches me as I pace, his eyes hot on my face, almost as hot as the magma traversing his gray skin. He doesn't speak, allowing me a moment to fall apart away from the watchful gazes of the others.

We have a plan.

But I worry it won't be enough.

Dev went over every aspect of how tomorrow will play out. I know exactly what I need to do and how to do it. Still, the fear persists, this white-hot pang in my chest where my heart should be.

Dev initially wanted me to remain behind, but I put my foot down before that idea could gain traction. There's no way in hell I'm allowing my guys to put their lives on the line while I hide away like a dainty princess in distress. It only took a few minutes for Dev to reluctantly change his mind, but I can tell he isn't happy about it.

None of my mates are happy about it, but they trust me—and my capabilities—enough to allow me to fight.

To end this, once and for all.

"Breathe." Tesq's deep, raspy voice drags my attention to where he stands next to a stump on the opposite side of the clearing. "Need to breathe."

It's only then I realize that my breathing is coming out in ragged gasps of air. I'm surprised I didn't pass out from the lack of oxygen to my brain.

I work to modulate my erratic breathing, my chest mimicking the steady rise and fall of Tesq's. The curiosity in his eyes from moments before has turned into concern.

"Everything could go to shit tomorrow," I blurt as I take a tentative step towards him. My breathing is still embarrassingly choppy.

"I know." Tesq watches me warily, almost like I'm a rabid dog foaming at the mouth and straining against my chain in an attempt to get to him.

"I could lose *everything* I care about. Everyone," I continue, something hot pricking the backs of my eyes.

Tears, I realize belatedly.

"So could we," Tesq points out. His tone is still cautious, still concerned, still soft.

It brushes my skin like the whiskers of a paintbrush, adding streaks of light and warmth that set me ablaze.

"I can't… I don't…" I'm hyperventilating. I know I am. Fear has grabbed my throat in an iron vise and is now cinching my airways.

But then Tesq's there. He's moved in front of me, and we're standing toe-to-toe. He lifts one cold finger and pushes up my chin, forcing me to meet his eyes.

"Breathe," he says again.

And I do.

Slowly and surely, the fear percolating inside of my chest begins to fizzle away like water on a blistering hot day. All that remains is an emotion more potent and consuming than anything else is capable of making me feel.

Love.

I *love* Tesq.

I love the gentle way he touches me.

I love the tender anxiety in his eyes.

I love the way his cheeks darken when he's embarrassed.

I love him, and tomorrow, he may be taken from me.

I flick my gaze to his lips, and his breath stalls. His eyes dart over my features, never really sticking, as he swallows.

"Aliana…" he whispers.

His fingers tighten on my chin, but it doesn't hurt. Pleasure migrates from where he touches my skin and shoots straight to my core.

"Tomorrow, everything could change," I whisper.

"Yes."

"I don't want to leave this world without letting you know how I feel." I press up on my tiptoes, trying to get closer to him. "Do you remember when you first saved me from Dev? When you protected and cared for me, even when I was afraid of you?"

This time, his answer is more hesitant. "Yes?"

"I think I started falling for you then."

And then I gently place my mouth over his.

ALIANA

I JUST MEAN to kiss him, to gently show Tesq how much he means to me because the brooding, silent gargoyle will never say anything aloud—and like hell if we're going to die tomorrow with words unsaid between us.

Out of all of my mates, my monsters, I loved him first.

He brings out a side in me that no one else does, a soft tenderness that causes me to cup his cheek and drag my palm gently over the stone-hard curve. He's so sweet and unassuming, this massive man with such quiet strength.

Our kiss gentles to a stop like a feather floating to the ground. When he sighs from my touch and leans his cheek into my hand, I pull back to stare longingly up at him, my gaze roving over his deep-set eyes, bone-white horns, and strong jaw.

I don't want tonight to be our last night together.

He's a Terror, a king in his own right. But I can see the exhaustion burdening him, weighing down his shoulders. All day long, as we planned and the horrors Barnabas is perpetrating kept filtering in from Uni's minions, the tightness in Tesq's shoulders grew more pronounced.

I'm not sure Barnabas has left a single monster under the age of five alive. He's swept through the city on a rampage, desperate to power up his league of beasts before the Terrors come for him. He knows they're coming.

My monsters could never sit idly by and let others take their power. But more than that, they refuse to stand by and let Barnabas and his bastards destroy their future generation.

They may have run a brutal kingdom full of wrongs, but I truly believe they've changed. I've seen their hearts expand, their minds forced to face realities they've never experienced because we all thought I was human and their mate. They've pushed through the idea that I should be a pet, a prisoner, a plaything. And I think they've come to realize that the world, while brutish and violent, is better with a little bit of love and loyalty.

Of course, Tesq was already closest to that realization. He's the most evolved of all of them. A gentleman among beasts.

I want to tell him that, to tell him how he unlocked this side of me that no one ever has before, that he makes me believe in things like soft smiles and fairy tales filled with glimmering sunbeams and dances in meadows. Things I would have dismissed as stupid before. Things I'll still dismiss as stupid if someone like Dev ever mentions them.

But Tesq...

I move my lips to the corner of his mouth and press gently, a kiss as soft and warm as a wax seal of approval. Moving along his jawline, I resolve to kiss every inch. I cannot only hear but feel his sigh of contentment as it rumbles through his massive chest, and it makes me smile.

But I don't want to be done. The pressing need to be honest with him transforms into a need to show him. I've always been better with actions than with words, anyway.

I pull away slightly and grab his hand, intertwining our fingers and marveling at how thick and huge his are. They're twice as large as mine, the skin so smooth but also so firm, with no give. Something about the simple act of holding his hand makes me feel both safe and cherished.

I stare down at our linked fingers for a long moment before glancing up at him and then backing toward the cave. He follows easily, without question.

The other monsters are sleeping under the cover of the trees, Creep snoring where he wedged himself underneath a fallen, rotting log. Turning, I walk Tesq away from the others. The cave will lend us a little bit of privacy if anyone wakes, which I think my shyest monster will appreciate.

I duck as we enter the dark space, and the shadows enfold us, only broken by the tiny streams of glowing orange criss-crossing Tesq's limbs. The heavy thumps of Tesq's footsteps echo in the tight space as I lead him over to a flat slab.

"Sit," I whisper, though no one is awake or near enough to hear.

But whispering feels right because this is a private moment, and I don't even want the stars above spying on us.

Tesq sits, one hand planted on his knee, the other still woven with my fingers as I stand between his legs. When he glances up expectantly, I can't quite read his expression in the dark, but it's better that way because the nerves inside my stomach are crumbling like a cracker gripped tightly in a fist. I want to do this right, and I don't want to scare him, my timid man. That means going slow, something that's never been my strong suit.

Slow.

I lift our joined hands and gently kiss his knuckles.

Slow.

I step closer and then carefully sit sideways across his legs, bringing our woven hands around my waist to hold me against his chest. His rapid heartbeat drums against me, and I realize that I'm not being quite slow enough. Tesq is a tranquil pond, and I'm causing ripples.

Instead of kissing him again, I lean against his chest, simply soaking in his warmth, waiting for the crash of his heartbeat to mellow. I let him get used to the idea of holding me, of our arms pressing together. I let him reconcile the fact that the rivulets of lava running along his body don't hurt me at all, merely cause steam to billow up around us, as if his fire and my ice are encasing us in a cloud.

Once I feel like Tesq has calmed, I turn my neck and place a feather-light kiss to the pulse on his neck. His breath catches, and I smile slightly as I drag my lips up and down the thudding vein. His heartbeat starts to quicken again, but this time, I make my intentions a little clearer—I dart out my tongue and trace a hot, wet path up his neck.

"Aliana." The way he says my name is so full of breathless worship that my stomach skips.

I drag my lips to the hollow of his neck and press a kiss there before whispering, "Tesq."

256

I'm certain he can hear the longing in my voice, the ache, when his fingers tighten their grip on mine.

His roiling veins seem to glow a tiny bit brighter, and the steaming mist around us grows thicker as I reach up with my free hand and wrap it around the back of his head, pulling his face down to mine for another kiss.

We spend several minutes that way, my hair growing damp and sticking to me as we gently kiss, not leisurely, but softly. Delicately. Our lips brushing, our breaths colliding as we inhale each other. Something fragile and sweet blossoms between us, like the first spring buds on a tree, tiny little pinpricks that become a burst of bright pink.

I trace my fingers in a pattern over the back of his neck, and as I grow bolder, I slowly sweep them down his spine, trailing across the massive muscles of his back. His strength sends delicious shivers through my body, and I pull him into me, letting my tongue dart out for the first time, cautiously testing the waters.

I can feel Tesq's gasp, feel his abs tighten and his back stiffen for a millisecond, but then he's kissing me back with hesitant swipes of his tongue, responding to my advances and filling me with eager optimism that he's going to let me guide him through this.

That's all I want. My core heats at the fact that he's responding to me, and I grow a little more aggressive, a bit more enthusiastic as I press up against him, my hardening nipples desperate for more.

I unwind our fingers and set his hand firmly on my hip, holding him tightly in place as I shift my body and move my legs so that I'm straddling him.

As I sink down onto his lap, I pull back from our kiss so that I can watch his eyes, drink in his expression, ensure he's okay with everything I'm doing. Shell-shocked, he blinks up at me, mouth slightly agape, until I reach behind myself and deliberately slide his hand from my hip to my ass.

"Squeeze," I instruct.

And he does. Carefully. Gingerly.

I want more, but we'll get there. My Tesq isn't Dev. He's not going to manhandle or maul me; it's not in his nature. It's going to be up to me to be rough with him.

As his palm gently glides over the globes of my ass, experimentally kneading, I grind against his erection, which is thick and full beneath his pants. It may be my imagination, but I think I can feel the spiral of his dual cock—and damn, does it do things to me.

I go back to kissing Tesq, and now I'm not as slow as before. I'm deliberate, swiping my tongue deeper, probing his mouth, thrusting in and out in a preview of all the things I plan for us to do shortly.

Tesq grows breathless, his grip on my ass tightening slightly as I start to shamelessly slide my body along his, gyrating as my core heats and I grow wet. That soft tenderness between us grows thorns, prickles of need that scratch and claw at me.

More. I need more.

Pausing our kiss, I wrench back, take my hands off of his body, and yank up my shirt, discarding it carelessly. I lock eyes with him, panting as I unhook my bra and throw it aside.

Slowly, his eyes dip down to roam over my body, and the sexual tension builds and shimmers until I can't stand it any longer. I push up onto my knees and reach for his head, grabbing him by the horns and pushing his face toward my naked breasts.

"Kiss me," I order—no, I beg.

Tesq is the only monster I'll ever willingly beg to touch me.

But I need his lips on my body more than I need air right now. I need this gentle monster to surrender and become mine. I need to bond with him in a way we haven't yet because I refuse to let another day dawn without claiming Tesq.

His lips hesitantly latch onto my nipple and suck, and I encourage him with soft sighs, moaning when his lips close a bit more and pull harder.

"Yes. Yes."

Confidence growing, his hands come back to my ass and knead it, squeezing tight. My grip tightens on his horns, and I arch my back, gazing up at the jagged rock ceiling, watching the spiraling curls of steam lift from our bodies as heat overtakes me.

I slide against him, rolling my hips, eyes at half-mast as I just let myself feel. The water droplets in the air collect on my shoulders and glide down, adding another layer of sensation to the already overwhelming fierceness inside. I try to remind myself that my plan is to be slow and gentle with Tesq, but my need mounts, and the feral bit of me that erupted when I tasted monster blood on Dev's cock rears its head.

"More," I hiss through gritted teeth before I wrench myself backward, reveling in the way Tesq

accidentally bites down on my nipple as I pull away and stand.

I strip off my remaining clothes and gesture for him to do the same. He hesitates, but when I hiss, "Tesq, I'm going to kiss every inch of your body. And if I have to freeze your clothes and then shatter them to do it and you have to fight naked tomorrow, I will."

His surprise makes him slow—he's clearly taken aback—and I end up helping him lift his arms and peeling off his shirt, a task I delight in as it reveals every sculpted bit of his eight pack to my wandering eyes.

He's quicker with his pants, having realized that I'm serious, though after he's naked in front of me, that twisted gray and black cock with its double head shining with dual droplets of purple precum, he hunches his shoulders.

His lips press nervously together, and then he confesses, "I've never…with a human. A part human. I don't want to hurt…"

He doesn't finish his sentence. He doesn't have to.

While I'm a bit shaken to realize my sweet monster has never been with a human, I can't say that I'm shocked. It makes sense that my shy recluse has never given in to the urges that seem to consume the rest of monsterkind. He clearly has a fascination with humans, given his collection, but he's never taken a pet, never bid on one at auction before…never kissed one. Never done what we're about to do with a human.

The fact that this is going to be a novel experience for him makes me all the more determined to make it mind-blowing.

"Lie back," I murmur.

When he's laid out on the slab of stone with his unicorn-horn shaped cock pointing at the ceiling, I clamber up between his legs and kneel, my hands bracing on his thighs. I glance up at him for a moment, catching his eye before I deliberately lean forward and stick my tongue out, lapping at his precum.

Instantly, he moans, his hips tightening and threatening to lift. He won't last long. I can tell immediately that it's been an age since he's been with anyone.

And somehow, that knowledge brightens my smile as I look up at him. "I'm going to suck your cocks. And I want you to come in my mouth. I want to swallow it all down and then crawl up your body and sit on your face, and you're going to kiss my pussy like you just kissed my mouth."

In response to my dirty talk, Tesq's dick bobs.

Before he can answer, I dive back down, parting my lips and deliberately dragging them slowly down over his twisting cock. It heats under my tongue, growing so hot in my mouth that I almost wonder if it will burn me, but it doesn't. In fact, the heat almost makes it easier to swallow him deep despite his width. I'm rewarded by a long, low moan from him that echoes off the rocks around us.

I grip his base and twist my wrist, trying to add sensation because there's no way I'm going to be able to get to the base of this thick motherfucker. Clamping down, my fingers glide over the evenly spaced diagonal ridges along his dual dick, and I can't help but wonder if this is what it feels like to suck two dicks at once. It's dirty and delightful to see how far I can go, feel how Tesq's hips rise automatically in response.

But I can't keep it up for long. My jaw will lock if I even think about trying.

So, instead, I pull up, my lips losing their suction with a light pop as I ask, "Unwind for me? I want to play with each of them."

Marveling at the sight as Tesq's dick seems to magically unwind before my eyes, I find myself growing hotter as I recall what it felt like to have both those dicks inside of me at once. Unlike when I was with Dev and Creep and the sensation was overwhelming—more about winning than pleasure in the moment—the last time I felt Tesq's dick, it was one hundred percent pleasure.

I feel a little twinge of anticipation, and my pussy lips tighten, my body aching for more. But I'm going to have to wait my turn because, based on the way his fists are clench and his thighs tremble, I'm not certain Tesq has ever gotten his dick sucked before. I want him to blow his load and his mind.

I scoot farther back so that I can rest on my stomach between his legs. Taking a dick in each of my hands, I slowly stroke up them in tandem, watching Tesq's chest, registering his shallow breathing. I gather some new precum on the tip of each and slide down to the roots, twisting lightly.

His balls tighten, and the black cock in my left hand swells. He's so responsive that I feel certain this is going to be quick. Good. We'll take the edge off and then have a nice, slow round.

I dart my tongue out, and I bring his dicks side by side, noting how the gray one is a little bit shorter and thinner than the black one, and the gray one is leaking another round of precum already, lubing itself. I can't wait to have them both inside me again. Using the flat of my tongue, I swipe upward over the underside of both cocks simultaneously.

Tesq sucks in a breath through his teeth, bringing a smile to my face as I repeat the process before leaning up and taking the heads of both into my mouth while I give my hands free rein to play. I end up alternating strokes, trying to give him as much sensation at once as possible. Down on one side, up on the other.

His chest heaves, and his leg muscles tense. Increasing the rhythm, I glance up at his face from underneath my eyelashes, relishing the way his eyes are closed and his teeth are gritted, his fists pressed tightly against his sides as if he's resisting the urge to grab my head and force-feed me his cocks.

Sweet Tesq.

The fact that he won't force me encourages me to try even harder, sinking down until my gag reflex kicks in. As I pull back, I try to stimulate the heads of his dicks with the tip of my tongue, spelling my name along them.

Instantly, Tesq starts to come, spurting into my mouth and flooding it so much that it's impossible to swallow it all. It drips down my chin, and I try to stay still, keep my lips in place, and draw this moment out for him. I only release when his entire body relaxes, gently uncurling my fists and letting his cocks sag against his stomach as I sit up onto my knees and stare at him.

I grin and go to wipe the excess cum from my chin, but Tesq crooks a finger. "Mate."

I crawl up his body, wet and excited to see what he'll do. When I hover over him on my hands and knees, he reaches up and pushes my hair behind my shoulder before gently gripping the back of my neck and pulling me down toward him. His tongue comes out, and he laps at the cum splatter on my chin like he's a cat.

A rumble in his chest reminds me of a satisfied purr, and I can't help but ask, "Like seeing your mate covered in your cum?"

"Love…" His second word is so soft that I can't catch it. I can't tell if he just said "it" or "you."

My throat grows tight at the possibility that he said the latter and I missed it. But he doesn't give me time to try to wrangle it out of him.

"You wanted kisses?" he asks, his massive hands coming to my hips, fingertips tracing soft patterns across my skin.

I debate whether I want his tongue or his confession more, but ultimately decide that my goal is to make this next round so intense and amazing that he'll say it again. Much, much louder.

I stare down at him, into the deep darkness of his blown-out pupils, and my breath catches because there is an intense, almost worshipful expression on his face that I'm not quite prepared for. It only lasts for a second before his hands on my hips lightly nudge me, urging me to crawl upward and sit on his face like I promised to do.

Teeth digging into my lower lip, I move and position myself above his mouth. Uncertain if Tesq has ever done this before, and not wanting to put undue pressure on him, I try to give him an out.

"If you don't want—"

He leans up and seals his mouth against my opening before I can get another word out. And damn. The lava running through him raises his body temperature in the most delicious way. His lips are so warm that I am momentarily struck dumb. When his mouth opens and his tongue darts out, that stupid feeling only spreads. My eyes flicker closed, and I can't focus on anything, can't hold a single thought in my head as he laps at me, carefully kissing my seam just like he kissed me earlier.

My hands reach down and gently close around his horns, and I cant my hips slightly so that his tongue laps at my clit.

Fuck yes. There.

His tongue is so hot it's just shy of painful, but the heat adds an intensity that I can't resist. The slow, deliberate strokes stoke a fire inside of me, one that has flames jumping up my spine. A swirl of that tongue adds to the intensity, and a burst of energy surges through me, bolting down my arms and erupting from my fingertips. Tiny ice crystals line Tesq's horns as my power manifests for a moment, though his body heat quickly morphs the ice into steam, which coils up around my face.

I press my hips down, grinding onto his face, need overpowering all my good intentions about being gentle. But Tesq's fingers on my hips dig in, and he presses me down even farther, his tongue parting my lips and diving inside of me. It feels like my pussy is melting in the most glorious, decadent, sensual way.

"Oh. Fuck. Oh. Fuck. Tesq. Yes." My words are choppy and broken, as are my movements.

Behind my eyelids, oranges and reds flicker, and I clamp down on Tesq's horns as I roughly thrust against him, fucking his tongue as my clit bumps against his face. I teeter like a skyscraper that's been swarmed by a herd of teeth, my foundation cracking, walls leaning. With a groan that can probably be heard miles away, I collapse into the most intense orgasm of my life.

When I come back to myself and release the tight grip on Tesq's horns, my muscles take a minute before they recall how to move. Lifting myself off Tesq's face, I slide down his body, anxious to see him, to make certain he's all right. Concern arrows through me as I wonder if I got carried away and was too rough with him.

I shouldn't have worried.

The second my hips hover over his torso, his hands are dragging my body farther down. As I peer up at his face, shiny with my cum, he slides me along his body until his rock-hard double cock is tapping at my entrance, spiraled back together into one massive monster of a dick.

He presses lightly down on my hips, almost as if he's wordlessly asking permission to enter my body, because Tesq is always thoughtful. Always gentle. Unlike me.

Responding to his request, I sink down onto him, and the stretch so soon after my orgasm makes me hiss because I'm still very sensitive.

"Does it hurt?" he immediately asks, concern lacing his tone.

"No. Not at all," I respond as I press down farther.

And it's true. Once he's in deep enough, my sensitivity ends, and all I can feel is the thick stretch, warm heat, and that spiral twisting against my pussy lips and making them throb with desire, ready for another orgasm because I'm greedy like that.

Pulling up and sliding back down, I plant my hands on Tesq's deliciously hard pecs as I slowly build up a rhythm.

"Aliana. Oh, Aliana." His soft murmurs are full of tenderness punctuated by short gasping breaths that tell me he's working to keep himself from coming too soon.

Honestly, I'm close already, so he doesn't have to hold out for long.

When I tell him that, his head arches backward, and he growls before responding, "No. It can't be over that quickly."

"Fine. But I'm orgasming now. And then you'll have to wait until I orgasm again before you come."

Any of my other mates would argue. Sass me. Flip us over and try to dominate me by fucking me into oblivion. But Tesq simply nods and raises one of his hands, reaching hesitantly for my clit. I pull one hand from his chest to help guide him so that his thumb swipes firmly over my swollen nub each time I sink down onto him and his deliciously thick double dick.

"Tesq. Fuck. Yes. Right. Fucking. There!" I nearly shout as I move faster.

His eyes lock on my breasts where they're pressed between my outstretched arms, and he watches them bounce lightly. Then, those deep eyes, which are dark as midnight and yet somehow filled with star-like glimmers, roam back up to my face.

"Are you going to come, Aliana?"

"Tell me to come for you," I tell him.

He swallows hard, and then in a low, rumbling tone that sends goose bumps across my skin, Tesq purrs, "Come for me, mate."

I do.

With my eyes locked onto his, I find myself clenching, my fingernails scratching along his pecs, my back arching, as pleasure as bright as a sunbeam fills me. I move faster, fuck him harder, trying to draw the sensation out until my entire body is little more than a puddle of overwrought nerves. I fall down, cheek to his chest.

His arm comes up around me, and his fingers lightly trace down my spine, letting me recover.

After a long moment, he asks in a quiet whisper, "Can I try something?"

I bite down on a proud little grin and rub my cheek against his chest. "Anything."

In a move that surprises me, his abs tighten, and he sits up without disconnecting us so that I end up on his lap, facing him, my legs wrapped around his waist. His hands slowly glide over my body, adjusting me slightly, almost as if he's making sure I'm comfortable.

"You want me to fuck you in this position?" I ask, still a bit noodley and not quite up for the task just yet but absolutely willing to do what he wants.

"No. I want you to stay as still as you can and let me fuck you." His arms wrap around me then, one of those massive biceps curling in front of my face within biting range. The other clamps down around my lower back, locking me against his body.

His gargoyle strength has never been more apparent than when he's boxed me into his chest, and I realize I can't move even if I wanted to.

Not that I want to. I'm more than willing to do whatever Tesq wants. I trust him completely.

But I don't expect what actually happens. Not at all.

At first, I'm not even sure what's happening, because he holds me in place and doesn't move. But then…then I feel it. There's a massive stretch inside of me, a sense of motion, and something glides over my G-spot.

I gasp. "What?"

But then the sensation swoops lower, along my lips, and I figure out what's going on. Tesq's uncoiling his dicks while they're inside of me. And once he has them unwrapped, they move along my pussy lips and coil back together in the opposite direction.

Fuck.

I've never felt anything like this before. It's intense, and there's a bit of strangeness, a bit of pain to it, but as he repeats the process and spreads those dicks wider apart inside of me, he also ends up rubbing more intensely against my G-spot, forcing a long moan to erupt from between my lips.

"Mate. Mate." Tesq chants the word almost under his breath as he speeds up his uncoiling and recoiling until I'm bucking and writhing in his hold, tears streaming down my cheeks because it's more intense than anything I've ever experienced.

"Tesq." His name is a plea—whether it's for him to stop or for more, I'm not certain.

But somehow, he knows. He pulls me in tighter and wraps his hand more firmly around my ribs so that his hand can glide along my lower belly. This time, without any guidance, he finds my clit. His fingers slide over either side of it, pinching it between them as he coils and uncoils even faster, so quickly that the sensations inside me become a quivering ripple of constant sensation.

"Aliana. Fuck. Aliana. I LOVE YOU," he roars, the words echoing through the cave, through my nerve endings.

His orgasm triggers my own, and I shake against him, trembling and clenching, gasping until—to my own surprise—the world becomes as hazy as the steam around us, and I pass the fuck out.

THE CREEPER

I IMAGINE the Empire State Building was once a grand skyscraper. I can see the ghost of opulence in the marble floors, intricate ceiling designs, and elaborate moldings.

But the marble floors are now cracked and covered in drying blood, dirt, and debris. The intricate ceiling designs are nearly unrecognizable, due to the wildlife growing down through it. And the elaborate moldings are beginning to shatter and crumble, unveiling a gray, dusky world outside.

A heady combination of fear and cocky adrenaline laces my bloodstream as I portal from shadow to shadow, counting how many monsters we'll have to face. There are over a dozen in the lobby—all Eights and Nines—which makes me immensely happy we decided to go through the basement instead.

My job is simple—find a clear pathway for the others to the top floor, and if I can't find one, make one. As soon as I give the signal, Dev will use his strength to tear apart the wall in the basement, allowing the others access.

And since Aliana is a part of the "others," I need to make sure there is not a single threat left alive that can harm a hair on her pretty, little head.

I portal down to the basement.

While the lobby and upper floors were a glimmering patchwork of gold and marble, the basement is nothing but cement walls, cement floors, and cement ceilings. Pipes run the length of the large room, though the majority of them have begun to fall with age. They dangle at odd angles, almost like metal streamers.

No one would expect someone to enter through here. There's not a door that I can see, nor are there any windows. It's nothing but a cement cube littered with broken furniture and rotted boxes.

But we have something others don't have.

The Devourer, whose strength rivals that of a dozen monsters.

Within the basement, there are only two monsters that I can see, both of them Fours, and they're sitting at a broken table playing cards.

I'm not the least bit surprised my father would have his weakest monsters watching the basement. He would have all of his strongest soldiers guarding the main entrance and the fire exits.

I can't help but smirk.

My father's cockiness in his own capabilities will lead to his death. A real death this time. I won't walk away. I won't have trouble looking. This time, I'll ensure his face is stomped in until his skull doesn't have a bit of bone left bigger than a chess piece, his brain rolled out under my shoe like cookie dough.

I remain in the shadows for a second longer, studying the two monsters standing between myself and my mate. She's just on the other side of that cement wall, standing in a tunnel that Uni found—one that was created by wayward sandworms.

"Got any fives?" one of the monsters asks.

He's abnormally tall with arms nearly the length of his torso. Two horns protrude from his bald head. His skin is a bright, stop-sign shade of red interspersed here and there with green veins.

I'm gonna call him…Christmasy.

"Go fish," the second monster says, waving a talon-tipped hand towards the direction of the pile.

This one reminds me a little bit of a scorpion, though he has human hands and a humanoid face.

Scorpion and Christmasy it is, then.

Christmasy bares his teeth. "You're full of shit! I know you have fives in your hand."

"Fuck you," Scorpion snaps. "I ain't no cheater."

Christmasy throws down his cards and lurches to his feet. He places his hands palm down on the table—he doesn't even need to bend to do so since his arms are that long.

"Prove it. Show me your hand."

"Fuck off."

"Show me your hand!"

Scorpion's barbed, serrated tail curls over his misshapen body as he bares his teeth.

"Fuck. You."

Christmasy lunges at Scorpion then.

Huh. Maybe I won't need to kill them. Maybe they'll do the job for me.

The two of them roll around on the ground, slashing and biting and clawing at one another.

For a moment, I allow myself to pretend that I'm in a different place, a different time, watching a stupid play about two idiots. Amusement fills me, bolstering my confidence, and a tiny smile touches my lips.

But then I think of the monster twenty or so floors above me, staring out at the Ebony Kingdom like a monarch over-looking his land.

Anger fills me, white-hot and blistering, and my hands ball into fists.

Barnabas will *never* rule the Ebony Kingdom. I'll make sure of it.

Deciding I've had enough watching, I step out of the shadows and fold my arms over my chest. It takes the two idiots a solid minute before they see me. They stop wrestling each other and blink up at me with wide, terrified eyes.

"I have to say, you two amuse me." I absently pluck at a piece of lint on my shoulder. "It's a shame you picked the wrong side to fight for. Now, you have to die."

"Creeper." Scorpion's voice is a pathetic whimper as he attempts to prostrate himself before me. "Whatever do you mean—?"

I wave a hand in the air dismissively. "Cut the shit, yeah? I don't know what Barnabas promised you to turn you into his little bitch—power, more than likely, and a chance to move up in the world—but whatever it is led to your death."

"Please, no!" This comes from Christmasy who has staggered to his feet and is now holding his long arms out in front of him, as if he means to fend me off. "We have information!"

"Yeah." Scorpion nods eagerly. "We know where Barnabas is and how many monsters he has protecting him and his right-hand man's—"

I feign a yawn, covering my mouth dramatically. But despite my nonchalance, my curiosity piques. I have a general layout of the building, but I didn't dare travel too close to where I suspect my father to be. Knowing him, he'll have his monster minions staking out every shadow, waiting for me to make an appearance.

He won't consider me working with the other Terrors to bring him down even though we all appeared in the meat-packing plant. He probably thinks that all they cared about is power and appearances because he stole one of the four kings of the kingdom. Or perhaps he believes that I lied to get the other Terrors there.

Even though I'm certain that his minions told him about our little human mate—correction, partially human mate—I doubt he could conceive how much having her has changed us. United us. Bonded us.

To him, friendship is a weakness. *Love* is a weakness. If you can't do something on your own, then you deserve to be eradicated from this earth.

He couldn't be more wrong.

"Give me something worth my while, and maybe I'll let you live." I pretend to examine my sharp fingernails using the light of the single hanging bulb.

"Barnabas is almost constantly with Tennious," Christmasy says eagerly. "He claims it's because Tennious is his second-in-command, but I think it's because he's scared and knows Tennious can protect him."

"And this…Tennious… What are his powers exactly?" I try to keep my tone casual and indifferent, not allowing either of these monsters to see the fear lurking just beneath my carefully crafted façade.

Most monsters we can handle with ease, but one powerful enough that my father feels the need to keep him by his side at all times?

My stomach lurches.

Christmasy and Scorpion exchange a long, eloquent look that I translate to: "We have no fucking idea."

"Is that all?" I tilt my head to the side curiously.

"They're on the top floor, and they have dozens, if not hundreds, of monsters surrounding them," Christmasy says. "An entire freaking army."

"Why do they follow him?" I can't help but crinkle my nose in disgust.

Scorpion scoffs. "Isn't it obvious? He's offering everything you and the other Terrors never did—power and humans."

"He promised us not only the city but the entire world," Christmasy adds. "Every monster who helps him will get territory of their own to rule over."

His eyes take on a wistful, glassy state, and this time, it's me who scoffs. My father would never hand out power to other monsters, especially ones as weak as these.

They got played, just as every other monster in this building did.

I have to give my father credit. It's ingenious, actually. He created an army of monsters who will kill and die for him, and that's exactly the outcome he wants. He won't shed a tear if every single one of these creatures is slaughtered by me and the other Terrors. Hell, I wouldn't be surprised if he's *planning* on us killing them.

He doesn't want to share his crown with anyone.

"Unfortunately for you two, you backed the wrong king." I allow my easygoing smile to slip, allow them to see the darkness in my eyes—a product of my father's cruel abuse and the continuous threats against my mate.

This is war, and there will be no mercy.

Without preamble, I reach for Christmasy's head and give it a tug, feeling a tiny bit of resistance as tendons and muscles hang on for dear life. I use a little more force and then—pop —I hold the monster's decapitated head up in the air.

Oddly enough, his body remains upright, green blood jetting up in spurts like one of those old-timey water parks humans had for little kids, where the water would shoot up out of a hole in the ground. I watch it for a moment before shrugging it off and turning to the other monster.

Scorpion makes a strangled sound in the back of his throat and lunges at me, his tail extended. I have no idea if it's poisonous like a normal scorpion, but I'm not going to stick around long enough to find out.

I portal to a dark corner directly behind the monster and watch as he rams headfirst into the wall. He staggers, appearing dazed, and if this were a cartoon, I imagine I would see birds flying around his head.

And then, like an angel of death, I step out of the shadows.

ALIANA

Only Tesq's hand in mine keeps me from completely losing my shit.

Creep is somewhere ahead of me, alone, attempting to clear a pathway to allow us easy access to Barnabas and his minions. Fear for my blue monster threatens to bowl me over, but iron determination and willpower keeps me upright. I can't afford to lose myself to the turmoil of my thoughts when we're seconds away from the largest fight of our lives.

I have my crossbow slung over my shoulder and my bag of magical jewels in a pouch connected to my waistband. They're merely backup, though. My true power—the one that will hopefully make a difference in this war—is my ice.

I'm also wearing a nearly new outfit. Creep portalled into an abandoned biker store somewhere in Jersey, and now I'm wearing brand-new calf-high leather lace-up boots, slick black pants, a black shirt, and a leather jacket that has neon pink stripes down both arms. The stripes call a little more attention to me than I'd like, but fuck, my old clothes were so full of either blood or cum that this outfit is far more comfortable.

I stare down at my free hand and think of how my life has changed since I was bought by the Terrors. Back then, I'd been terrified of them—and even more afraid of my growing feelings for the four monsters. I thought I was betraying humankind by allowing them to touch me, care for me, love me.

Now, I can't imagine life without them.

Tesq stands directly beside me, cold fury paving its way across his stone face. The heat of his palm in mine is a startling contrast to my cold skin.

Behind us are Dev and Em, the former pacing and the latter standing with his hands clasped around a gun. Since the Empty Man is trapped inside of Chase's body for the time being, it was decided that he would have a weapon. Em doesn't know the first thing about shooting a gun, but Chase is a skilled marksman. I have no doubt my cocky human will be able to protect my monster mate.

Wait...*my*?

I shake my head at such a ridiculous thought, even as my heart increases speed.

Uni stands the farthest back, his gray face nearly hidden in shadows, his tentacles wavering in the air as he whispers to his two dolls, who have both been shoved into a makeshift baby carrier that wraps around his chest. At first, I tried to hear what he was saying to them, but then the words "orgy" and "monster cocks" flitted to my ears, and I zoned the fuck out.

Yup. Nope. Not happening.

The radio connected to my shoulder begins to crackle, and then Creep's voice echoes through the tunnel, staticky and tinny.

"Beautiful, this is Blue Lightning. Are you in position?"

Nerves war with relief at hearing Creep's voice.

I press down on the radio button and lower my chin to speak to him. "Yes. I'm here with..." I hesitate briefly, remembering the code names Creep gave my other mates, before continuing. "I'm here with Stoned AF, Mostly Ghosty, and, um, Hairy Boy. Water Man and the Two Misses are ready as well."

All three of my mates glare at me, and I hold my hands up in the air to fend off any impending arguments. *I* didn't pick the code names.

"Roger that. Basement has been cleared out. I'm ready for Hairy Balls to make his move."

Dev growls. "I thought it was Hairy Boy."

"Isn't that what I said?" Creep asks innocently.

"I vote we change my code name," Dev barks out, his voice a low rumble.

"Too late. We're already here. There's an unspoken rule that code names can't be changed once we're in the middle of battle, Hairy Boy."

"I swear to fuck, if you call me Hairy Boy one more time, I will eat you." Dev steps forward so he can glare at the radio on my shoulder, as if he's visualizing reaching through the radio waves, gripping Creep by the neck, and wringing it like a chicken.

"I suppose we can change it…"

Dev puffs out his chest.

And then Creep continues, "Hairy Balls, we're ready for you."

Dev bristles, and I have to bite back my smile. Trust Creep to bring levity to one of the scariest moments of my life. Only my crazy mate could make me smile at a time like this.

Tesq rolls his eyes and tugs at my hand, moving me away from the wall. He then positions himself so he's standing slightly in front of me, protecting me. Em claims Tesq's previous position at my side.

"Stand back," Dev growls, rolling his neck from side to side, his pointed monster ears flicking, tongue grazing over his sharp teeth as he opens his muzzle and bares them at the wall as if he can intimidate it.

Then, he charges at it with a roar.

There's an audible cracking sound, and I'm filled with an inexplicable amount of fear at the thought of that noise belonging to my mate's bones. But then chips of cement begin to rain down around us, and a hole appears in the wall the size of the Devourer.

My jaw unhinges, and I blink in surprise.

He did it.

He really fucking did it.

He ran through a wall of pure cement.

He now stands on the other side, flicking his head from side to side as he attempts to dislodge stray pieces from his dark mane.

Creep's head materializes above Dev's shoulder, and his eyes home in on me, checking me for injuries. I flash him a smile to assure him I'm okay, I'm ready, and I'm prepared to fight like my life depends on it.

Because it does.

This is it. The end. What we do now determines the rest of our lives. If we fail today, then there'll be no happily ever after for us. There'll be no fairy-tale ending or wedding or children—things I never even considered before but now can't imagine never having.

Oh god.

My heart ricochets off my breastbone as I turn to stare at each of my mates.

The Devourer, fierce and possessive, but with a gentleness that belies his rough exterior. He's gruff and domineering, yet he's also protective of those he cares about.

The Creeper, whose charm and sharp wit hides a broken boy who just wants to be loved. We taunt and tease each other, but I know he'll always have my back, no matter the situation. I can trust him to make me smile when all I want to do is cry.

The Grotesque, the first of my monsters I fell in love with. He calls himself ugly, but he fails to realize he has the most beautiful soul anyone could ever hope to possess. He exhibits a type of gentleness I've never seen in another monster or human before.

The Empty Man, who tried to kill me and then took me on a romantic picnic, all within a span of a couple of weeks. I can't quite decide how I feel about him, but I know a future without him in it seems unimaginable. He makes me laugh nearly as much as Creep does, even if he's borderline insane.

Then there's Chase, a human trapped in a world of monsters. I once thought him to be cocky and self-involved, but I'm now beginning to believe that was all an act. Sometimes, when he thinks I'm not looking, he stares at me like…like he loves me. Like he can't imagine a future without me in it.

We're a broken, misshapen bunch, but I wouldn't have us any other way. I'll fight for these monsters, just as they'll fight for me.

And maybe, once this is all over and Barnabas has been removed from his blood-soaked throne, I'll be able to worship my monsters.

And be worshipped in return.

3 5

ALIANA

WE BURST onto the floor of the lobby like a series of fireworks—bam-*bam*-BAM-BAM.

But it's very anticlimactic because the monsters Creep spied on this floor earlier have moved. The space is now eerily silent, and our footsteps echo against the marble floor as we walk.

I have my crossbow lifted and ready, scanning back and forth as I try to keep two paces in front of Chase, who's most defi- nitely the weakest member of our group right now. The kidnapping clearly showcased that.

A tiny part of me regrets the fact that we haven't had time to visit the Bell Witch and see if there's a spell to reverse the potion that Tesq gave to Empty, the potion that Barnabas and his crew apparently also fed him in captivity.

I'd feel so much better right now if Empty could float ahead of us from room to room, invisible, scouting, using objects to attack people. Meanwhile, Chase could be snuggled up with Fluffy deep in the forests of Jersey somewhere safe.

Unfortunately, time isn't on our side, just as most of the fucking monsters in the kingdom aren't on our side either.

As Creep portals ahead of us into a shadow in the stairwell to check and see if it's safe to head up, I briefly think about the humans in the resistance. I wonder where they are and what they're doing. If anyone I know is still alive. I'm not sure what will happen after today, but I am certain that as awful as life in the Ebony Kingdom has been, Barnabas will ensure it gets far worse.

Creep makes a clicking sound that resembles a common scavenger tooth species called ings. Beatle-like, football-sized creatures, they scour buildings for dead things to eat, so no one will think twice about hearing an ing rustling around. At least, that's our hope.

Dev insists on going in front of me, even though he's so massive and his fur is so dark against the white walls that we've got no hope of going unnoticed if someone spots him. Of course, my dark outfit isn't much better, but I'm not quite so hulking, and for once, my white-streaked hair may help me blend a tiny bit with some of the marble.

My heart wails against my ribs, and the pulse in my throat throbs so hard that I have difficulty swallowing. I count the steps as we climb, muscles growing tighter with each one until I have to deliberately uncurl my finger from the crossbow trigger so that I don't accidentally set it off.

Unlike the last mission, where rescue was at the top of my mind, this time, violence is our only objective. Violence—and hopefully—survival.

It's hard for me to peel my emotions away from my mind, separate them out and then toss them aside. So much harder than it's been for any prior mission. Last time, I couldn't bear the thought of Chase suffering an awful fucking fate when he was innocent. This time, we're all here together and—

I'm just repeating myself. Thinking the same damned dark thoughts on repeat. It's not helping.

I try to focus. Remember things my father taught me.

But memory is tainted by my new reality.

My father probably isn't my father.

Fuck, Aliana. It's not the time for an existential crisis, I scold furiously, heat rising along my neck because I'm so angry with myself.

But if not now, when?

Behind me, Chase trips on a step and grabs at the railing. I turn to see him cursing at himself under his breath, and I wonder for a second who has the reins right now. I'm guessing Empty, since Chase may be a lot of things, but clumsy isn't one of them.

"I've got this," he mutters.

"Mate?" I call out in a whisper.

"Yes?" His forest-green eyes flash up to mine with an adoring yet slightly psychotic look.

"Let the human drive right now. Keep yourself safe for me."

His lips twist, but then his body relaxes before it takes on Chase's familiar, cocky, chest-puffed posture.

The human man's eyes are steady as he glances up at me and mouths, "Thank you."

I give him a wink that probably looks far more sassy and relaxed than I feel before turning forward again and following Dev onto the emergency landing for the second floor.

Creep waits until we're all huddled on the landing before he steps into the corner and disappears, going to check the floor. I wait, pressed between Dev at my front and Tesq at my back, the heat rolling off of both of them stifling in the small space.

Crash!

The door in front of Dev smashes open, and a bright-green, snakelike appendage wraps around his head, dragging him through the door before I can blink.

FUCK!

I race after him, all thoughts and worries wiped from my mind, my body taking over, intent on action.

I spot a blur of movement to my right and immediately pivot, pressing the trigger and sending a bolt in that direction before my vision even confirms that I'm facing a goobed—a ridiculously immature name for a slime monster. My aim is true, but my bolt darts right through the jelly of the fucker's body and lodges in the wall behind it. Waste of ammo.

Frustrated, I raise my hand and send icicles flying his way. The smug monster smiles at me as they enter his body, pricking it in six different places. He's certain they're going to fly right through just like my bolt, and he oozes forward.

Unsure if my plan will work, I simply wing it, clenching my fist and then throwing my fingers wide, imagining the ice inside of him expanding, shooting outward, sharp crystal spikes growing out in every direction until the icicles resemble throwing stars or saw blades that will chop this bastard to pieces.

He lurches in place, and his grin droops while I tick up the corner of my mouth.

On the outside, I'm smirking, but internally I'm punching my fist in the air and jumping up in excitement.

Next to me, Tesq throws a creature that looks like a yellow orangutan with bat wings for ears. It soars across the room and crashes through a window headfirst. The monster's body starts to disappear, but its leg gets caught on a shard of glass. It howls in pain as it ends up dangling outside the window, suspended and stuck, slowly bleeding from the gash in its leg.

Good. Motherfucker deserves a slow, painful death. They all do. They've chosen to stand against my mates, and we're going to wipe every last one of them out.

Finally, battle mode seems to click on inside my head as I settle into the fight and send another round of ice spikes at the slime monster. This time, when I spread my fingers wide, I lift and lower my hand, sawing up and down inside of him until he wavers in place and then melts into a sticky green puddle.

I can't help it. I make a finger gun and blow imaginary smoke off the top of it before winking at the puddle and stepping forward to find my next victim.

Who else wants to play?

I scan the room and do a quick check to ensure my mates are doing okay. The confidence and bloodlust of war have seeped into me, and I'm not really worried. They're Terrors after all.

My confidence is proven right.

Dev is clawing at the monster with a head that looks like a face smashed onto a tissue box and eight snakes for limbs, the same monster who pulled him through the door. My beast mate's massive nails are ripping through the other bastard's scales. Two heads are already hanging limply, half detached—probably the limbs that wrapped around his neck. A giant centipede-shaped monster charges at him, but he backhands it and sends it onto its back, where its legs uselessly struggle and squirm.

A gunshot sounds, and a purple monster whose body looks like a bunch of grapes falls from the ceiling and smashes into the floor. Chase doesn't make eye contact with me, just spins and shoots at another.

Tesq is crushing the skull of a short monster with leopard-print skin. His hands are on either side of the monster's face, and I watch in satisfaction—and a sliver of desire—as his hands smash together. Goddamn, he's strong.

Meanwhile, Uni stands in the doorway we rushed through, not fighting but whispering frantically at one of his dolls, his gaze darting in every direction.

A sliver of worry creeps into my chest that he's about to betray us, but a monster that's shaped like a heart barrels toward him. Uni's tentacles scoop it off the ground, squeezing until it turns an ugly shade of blue reminiscent of a bruise.

Fuck, yes. We're kicking ass!

I feel confident that we'll blast through each floor of this 102-story building until we get to Barnabas and take him out.

But then a red cloud rolls across the ceiling of the room and descends on us in very unnatural columns, shooting down to engulf each of our heads. Instantly, the second I inhale, a mindless sort of anger fills me, and a psychotic craving for blood coats my mind.

I lash out at whoever is nearest to me, and that happens to be Chase. My mind doesn't register that fact, overridden by a strange, foreign need to kill that chokes out everything else. My palms ice over, and I shove cold into his arms.

Bam.

His gun goes off, and I feel a burning sensation in my left shoulder. Pain ricochets through my body and distracts me momentarily, but the all-consuming need to destroy soon rears its head and roars inside me. Almost as if it insulates me from my senses, the pounding trauma of my shoulder wound disappears, and that hunger for violence resurges.

I shove an icy hand at Chase's cheek and feel an ice spike start to form in the center of my palm. A vicious smile carves my lips upward as I anticipate blood. Lots of blood.

A surge of heat like I've never known fills the room along with an orange glow. In under a second, a river of lava surges out of Tesq's body and crosses the floor. An agonized, high-pitched yowl sounds…and the red fog around me clears. Evaporates.

The ice dagger that I nearly used to stab Chase melts, dripping down my palm as I stare, horrified, into his bright-green eyes.

His blond hair is plastered to his forehead, and his slack-jawed expression is just as distraught as he takes in my bullet wound.

"What the fuck was that?" I whisper.

His head jerks slightly, and his expression changes. He goes from wrecked to matter-of-fact in moments.

Em's taken control.

"That was a rage monster," he states simply.

I blink.

All the confidence that I just had vanishes.

I'm not sure we're going to make it through this after all.

ALIANA

FORTY FLOORS. We make it up forty floors, fighting through each one.

I'm sagging. My thighs are burning, and my arms are aching, and my ferocity is flagging. The wound in my shoulder doesn't bother me as much as I expect, perhaps because it was a glancing wound or because I touched my hand to it and numbed it with a coating of ice crystals that haven't melted off.

Whatever the case, it doesn't ache or throb unless I try to lift my arm, which I don't. I've tossed aside my crossbow and focused on weapons that I can use one-handed. Namely, magic and that mysterious bag of jewels. The pouch at my hip is now empty save for one final emerald, which I finger through the material of the pouch.

I cleared the entire tenth floor tossing a diamond at a group of monsters that shrank them to the size of ants that Creep took pleasure in stomping. A ruby turned the walls of one room into giant spikes, and we barely made it out of there before we were pierced through. If Tesq wasn't made of a substance as hard as stone…I can't even bear to think about the way the spikes scraped against his back as he escaped.

Jewel after jewel helped us this far…but we still have so much farther to go.

Breathing hard, I glance up the stairwell, which seems to go on forever, bending and turning.

My heart sinks knowing we have so much farther to go before we reach Barnabas. If we can reach him.

I'm certain that's the bastard's plan. Wear us down before we face him, whittle my monster's nearly impenetrable defenses down to nothing.

"This reminds me of a video game from the before times," Creep says with far too much enthusiasm as he appears out of nowhere, popping into existence in the shadows next to me. "We're working our way up to the big boss fight."

He's grinning and his posture is relaxed because he hasn't climbed every single stair thus far. No, he's just portalled along, sailing through space like it's nothing.

Jerk.

I may be a little bit grumpy.

Possibly hangry.

"What the fuck is a video game—" I start to ask, but Creep's in his own world as he rounds the landing and takes the stairs in front of me, Uni at his side.

"I remember those," the water monster announces. "Love them. Except the electrical shorted out a lot. Water monster hazard."

They share a laugh.

"Wish we had a cheat code," Creep murmurs.

Uni stops walking, and I nearly smash into his spine. He turns sideways on the stairs, mouth twisting as his head tilts, almost as if he's listening to something. "I don't like it."

He doesn't like what?

Immediately, we all tense, eyes scanning, hands extended to blast magic at any new threat. But nothing's there. There's literally only our little group in the empty, white stairwell.

I take a step down and share a concerned glance with Creep. A glance that says, *Ummm, is this guy losing it? I mean, more than usual?*

"Fine. FINE, I said. But you'd better—" Uni cuts off his imaginary argument and stomps the rest of the way up the stairs to the forty-first floor, leaving the rest of us gaping at his back.

"What was that?" I ask Creep in a loud whisper.

"No clue." He shakes his head.

Tesq's warm hand comes up to touch my spine. He's been walking behind me the last few floors, offering every so often to carry me. I haven't given in yet because I don't know if I could bear the smug look on Chase's face if I did. He doesn't look fucking worn down at all, despite fighting at least thirty monsters himself. As a full human. Or human/poltergeist. Semantics.

"Stay by me," Tesq intones. "Just in case."

I nod. I may be stubborn, but I'm not stupid. If Uni's brain has gotten waterlogged, lava is the best way to counter his powers.

We head up the stairs in a tight cluster, my mates boxing me in. But when we reach the next floor, I'm shocked to see Uni kneeling on the floor, ignoring the monsters rolling in his direction as he carefully sets his precious dolls down and straightens their little skirts. And I'm even more taken aback to see them remain standing when he pushes to his feet and then backs up.

What the hell?

Though their faces are as placid and porcelain-looking as ever, though their eyes don't blink, their chests don't move with inhales and exhales…somehow, the two dolls start to walk forward stiff-legged. Two tiny, eighteen-inch-high porcelain dolls heading straight into a room swarming with giant egg-shaped monsters.

Holy shit! They're alive!

The revelation smacks me across the face with all the potent sting of a slap and makes me reevaluate my judgment of Uni as unhinged for a moment.

But that's before the dolls slowly raise their ceramic arms and Uni shouts, "Fuck, Brittany, I love your ass in that dress."

Ew.

Wrong. That's just so wrong.

Simultaneously, the dolls lower their arms, and every egg in the room cracks as if they've been smashed against the floor. The faces of the egg monsters freeze in expressions of horror as lightning-bolt shaped cracks cover their bodies and yellow goo spills out, coating the floor.

I gape, mouth slack.

The dolls have frozen back into their original positions. They remain completely still as my mates and I walk around the room, verifying that each of the other monsters is indeed dead. Nothing could be worse than missing one and having it sneak up behind us. There's not a single shell left uncracked. With one gesture, the room has been obliterated.

I glance over at Brittany, the blonde doll with glasses, and the other one…whose name I can't remember. They both are just standing there, looking as unalive and doll-like as ever. It gives me the heebie-jeebies. Then again, I was about to have to fight a room full of oversized sentient eggs…so…

I'm torn between gratitude and wanting to ask why the fuck they made us fight through all the floors beneath this one. But seeing as I'm not an idiot, I bite the inside of my cheek and say nothing.

"Anyone feel like scrambled eggs?" Creep jokes.

My stomach growls in response.

When he turns to me with a raised eyebrow, I quickly shake my head. I need to win this fight more than I need to eat. More than I need anything. I just want to get this shit over with.

"Let's keep moving," Dev says, because he's in full bossy mode —his alpha instincts flipped to high and so intense they nearly cast a shimmering aura around him. His tail swishes as he turns to lead the way up the stairs, and we follow him.

Uni scoops his girls into his arms and speckles them with kisses as we walk, which at first is cute. Until I unfortunately see his tongue dart out and swipe over Brittany's mouth. Then it just gets weird again, and I avert my eyes because if I don't, I'll be forced to carve them out with rusty spoons, and I like being able to see. Usually, that is.

"I wish there were some other fucking way to get to the top," I moan as we tromp up to the next floor.

"There used to be these music boxes that floated up and down inside the building," Creep states, painting a beautiful, fantastical picture for me of mechanical music boxes with humans that danced inside them as they rode up and down.

Finally, once my thighs are on fire, we're on the landing, and Uni gestures for us all to wait again.

His dolls end up taking out the next sixty floors for us. Uni says they insist on helping so we can save our strength.

"And because they like to show off. Nothing gets them horny like an awed audience," he whispers confidentially to Tesq, who blushes furiously.

Is there some kind of bleach for ears? Something that erases what you just heard? If so, I fucking want that right now—a gallon of it.

Ultimately, I let Tesq carry me up the second half of the stairs, but only after Creep scoops Chase up with a cheerful, "Piggyback time for the humans and part humans! Gotta rest those legs… Now wrap them around me, pretty boy."

He gives me a wink as he says it, making me embarrassingly aware he's doing it for my benefit. But…I can't let pride win out in this situation, not when I'm pretty sure I won't even be able to stand once we make it to the top floor.

Begrudgingly, I let Dev take the lead as Tesq scoops me up and gently cradles me against his warm, cozy chest. He smells so good coated in monster blood, and the warmth of his lava veins is so soothing to my sore legs that I curl in tightly against him, the steady pace of his footsteps comforting.

I may doze off, but I'll never admit it.

I just know that the final ascent seems to go a million times faster than any of the floors in the lower half of the building. When Tesq gently sets me down on a landing that's brimming with light so bright that it could be the stairway to heaven, I glance around at my guys, and I'm feeling reinvigorated. Refreshed. Renewed. Ready to fight.

"Two floors left," Dev announces, as if we don't all know. His posture is tense and ready, his black fur gleaming and his red eyes casting a glow across his muzzle.

"Thank goodness." Creep sets Chase down and then puts his hands on his lower back, stretching until there are several pops. "This one's constant boner has given me sciatica."

"Fuck off!" Chase retorts with narrowed eyes.

"That seems like exactly what you were trying to do against my spine," Creep waggles his forked tongue, clearly enjoying getting a rise out of the other man.

Chase's fists ball up, but I step between them, my eyes steady on the human I've known all my life.

"Hey. Save the fighting for the other monsters and the fucking for me, okay?" I wink.

I tried to break the tension with a little bit more levity, but Chase's expression immediately becomes gobsmacked.

Did I go too far?

"Showtime," Tesq calls out, and Dev smashes through the door, sending it flying, before Chase and I even have time to turn toward it.

The others surge ahead of us in a rush so strong that it creates a wind that rustles my hair.

Chase leans forward and tucks a whipping strand back behind my ear. "Stay safe."

"You too," I respond.

And then, suddenly, we're part of the melee. I'm throwing icicles at a seven-foot-tall monster that looks like a frosted wedding cake. Tesq is facing a monster made of pebbles who crumbles and reforms behind him. Dev goes crashing through a wall with his opponent, and dust flies everywhere, getting into my mouth as I lift my hand and instinctively form a giant sword made of ice.

"Do you taste as good as you look?" I ask the cake monster, swinging the sword in my hand and getting a feel for its balance.

All right, and showing off a little, I admit.

The cake monster doesn't have a mouth or a face, just pink arms and legs, but the frosted roses on its edges spin angrily, and I grin in response.

Come at me, motherfucker.

It charges, and I slice down, watching in satisfaction as my blade sinks into the thick beast, not even bothered by the reverberating sting that travels up my arms at the impact. No, I'm focused on the chunk of spice cake that falls to the ground. Holy shit. It really is made of cake.

Fuck.

I used to be disgusted by cannibalism, but this fight just got a whole lot more exciting.

My stomach growls in anticipation.

The cake charges again, and I brandish my weapon, arcing it sideways like I'm swinging a baseball bat. I sever that motherfucker's bottom layer off. It collapses into two piles, an upper and lower half, legs and arms twitching violently for a second before growing still. The fresh bakery scent of its body makes me step forward, stoop, and scoop up an experimental bite with my fingers.

Something shoves me from behind, and my lungs compress, my breath fleeing as I go sprawling. Icing coats my jacket and pants, and a pink frosting rose gets smashed into the strands of my hair as my heart jumps with fear.

Too smug. I was too smug, I curse myself as I whirl clumsily, lifting my sword as I try to force air down my windpipe.

An alien-like monster with a giant forehead and bulbous black eyes stares down at me. An eerie, breathy but high-pitched noise erupts from its mouth, revealing jagged teeth and a black tongue.

"Hello, princess," it says.

But not aloud. Inside my fucking head.

I rear back, and my sword tilts too far. I'm forced to grab it with both hands to steady it.

The alien creature lifts its hand, and I realize that it has blades for fingers.

The trickle of worried sweat trailing down my spine becomes a waterfall of *oh-fuck* freakout.

I toss my sword roughly at it as a distraction strike and struggle to clamber to my feet. But the cake is spongy underneath my boots, uneven, threatening to roll my ankles in its moist crumbles. The fucking frosting is almost a gluey barrier when my left foot slides into it and I'm unable to pull out.

Panic tightens my throat, and I shove my palms out, sending ice daggers right at this motherfucker. But his alien skin must be made of rubber or something hard because my ice doesn't penetrate, doesn't even dent him, simply bounces off and clatters to the ground.

I scramble for my pouch, though I really wanted to save that fucking emerald, but the stupid opening is covered in frosting, and my hand is stuck. A dark web of horror descends over my nerve endings and wraps me with a sense of impending doom. The silver blades on the monster's hand gleam. Time seems to slow.

The bastard chuckles inside my head, his laugh ricocheting off my skull and echoing down my spine.

The alien raises his hand, and it hovers several feet above my heart, fingers splayed as he prepares to rip the organ from my chest.

I don't presume it. I *know* it. Because he's whispering his plan inside my head.

A horrified gasp escapes me as I lift my right leg, attempting to kick him—but a shadow flies through the air, diving across me, between us. Instead of sinking into me, the bastard's blades sink right into Chase's stomach.

His face contorts in surprised pain before his gaze lands on me, expression softening for a second, before he falls to the floor.

Chase!

I'm scrambling, slipping, panicking, covered in cake as I try to reach him. The fact that his attacker is still attached to him is one I'll deal with when I get to—

Tesq stomps forward and grabs the alien by the neck, squeezing until I hear a pop. The brain of the other monster erupts from its head like a piece of popcorn and flies across the room. For two distracted seconds, I watch it before I'm on my hands and knees, crawling toward Chase. Toward Em. Toward both of them.

I stretch my hand out in front of me, soft snowflakes streaming from my palm to pack around his wound.

Beside me, Tesq stomps off with a roar to face another threat.

In front of me, Chase pants, gasping.

Fuck. Oh fuck. How bad is it?

I crawl closer, reaching for him, when suddenly, my shoulder's wrenched from behind. I'm picked up and tossed over a shoulder with a thump that knocks the wind from my lungs a second time. I can't cry out, can't speak, can't make a single noise, as I'm carried out of the room by some unknown foe.

ALIANA

"Let go of me, asshole!" I struggle futilely to escape the monster, but it's no use. Beating on his back has zero effect. He's so much stronger than me that I feel like a rag doll in comparison.

And, not for the first time since we entered the Empire State Building, I feel fear. True, genuine terror that siphons the oxygen straight from my lungs. I can't reach for my final jewel, and when I shove ice magic at him, my power fizzles ineffectively against his spine.

He chuckles but doesn't stop moving. Instead, his entire body turns crystal clear, and his footsteps start to clink. The cold radiating from him chills the air, and I realize that he's turned himself to ice—my powers are useless against him.

What the fuck am I supposed to do?

When I was a member of the human resistance, I didn't give a lot of thought to my mortality. It was a given that I would die at some point in my line of work. It'd be a miracle if I made it to forty. I can't say I ever really feared death. It was *life* that scared me—the horrible possibilities of what would become of me if I were to get captured.

But that was before I met my mates.

Before I realized what it meant to love someone and be loved in return.

Before I knew what it felt like to be a part of a team.

And right now, it's not *my* life I'm worried about. No, I could give less than a damn about that. Sure, I don't want to die, and I'll fight with everything I have to survive, but my impending demise isn't what freezes my joints in place and sends chills down my spine.

I can still see Chase's handsome face etched in agony as he falls to the ground, bleeding profusely from the wound in his stomach.

Oh god.

Chase…

Em…

What were those idiots thinking? How dare they throw themselves in front of me? How dare they sacrifice themselves for me? How fucking dare they? They can't die! Don't they know what that'll do to me?

A startling revelation settles in my gut like a lead weight.

I forgive them.

I forgive the Empty Man for trying to kill me when he misguidedly believed that doing so would save my existence.

I forgive Chase for being an arrogant asshole who put my life above everyone else's in the resistance.

And more than any of that, I care for them.

Maybe even love them.

And I'll never be able to tell them.

Terror scuttles up my throat like an overgrown, hairy spider, and every time I swallow, it's all I taste.

Oh god. I love them. And they'll never know the truth.

Fuck. Fuck. Fuck!

Think, Aliana! Think!

How can I—an ice monster—defeat another ice monster? Maybe if I could just reach for my jewels…

"You need to get out of here." The monster's voice is cold and unfeeling, even as his grip tightens nearly imperceptibly around my wrist.

He continues to drag me forward like a sack of grain, but I dig my feet into his hard belly in an attempt to stop our forward momentum.

"If you're going to kill me, at least have the decency to look me in the eyes," I hiss.

And that… *That* seems to get an emotion out of the strange monster. To my surprise, he sets me down, though he keeps hold of my arm. Shock flickers to life in his glacial eyes, and he opens and closes his mouth repeatedly before transforming from ice sculpture back into a monster that closely resembles a human except for his incredibly pale skin and shockingly white hair.

"I'm not going to kill you." He stares at me as if I've got a few screws loose.

We stand in the middle of a hallway, dead bodies strewn in all directions, the stench of death clogging my nose.

"I'd rather die than be your slave," I bark.

And that's the truth. I'd jam my own icicle into my chest if it meant freeing myself from him.

His white eyebrows arch downwards, though his eyes remain impassive, and his lips firm into a thin line. "I apologize. I do not quite understand how to go about doing this."

Go about doing what?

But I don't ask that question. Doing so will involve an answer, and I don't have the time. I *need* to get back to my mates, to Em and Chase. I need to make sure they're okay.

"Please, just let me go." I don't care that I'm begging a monster. I'll willingly get down on my knees if it means he'll release me.

"My name is Tennious." He stares at me expectantly.

Tennious?

Why does that name sound so familiar?

Then it hits me.

"You're Barnabas's second-in-command." A new type of terror grabs hold of my throat and squeezes until I fear I'll pass out.

Is that their plan? Use me against my mates?

It'll work. God knows it'll work. All four of my Terrors will stop fighting if my life is on the line.

You can't let that happen, Aliana.

They need to live.

There's no other choice.

I struggle against Tennious with renewed vigor. I refuse to be a pawn to utilize against my mates.

In my free hand, the one not currently gripped by the monster, I attempt to form an icicle. Maybe I could try to stab him in the throat—

"Your parents never mentioned me." It's not a question. Tennious cocks his head to the side curiously, his lips curving down slightly. It's strange to see on his face, almost as if his facial muscles don't quite know how to work properly.

"My parents?" His words are shocking enough for my magic to fizzle out. The icicle becomes nothing but water that drips from my fingers to the floor.

"Illy assured me that her sister and husband would take care of you." Tennious's frown deepens, creating taut lines on his handsome face. "Was that not the case?"

"Illy?" Nothing he's saying is making a lick of sense.

My head threatens to explode from the sudden onslaught of information. I feel like a balloon full of helium. Any second now, I'm going to burst.

"Your mother." Tennious says this matter-of-factly, like he's merely discussing the weather outside.

"My mother wasn't named Illy—" I begin.

"When Illy got sick, she begged her sister to look after you. As much as Illy and I loved each other, she knew I wasn't…fit to be a father." A tiny crease materializes between his brows.

"I struggle with certain emotions." He pauses, considers his next words, and then says, "But I know I don't want you to die."

Father?

That one word plays on a loop in my head, even as I try to find a new meaning for it. This male—this terrifying, monstrous male—can't truly be my father, can he? The mere idea is laughable. He works for the enemy, for fuck's sake.

And yet…

I can't help but take in his white hair, so much like my own, and his glacial-blue eyes.

And then I remember the tracker found dead in the visitor's parking lot, covered in ice…

No. No. No.

I don't realize I'm saying those words out loud until Tennious eyes me quizzically.

"Most humans are happy to be reunited with one of their parents, yes?" He sounds genuinely confused by my reaction.

"I'm not human," I manage to say around the hysteria taking root.

"No, you're half monster." Tennious continues to regard me with cold eyes—eyes that look similar to my own and yet nothing like mine. Even on my worst days, I don't think I've ever looked so…empty before. So emotionless. So cold. "But we need to leave—"

"No." I shake my head adamantly as sheer determination rushes through me. I once again form an ice blade in my free hand. "I'm not leaving without my mates."

"But—"

Quick as a whip, I press the ice blade against his throat. My heart rams against my breastbone with frightening velocity.

I know there's a lot I need to discuss with him, especially if what he claims is true, but now isn't the time. He's not the priority. My mates are.

I won't hesitate to slit his throat if it means getting back to the monsters I love.

"I'm going back for my mates with or without you." My words are a soft caress, potent and deadly, both a vow and a threat.

For a brief moment, I swear I see *pride* flash in the monster's eyes, but it's there and gone in less than a second.

He dips his chin in acquiescence. "Very well."

I hold the blade against his cold flesh for a second longer, making sure this isn't a trick, but he simply regards me with cool, unfeeling eyes. Only when I'm certain he isn't going to attack do I allow the ice to dematerialize. He releases my arm and steps back.

Without another word, I turn on my heel and race back towards my mates. I notice somewhat belatedly that my so-called "bio dad" doesn't follow me.

Hang on, my loves.

I'm coming for you.

3 8

CHASE

A STEADY HUM of pain reverberates through my stomach, though it's far more muted than I expect it should be. I don't know if it's Aliana's ice magic soothing it or—

Give me some credit, please, Em snarks inside my head. *I am a fucking Terror.*

Yeah, you are, I mutter as I scan the room and witness Dev throwing a triangle-shaped monster up at the ceiling and shattering its corner.

Are you twisting Terror into an insult?

Are you taking it as one? I shoot back as the sounds of bones breaking fill the air.

I turn, glancing around, but I don't see her. Not on the ground, not standing over any of these bastard monsters.

Aliana isn't here! I mentally shout in panic just as she bursts through a side door, breathless, her hair whipping around her as she slides through a puddle of green blood.

A warm sense of relief heats my stomach at the sight of her, safe and whole. But then, the warm feeling turns wet, and I glance down to see a dark patch of blood blooming on my shirt. Aliana's ice magic seems to have worn off.

I lurch forward a step, clutching my wound. But suddenly, she's there, those beautiful eyes sparkling with concern for me. Numbing cold immediately replaces the slamming thump of pain that welled up in my gut, and I breathe a soft sigh of relief that's short-lived.

"Next floor," Dev calls out, indicating this one's been cleared. "Be ready. If he's in the building, that's where he'll be."

Ominous silence descends over the room as everyone turns to stare at Creep.

The antlered monster from under the bed looks two shades paler than normal, almost a sky blue. If I'm not mistaken, there's a bead of sweat on his brow.

But he forces a stern look and says, "Let's get it over with."

"Wait," Uni calls out, pointing to the window.

I turn and glance at the sky, which has darkened considerably in the last hour. Clouds of every color blot it with steel-gray puffs and lavender tufts along with a solid sheet of dull milky white.

A storm's rolling in.

We are the storm rolling in, Em corrects.

I don't argue with him because I want that to be true. I want us to roll in like a fucking hurricane. We have thus far…but a small part of me wonders if this Barnabas isn't trying to wear us out but also bolster our confidence so that we swagger right into a trap.

"If we wait a minute, I can use the storm water," Uni offers with a nonchalant shrug as if it doesn't matter either way.

I vote we wait. We need every advantage we can get.

No, Em argues.

"He'll think we're hesitating," Creep replies, his tone flat and dead, just like his eyes, which are focused on the stairs. He holds a whip that he stole from another monster limp in his hand.

I don't think I've ever seen the cheerful monster so withdrawn.

Barnabas nearly destroyed him, Em informs me. *I'm surprised he didn't end up like me.*

An uncomfortable feeling slithers across my chest. I think it may be pity. For a Terror. A monster Aliana loves.

Fuck off. I'm driving if you're going to feel this kind of sappy crap, Em threatens me, yanking at my brain and limbs and making me stumble.

I wrest the controls away from him with a bit of a struggle that jerks my arms wildly around in front of me. Then I force myself to turn from Creep to the stairs. Shoving aside my emotions so that Em won't keep struggling against me, I shift into raid mode—light on my toes and heavy on the trigger finger.

It's go time.

Barnabas won't know what hit him.

Why? You going to throw something surprising at him? Em pouts. *He's the world's strongest fucking greed monster. I'm pretty sure he's anticipated our attacks.*

Greed monster? I've seen a ton of different monsters over the years, but I can't say I've ever heard of a so-called greed monster.

They fuck with your mind, Em responds, and I detect a sliver of fear in his voice that normally remains hidden.

Is Em…afraid of Creep's father? That doesn't really bode well for us. Em usually isn't afraid of anything.

Fuck with your mind? I mentally urge Em to continue.

I need to know exactly what I'm dealing with. We talked about it a little bit back at our base, but I always felt stupid asking for more information when the others seemed to know everything already. Now, I'm berating myself for not speaking up.

He makes you want things. Em pauses and then amends his previous statement. *He makes you want things so badly that you'll kill others to get it.*

That sounds ominous as fuck.

We've got a plan, I remind him.

The plan requires us to stay united, Em retorts. *Barnabas is going to try to fuck that up.*

Don't get greedy, then.

His only response is a dark chuckle, and a sense of foreboding crawls slowly up my spine.

Everything I've seen about monsters thus far has been defined by greed. The desire to level up, to own humans, to increase their own sense of self-worth.

We may be fucked.

Now you get it, Empty says, almost jovially.

What the fuck? Is that supposed to be your pep talk before we head up?

That's supposed to be a reminder not to let that gold-tailed bastard get inside your head. Only I'm allowed in here, he retorts scathingly.

Yeah, well, you're more likely than I am to screw us all over. You're the one who tried to kill Aliana to keep her for yourself.

Psht. That was weeks ago. I'm a changed poltergeist.

So you don't want her all to yourself, then? You don't dream about slitting all our throats and having her to yourself— I start to vividly picture doing just that. Killing each of the Terrors in gruesome but satisfying detail.

FUCK! Empty steals the reins, and my body jerks roughly to a stop, my neck lashing forward and back.

What the hell is your prob—

He's already in here! Em hisses in a panicked tone.

My neck twists as Empty swivels my head. I can already see Dev's claws extended, his beady red eyes focused on Creep as if the monster is his next target instead of his closest friend. And I was just picturing killing all of them to keep her.

Dammit to fuck. Empty's right.

Even Uni is clutching his dolls tighter, muttering to them under his breath, his expression suspicious as he darts glances around at the rest of us.

How do we stop it? What can we do? Bile rises in my throat, my cheeks flushing, panic making me feel like I'm going to puke.

We have to break their concentration, Em asserts.

And all of a sudden, my body is contorting and twisting, my mouth is opening, eyes are widening—Em pulling each piece of me as if he's a puppet master. Words spring from my lips, and I'm shocked into silence as Em sings, "I'm a little teapot, short and stout…"

All eyes swivel to us.

Em sings louder. Exaggerates his movements. And changes the lyrics to "here to fight Barnabas and kick him out."

A stunned silence fills the space in the wake of his weird song.

What the fuck was that?

Attention breaking. It worked too, Em retorts with an air of superiority that's completely at odds with the idiotic song and dance he just did. "Remember, he's going to try to turn us against each oth—"

"We know," Dev snarls, racing for the stairs as if he's bound and determined to punish Barnabas for getting inside his head.

I kind of want to do the same.

"Try to keep your thoughts neutral. Don't think about anything you truly care about, or Barnabas will warp your feelings until it becomes an obsession," Creep adds, his tone monotone and his eyes distant.

I wonder how many times he had to deal with Barnabas's twisted mind games.

My turn, I tell Empty.

Then I take over my limbs and reach into my pocket for a new magazine so that I'll have it at the ready when the current one runs out. I want to unload every single bullet into the bastard upstairs.

Licking my lips, I follow the Devourer.

My heartbeat doubles, and my palms sweat against the grip of my gun. In the distance, thunder rumbles, and I think I may hear the soft plink of raindrops on the glass windows of the building, but I pay them no mind as I try to control my breathing, keep my pulse from going haywire as we hurtle up the stairs for our final faceoff.

Remember—neutral thoughts. Rocks. Grass. Puppy dogs—no, scratch those. I fucking want a puppy, and those fluffy little tail-wagging assholes hate ghosts. Not that one, Em coaches.

You work on thoughts. I'll work on shooting the motherfucker until he's as holey as church water.

What the fuck does that mean? Em questions.

I don't have time to tell him that it was a saying I picked up from my grandfather because we emerge on the top floor of the building, which has floor-to-ceiling windows all around and these strange, oversized badge-shaped metallic contraptions on poles in front of each one.

The center of the room is filled with a cluster of monsters packed so tightly that, initially, I can't tell if it's one giant monster or a bunch of them. But they detach when they see us, rolling out one by one, and I spot at least thirty of them.

Yes, we're outnumbered…but it's not nearly as bad as I expected it to be.

Until I note one monster who clones itself, quickly turning from a single humanoid figure into twenty.

Well, shit.

Shit stains, underwear, lace doilies, wagon wheels. Em keeps up his chanting of random objects while I search for a target.

But I don't have more than a second to search before I find that I'm the target.

A massive roar attacks my ears as a Minotaur charges at us, steam erupting from its nostrils. I raise my gun and start shooting as, out of the corner of my eye, I see Dev leap on some pink monster woman.

Aliana rushes in from behind me and lobs one of those jewels she's got into the crowd of monsters. Green puffballs appear in the air above the clones, which then fall onto a half a dozen or so heads, the giant cotton balls encasing monstrous faces. Their arms rise, and they try to claw the strange items off their heads with no luck. The other clones snarl and quickly repopulate.

My love curses because that jewel definitely didn't have the massive effect she was hoping for. There are still tons of monsters in the cluster, and the center of it contains Barnabas.

I wish we could just get a direct line right to him. Not face all these pricks, I grumble.

But Empty is quick to chastise me. *Don't get greedy about the fight. Remember what Creep said. Think about duct tape. Dirt. Toilet paper.*

His idiotic chatter distracts me, and we go sprawling when a waxy-looking shape shifter clobbers me in the side of the head. At the same time, the Minotaur lowers his head, horns glinting ominously, and charges in my direction.

Your job is supposed to be fighting. Do I need to do everything around here? Em snarks.

I snarl at him as I lurch back to my feet, firing off a shot to the side that's a waste of a bullet because the wax man just morphs his body so the damn thing misses. I crouch, ready to leap aside when the Minotaur reaches me.

"Fuck off!" I tell Em.

Of course, my opponent thinks I'm talking to him.

"Maybe I will fuck you after I kill you. Thanks for the suggestion." A creepy smile snakes across the Minotaur's face.

Until, from out of nowhere, Tesq's hand slams into him. A single punch cracks the Minotaur's horn from the tip to the base, and the monster lets out a girlish scream of agony before curling up on the floor in the fetal position.

Tesq spins around and grins at the wax monster that attacked me. The wax bastard spies the orange lines of magma on Tesq's arms and takes a step back, retreating slightly.

Behind Waxy, Creep steps into the room. Unlike the rest of us, he doesn't join the fray. He simply stops walking to stare across the room at a man with golden horns and a golden tail. A bastard I'm very familiar with because he participated in my fucking torture.

I glance between the two of them. There's not a ton of resemblance, perhaps their noses. Maybe chins. But the way that Creep's entire body stiffens screams of trauma. The way his chest stops expanding as if he's holding his breath. How his eyes shutter and his expression blurs into something unreadable, but it's so vacant compared to his normally boisterous self that I'm not certain Creep's still all there.

"Hello, son." Barnabas's lips stretch into a toothy grin. "I knew you would show up."

Creep doesn't respond. He simply...stares at the monster who tortured him for so many years.

"I have to admit..." The golden monster begins to pace, his hands clasped behind his back and his chin hefted upwards imperiously. "I didn't think you would come with the other Terrors. That certainly was a surprise. I thought my sources were overexaggerating when they claimed you guys had become...friendly."

His upper lip curls away from his teeth as if the idea of befriending other monsters is preposterous.

Creep still doesn't respond, his expression blank, his arms limp.

"I suppose this just makes my job easier." Barnabas snaps his fingers in the air dramatically. "Poof. All the Terrors dead. I should thank you, son, for bringing them here to me. You saved me a trip into the city."

Creep just continues to stare.

And stare.

And stare.

Fuck. Is he out? I ask Empty.

No. He just needs to have some sense knocked into him.

My hand jerks, the ghost attempting to take control of it. I relinquish the hand to him, and he swipes it toward Creep, reaching.

He's too far away.

But then, to my shock, the whip in Creep's hand lifts of its own accord. Without him moving a finger. The tip curls up until the entire thing is suspended in midair.

A frisson of shock rolls over me.

Are you doing that? I ask in wonder.

Shut up! I'm concentrating, Empty's voice has never sounded so strained.

I can almost imagine him grunting and breathing hard as he flings the tip of the whip so that a crack sounds in the air.

The noise seems to startle Creep into action, and his stance changes. He puts one foot back and then lifts his arm again, snapping the weapon at a two-legged turtle running at him.

Thank fuck.

There's no real time for relief because Waxy is charging back at me again since the clone monster has surrounded Tesq.

Can you do that thing again? I ask Em.

What thing? Plum jelly, lucky penny, shark teeth—

Reach out...through the air, I ask between shooting and dodging the swipes of a monster that's trying to drip hot wax onto my head. *We need to throw him out the window. Or into the other monsters. Something drastic. I'm wasting ammo.*

Fucking hell, I knew I'd have to do it all. You keep us neutral, he grumbles.

Fine.

Fine.

But before he can take over my gun hand and we can switch places—before he can even start to summon his magic—a stream of magma cuts through the air. Waxy's face puckers and melts, his body sizzling as he drips into a puddle at my feet.

I turn to Tesq and raise my chin in thanks.

He returns the bro nod before turning back to one of the clones and punching a fist through its stomach. Straight through.

I inhale deeply, forcing oxygen into my lungs and turning, lifting my good hand and taking careful aim to avoid Uni. He's broken a window out and is summoning rain inside, creating a column of water. I leave him to it.

Together, Em and I move farther into the room, and I'm lost again to fighting. Shooting. Punching. Ducking. The spray of green blood through the air above me, beside me. A glancing blow that leaves my cheek stinging in pain. Blood fills my mouth, and adrenaline irradiates my veins, making me nearly glow with savagery.

Rain and wind funnel into the space from the broken window, and everyone's hair grows damp, eyelashes splattered with droplets barreling sideways. Thunder cracks and lightning illuminates us all in eerie, unnatural colors.

A monster with double-sided battle ax arms comes at me, and I have to duck and dodge the fucker like I've never had to do before. The slice of his arms creates a whizzing sound that makes my asshole pucker so hard I can feel it all the way up my spine.

There's an edge of death that starts to hover over me, this strange sensation that I've had a few times before. Most recently, when Em and I were tortured. When I was certain we wouldn't make it out.

Don't go there. Don't fucking go there! Em shouts inside my head as a chop from the blades rings true and skims off a bit of my left arm.

Misery splatters through me—from the pain but also from the direction of my thoughts. *Bullets didn't matter against a wax monster. They won't do jack shit against a blade-armed monster either. I'm useless.*

Think of ponies. Number two pencils. Chewing gum on the sidewalk!

I thought neutral thoughts were to counter greed.

They're for that shit too. Now, stop with the negative thoughts, Em scolds.

If I die, you'll be free, I tell him, my mind diving into morose acceptance.

He yanks away control from me, forces my limbs to dive to the ground, and do a painful summersault to escape the blades.

If you die, I'll be fucking alone again! Don't leave me alone.

Em's truth rings inside my ears. Inside my soul.

It makes me swallow hard because it drags up an entire set of soft vulnerabilities that I didn't even know existed inside myself.

STOP THIS FEELING SHIT! he commands.

If you want me to live, do what you fucking did with Creep earlier. Reach out past me and control this bastard's arms. Make him split his own head open.

Em wrenches control of my right arm away from me and extends it, gun and all. I can feel his presence stretching thin inside of me as he pushes himself through space. Unsure what the hell I'm doing, I imagine his essence like it's a body. I imagine holding his hand and stretching along with him, helping him move farther than before.

The ax monster's arm pauses mid swing.

I hold my breath.

Slowly, the ax moves a trembling inch backward. And another.

Fuuuuuuck, Em says, and I can feel the strain as if it were my own muscles shoving down on that huge bastard's arm.

Another inch, but we're slow, and the monster's face is contorting as he pushes back against Em. Has being inside of me weakened the Terror? Are we failing? Is it my fault?

The monster lifts his foot to take a step toward us, his other arm preparing for a swing. But his foot pauses in midair. His ax arm tilts farther back, and it gently bops him on the head, nicking lightly.

Not the destructive force that I imagined, but still, something akin to pride swells inside of me, and I cheer Empty on.

Hell yeah! You're doing it. Keep going.

The ax monster's arm rises up again, and I watch with rapt attention as the ax swings down and deftly splits the monster's own skull. The two halves open like an orange, and juice spills down over the fading gleam in his eyes.

Victory is short-lived.

I expel the old magazine in my gun and use my bad arm to shakily load my new one. That's when I see a murder of crow monsters surrounding Aliana and pecking at her, their beaks gleaming with razor-sharp metal.

I raise my gun and yell, but they're too close to her. Shooting is, once again, useless.

Charging at them instead, I attempt to ignore the way my entire left side feels like it's been engulfed in flames.

I can feel Empty reaching out, but we're both weakened.

To my right, Creep and Dev snarl at each other.

Fuck.

Is Barnabas getting to them?

My left side seizes up, and I can't take a single step more, the pain in my arm and stomach and the consistent blood loss finally catching up to me.

All I have left is my voice. "Save Aliana! And fucking kill Barnabas!"

Uni sends a jet of water at the two Terrors, dousing them. They both sputter and turn toward the golden monster whose tail is lashing behind him. With lightning cracking apart the sky in the background and his expression dark as night, he looks every inch the monster he is.

Horrifying.

Intimidating.

Evil.

Goose bumps cover my arms, and my stomach tightens as a man made of pure ice tromps through the room from a side door and comes to stand beside Barnabas, facing off against us. Gold and ice, their power practically shimmers in the air like humidity, making it hard to breathe.

The heavy patter of rain pelting the roof is overshadowed by Aliana's broken cry. "Dad?"

I swivel to see her face grow wretched with betrayal, her concentration faltering from the collection of frozen birds at her feet and the live ones still circling her head.

A bird takes advantage of her distraction, and the world seems to slow as it plunges right for her stomach, metallic beak sinking in, twisting, ripping out.

Blood as red as a rose wells up as she stumbles.

"NOOOOO!" The sound rips out of me and Em simultaneously, out of Creep, and Dev and Tesq.

The stone monster dives across the room, catching our love as she falls backward, breath sputtering, choking.

"Aliana, Aliana, no," Tesq murmurs as he holds her close.

I can't breathe. Can't think. For a solid minute, I think I lose control of my limbs and float above my body in utter disbelief. This can't be happening.

But Aliana gives a pained gasp. Her hands shakily clasp at the wound on her stomach, covering it, trying to staunch the flow of blood that stains her fingers. Running red. Glistening. Her gaze shoots up toward Tesq, and then...she stops moving.

Her chest doesn't rise. Her eyelashes don't close.

An agony that can only come right from the darkest pits of hell ignites inside my chest. Glowing hot like a fire, it feels as if scorching smoke is curling up my throat. My mouth opens, but no other sound erupts, emotion weighing down my tongue.

But my hands twitch, not quite as empty as the rest of me. I start shooting at the fucking bastard birds still flittering around the room without any regard for who's behind them or who I may hit instead.

They fall with fluttering feathers, caws cut off mid sound, but there's no relief. No peace.

Only a roar inside my head that seems to be mimicked by some noise outside.

Perhaps the foundation's crumbling like at the meat factory. Maybe a sandworm's come to eat us all.

I don't care.

It doesn't matter.

Nothing matters without her.

THE CREEPER

I TURN TOWARD BARNABAS, the sperm-donating motherfucker who tortured me and twisted me into the fucking bastard I am today. His expression is warped by pleased malice as he drinks in the absolute anguish all around him.

That golden fucking goat man's antlers are glowing from a ring light he stands inside, as if he's got a full-body halo. He may pretend, but he's anything but an angel.

He's the worst of us.

And that light won't protect him from me.

Nothing will.

If I have to raze the entire world to the ground to destroy him, I will. Because he just destroyed my entire world.

Those birds might have done the damage, but he was the puppet master pulling the strings.

"YOU DID THIS!" I scream, my voice cracking as my rage and anguish collide internally, both fighting for control.

"No, son." He uses that word with the utmost irony. "You did."

His words slice me open, tear exactly at that tender part of me. I would never have refused my little warrior when she asked to fight—always knew she could hold her own. But against him? Against the evil that almost destroyed me a thousand times over?

It is my fault.

A scream lashes through me, and suddenly, I'm in motion.

Sprinting and leaping five feet into the air, my stomach flies up, and my torso hollows.

My father's eyes widen infinitesimally, as if he didn't expect a direct attack.

I don't give a damn what he expects.

I body slam into the bastard, my elbow connecting with his nose and sending a gratifying jolt of pain up my arm as I tackle him to the ground.

His tail lashes at my side, breaks a rib, and makes me suck in a jagged breath. But even the knife-like pain of my own bones stabbing me doesn't make me stop.

Inside my head, I can feel the effects of his magic, digging at my thoughts, rearranging them, winding around my brain like ivy on a rosebush in search of a branch to cling to and choke. His magic is predatory, always has been. Unfortunately for him, all of my greed was extinguished with Aliana's final breath.

I want nothing but his death.

And I don't want to kill him to regain Ebony Kingdom. I don't give a shit about that any longer.

I want to watch the light seep from his eyes because it's what he deserves.

Scraping my ragged claws over his eyes, I dig in until I feel one of them pop beneath my fingers. His scream is satisfying enough that even when he throws me off of him and I go flying into something sharp that stabs at my back, I can't help but chuckle.

When I rise to my feet, I don't see anyone but him in the room. The light around him is partly smashed, but there's still not enough of a shadow for me to portal, so I stare at him.

"I did you a favor. Females simply get in the way. Like your mother. Now you don't have to cater to that bitch's whims. No, you can have whatever you want, do whatever you want…" His tone is slick as oil, trying to tempt out the greed in me, even as his breathing hitches from pain. Blood pools from his eye socket like rivers of red.

I just tuck my head lower and ram my antlers into my father, shoving him into the floor with a smash so violent that a piece of my horns chips off. "Without her to share it with… there's nothing."

"Looks like I'll have to kill you the old-fashioned way. With violence," he murmurs, having realized his magic no longer has any effect.

He shoves at me, his tail lashing at the side of my head and knocking me off him so that I go sliding across the floor.

I don't bother responding to him, simply launching myself at him again. Scrabbling and punching, ignoring the pain billowing up inside each of my muscles, I slowly work him backwards across the floor until I have him pressed up against a window.

For all his magic and manipulation, he's an old monster. His fight isn't what it once was.

When he realizes that I have him pinned, his good eye widens, and he starts to spit out manipulative pleas. "They're all here. We could take them all out, and you could be the king—"

"I don't fucking care!" With a torching yell that burns my insides as if an inferno's sweeping through me, I squeeze my father's neck. "She was my mate!"

A swipe.

Barnabas wears a necklace of red ribbons.

I swipe again because it's not enough.

The flesh peels away and reveals muscle. Still not enough.

His artery bends forward, the opened tube spurting green blood into my face with all the force of a fire hydrant from the before times.

Still not enough.

I swipe until I see bone.

Until his spine is exposed.

And then I grab hold of it with two hands and crack it.

Still, I'm not fucking appeased. I start to stab him with my claws, perforating his skin wherever I can reach.

To my horror, the ice monster beside Barnabas creates an ice sword out of thin air, and my stomach twists, certain I'm about to die by his hands. And I don't even care enough to move out of the way.

"Try this." The ice monster that Aliana called "Dad" startles me when he hands me a clear sword, hilt extended in my direction.

Without caring whether it's a trick, without bothering to think, I grab the frozen sword and plunge it straight down into my father's chest.

Empty.

His face is empty.

Body a shell.

Empty like I am as I slink down to my knees, covered in blood, sliding into a puddle of it, and not caring a whit about either one.

She's gone.

He's gone.

But mostly, she's gone.

What does that mean for me? Who am I without her?

My wondering is cut off as all around us, a raging, sucking, crushing sound surges.

At first, I think that it's simply Barnabas's warped essence disintegrating, his horrible power and evil animus twisted and pulverized into nothing.

But then, I see a nearby building quake and fall, making the floor beneath my feet tremble. And I detect the distinctive rush of water.

I glance over at Uni, whose arms are lifted as he gazes out the window. Following his eyes, I see a muddy tide sweeping down the streets, spinning cars like children's tops, collapsing old electric poles.

Looking at the tentacled monster in askance, I crook a brow.

"Your father had back-up forces coming," the water monster confesses. "My girls spotted them. I've got them."

I jolt as the building sways, and the crushing force of Uni's summoned flood water fills the bottom floor.

My stained soul hopes that it brings this entire building down. Because I have no more reason to live.

Without Aliana, there's no light.

And so I wish for darkness.

If I would've known the price of killing my father was my mate's life, I never would have taken part in this senseless crusade. I'd rather hand him this world on a silver platter than live a single moment without Aliana.

Pivoting, I turn from my father's body to face her. God, she looks so beautiful even when she's broken and her soul has fled. Something about her still calls to me. Pulls at me. Reminds me how I failed her.

What a way to discover that kingdoms and power and armies… None of that matters. Not anymore. Only Aliana does. She's my horizon, and nothing exists beyond it for me.

"The entire city's destroyed," Uni murmurs as he gazes out the window steadily, but I don't tear my gaze away from a motionless Aliana.

Does it really matter that we took back our kingdom? Or that the kingdom itself has been wiped out?

No. No, it does not.

I once thought I wanted the world, but that was before I realized *my* world is Aliana.

A tiny, tentative smile touches the corners of my lips when I think about the first time I saw her—a feisty, angry thing stuck on stage at the auction.

Who would've thought that the beautiful little warrior would come to mean everything to me?

Tesq whispers something to Aliana, but his voice is too low for me to hear. Behind me, Dev snarls and snaps at the white-haired monster.

I turn to look out the window, but my gaze lands on my father's sleek black combat boots. Anger wars with my grief at the sight.

I wish I had taken my time killing him.

He died too quickly.

Funny, the first time I attempted to kill him, I was slow about it. Methodical. Dipped his tail in acid so he could feel what he'd done to me. I glance over at his tail, which looks the same as ever now, covered in new scales. I can't even muster up the curiosity to wonder if there are scars beneath them.

This time, any grand fantasies I had went to shit.

The freight train of my rage collided with my grief, and there was only smashing chaos during the fight we just had. Panicked need. Not even desire, but something far more basic. The need to ensure the monster who was ultimately responsible for Aliana's death died.

He wasn't even my father to me any longer.

He was the orchestrator of my mate's murder.

The conductor of her agony.

He brought her song to an end.

And for that, his sounds needed to be snuffed from the world.

Slowly, I rise to my feet, never peeling my gaze from his damn shoe. The shoe leads to a leg, then a waist, then a torso, and then finally a head, his one good eye wide and vacant but lacking the horror he should've felt.

My movements are icy and mechanical, so unlike me, as I lower myself beside his still form. The rage is still there, bubbling and fizzing like water in a kettle, but it's been pushed behind a wall of pure ice.

He needs to pay.

With a cry, I throw myself at my father's body and hit and scratch and attack all over again. I don't care that he's already dead. I don't care that he won't fight back. I don't care that brutalizing his corpse won't return Aliana to me.

None of that matters.

Nothing matters anymore.

Tears stream down my face as I rip off one arm and fling it across the room and then continue to destroy the body of the man I hate most of all. By the time I'm done with him, he's nothing but a lumpy mass of skin, bones, and blood.

But it isn't enough.

Nothing will ever be enough.

I throw my head back and roar.

THE DEVOURER

I DON'T RECOGNIZE the sound I'm making.

It's not a scream or a growl or even a cry.

Everything inside of me rebels against what I'm seeing. I half want to close my eyes and blanket this unforgiving world in darkness. Maybe then, the sight before me won't be real.

But no.

Aliana's still lying in my arms.

Dead.

Dead.

My mate's dead.

Before I even realize what I'm doing, I'm slamming my fist into the floor hard enough for the entire building to shake and tremble. Pain reverberates from my busted knuckles, but it's a small ache compared to the gnawing pit in my chest.

Aliana's dead.

Dead.

Dead.

Dead.

I'm belatedly aware that Creep has dropped to his knees beside us, staring at Aliana's prone form and Tesq has begun to cry, his granite shoulders shaking. Em merely stands there, holding his wounded arm, his eyes glazed and unseeing.

From somewhere behind us, that white-haired fucker who helped us win the fight takes a step closer. I'm dimly aware of Tesq asking the monster who he is.

And everything inside of me goes still when he replies, "Her father."

A mind-numbing rage propels me towards him. I can't think through the agony squeezing my airways. Can't breathe. All I know is someone needs to pay for this, and since Barnabas is already dead, his second-in-command will have to do.

I shove my entire arm, covered in coarse black fur, against his neck, cutting off his air supply, but he simply stares at me blankly. Those blue eyes of his—so much like my sweet mate's—hold my own. But while Aliana's always glimmer with mischief and warmth, his are an icy tundra, devoid of any emotion.

"I'm going to kill you," I rasp as something wet touches the corner of my lips.

It takes me a second too long to realize it's a tear.

Am I…crying?

I've never cried before.

The monster doesn't even react to my threat as he continues to stare at me apathetically. But his impassive expression only infuriates me further.

His daughter is *dead.*

Dead.

Dead.

And he doesn't even fucking care.

With a roar, I swing my claw at his head.

THE GROTESQUE

IN ALL MY years of existence, I've never cared enough about anybody the way I care for Aliana. The only creature that managed to weasel her way into my heart was Fluffy. But besides her, there was no one.

Until Aliana.

I glance down at the woman clutched in my arms. With her streaked snow-white hair, haunting eyes, and a smile that never fails to make me weak at the knees.

But just now, that hair is tinted red with blood, her eyes are vacant, and her smile is nowhere to be seen. Her parted lips seem to be mocking me—they promise a smirk or a witty retort she'll never make again.

I half expect her to sit up and demand to know why we're all huddled around her like overbearing mother hens. She'll then check in on each and every one of us and ensure we're okay.

But she doesn't move.

"The entire city's destroyed." Uni's voice drags my attention up to him, where he stands at the window, overlooking the world below.

All I can see are white-frosted waves lapping at the first floors of all the skyscrapers and eating away at trees. Monster screams and roars sound in the distance, but it doesn't matter.

Nothing matters anymore.

We fought for this new world to be with our mate, but now our mate is dead.

And soon, I'll join her. I have no intention of living in a world where she doesn't exist.

Somewhere behind me, Dev begins to fight with Tennious, but it's background noise. In one ear and out the other.

I place my forehead against Aliana's, hating how unnaturally cold her skin is. How pale.

"I'm sorry, my beloved," I whisper huskily. "I'm sorry you couldn't see this new world you fought so hard for. I'll do what you couldn't—I'll make this world safe for the humans. Then, I'll join you."

My tears brand her smooth skin—imprinting my promise onto her flesh.

Soon, my love.

We'll be together soon.

THE EMPTY MAN

I THINK this pain might extinguish me.

And no, I don't mean the pain radiating from Chase's stomach. That's a physical type of ache that can be healed over time, with bandages and stitches and antibiotics.

But this? This agony searing my very soul?

It's a wound that will never heal.

I never even got the chance to tell Aliana I loved her.

Love her.

Because even though she's pale and still, even though her cheeks are white as snow, I still love her fiercely. It's the type of love that's pumped directly into my bloodstream, changing me irrevocably. There's no going back.

This can't be real. This can't be. Em, do something! Chase's voice is a desperate rasp in my head.

He gave up control almost as soon as Aliana fell, his thoughts running over themselves. His despair joins my own, compounding this foreign feeling inside of me.

I think…

I think I want to die.

It's an odd feeling for a being who has been around for hundreds of years.

My knees feel weak, or maybe I'm just queasy from blood loss. Does it even matter? Aliana's dead.

Em, please! You were able to come back as a ghost, weren't you? Maybe you can help Aliana—

It doesn't work like that. I thought it would, but I was being too optimistic. I don't recognize my own internal voice. It's dry and monotone. Curt.

Numb.

You need to save her! Chase begins to sob, and a part of me wants to drown him out, erect a wall between us.

Another part of me wants to take comfort in him and our bond.

Who would've thought I'd come to care about the pesky human whose body I inhabit?

She can't be gone. She can't be. It's impossible. She can't be. Chase is nearly incoherent.

I suddenly wish I had a body of my own so I could…hug him. Comfort him.

Or maybe I want him to comfort and hug me.

My legs finally give out, and I collapse on the ground. The sudden movement pulls at my wound, but it's a pain I welcome.

Something crashes into the wall just behind me, and I turn my head to see Dev pinning Aliana's biological father by the throat.

"Do you even care that your daughter is dead?!" Dev roars, and the force of it stirs the white-blond locks of the monster's hair.

Tennious simply blinks, nonplussed. "She's not dead, you overgrown, hairy imbecile."

Tesq slowly lifts his head from where he pressed it against Aliana's.

"She's not breathing," the gargoyle rasps out.

"Because she's frozen." All of this is stated in a stoic, no-nonsense voice. "Now, if you'd be so kind as to release me…" Tennious glances pointedly at the arm banded around his neck.

Slowly, almost reluctantly, the Terror releases him and takes a single step back.

"Explain," he growls, his hands balled into fists.

Tennious sighs as if this entire conversation is beneath him. "When she was attacked, her body froze itself to protect her from injury. It's a phenomenon called cryobiology. She'll wake up as soon as she unthaws."

What? Chase asks shakily.

I can feel him perk up and begin to pay attention to the other monster's words. Heaven only knows I am.

Frozen? Is it possible?

Tesq once again lowers his forehead to Aliana's, his massive shoulders shaking, and Creep twists his body from where he's straddling his father's corpse.

"If you're lying—" Dev threatens.

Tennious blows out another irritated breath. "You'll what? Maim me? Kill me? I've heard that all before, boy. I've lived thousands of years and seen things you can only imagine. Not a lot scares me."

But as his frosty gaze slides in Aliana's direction, I realize that he isn't being entirely truthful. Something *does* scare him.

The death of his daughter.

"What do we do?" Creep shakily rises to his feet. Blood coats his hands and face, but he doesn't seem to notice.

"Now," Tennious begins, his gaze homing in on Aliana, "we wait."

ALIANA

WARMTH. I'm aware of a gentle heat that feels like it starts at the tips of my toes, runs along the outside of my arms, and then drips down over the top of my skull. It soaks into me inch by inch until my chest is sweltering inside and a jagged beat begins to pulse.

The heat transforms into need, and my lips part automatically, sucking in a sharp breath.

Suddenly, there's not only heat, but a buoyant lightness to my limbs. Limp contentment controls my muscles, keeping them soft and compliant in a way I'm pretty certain they've never been before. It's strange, but I don't believe I've ever felt safer than I do right now.

My eyelids flutter open, and I'm surprised to find myself on a soft mattress, tucked into clean sheets, inside a small room with plastered walls that's filled with lemon-yellow light. At the far side of the room, six monsters are gathered, talking in hushed tones.

I clear my throat, trying to call out, but that miniscule sound is all they need. As one, my four mates turn to look at me, leaving Uni and my father behind. Dev's red eyes seem to boil over, tears dripping down his cheeks as he races to my side in his human form, his giant hand diving beneath the covers to grasp one of mine.

It's a struggle not to cry as the giant monster breaks down in front of me, wracked by silent sobs that scream relief.

Creep, whose beautiful antlers are chipped, strolls over, tipping up one corner of his mouth. "Decided to finally put us out of our misery, huh, little warrior?"

His tone is light, but his eyes are glossy as he reaches out and puts a hand on the blanket, gently touching my shin through the fabric.

I force a wry smile, but it wobbles slightly, so I'm not sure he believes the front I put up. Still, I push through and manage the tiniest sliver of sarcasm. "Did you sleep under my bed the entire time I've been here?"

"You know it. Though, it did make me decide that mattresses and bed frames should really be clear so I can stare right up at your panties."

That wrings a laugh from my tear-clogged throat. "Creep," I say fondly.

Tesq's heavy footsteps thump against the carpet as he trudges closer. He doesn't speak, but he doesn't have to. We share a gaze that sings like a wren calling to its mate. A song with gentle high notes that mean *mine* and *pair* and *forever*.

My gargoyle and I don't need many words. What we are to one another is carved in stone, unchangeable, everlasting.

My chest tightens, but not with pain—with a joy so bright it hurts. I'm so fucking happy I get to see him again.

Chase and Empty move more slowly than all the others, hand clutched to stomach. The other monsters leave space for him to sit down on the bed at my side. Once he's settled, I realize that Empty's in control, because his head dips a certain way, and his smile is a little wider than Chase's. His right hand reaches out and cups my cheek, and I lean into the soft touch.

"Aliana. I'm glad you're back. Even if it's not as a ghost and I can't have you all to myself."

I chuckle.

"Not funny." Chase wrests control from Empty and leans closer, green eyes glittering earnestly. "He doesn't even mean that, you know. He just likes to get a rise out of the rest of us."

I pull my free hand out from underneath the covers and put it on Chase's knee, needing to reassure him. "I know."

I squeeze his knee slightly, which makes his eyebrows rise.

"How are you feeling?" I glance meaningfully at his stomach. "Looks like you should be in bed here with me."

His lip twitches.

Suddenly, the blankets on top of me wrench back of their own accord as if pulled by invisible hands. They float a foot above me, hovering in midair.

Shock momentarily renders me immobile. Is *Em* doing that somehow? How? But I don't dare look a gift horse in the mouth. If Em is able to utilize some of his powers while in Chase's body, then that means they have an additional way to protect themselves. And all I want in this world is for my mates to be safe.

Chase blushes when he realizes that I'm only in a set of red panties underneath the covers.

I simply tease, "Well, are you getting in or not?"

He doesn't hesitate after the invitation, lying on his side next to me, face toward me, one arm wrapping gently around my waist as the covers tuck back down around us and cocoon us in that soft warmth once more.

Reaching my hand to his stomach, I gently press a tiny bit of numbing ice magic into him where I can feel his bandages. "Better?"

He ends up curling into me, his head pressed against my shoulder, his legs curving over mine until he's holding me like I'm a lifeline.

"Better than ever," he whispers in a hushed but sibilant tone.

"Me too," I murmur.

And it's true. In this moment, no matter all the questions floating in the back of my mind, I know one solid truth—we all made it through the fight. We're all together.

That fact alone means that we're better than ever.

ALIANA

THE HUMAN GLANCES in both directions anxiously.

She appears to be a few years older than myself, with scarlet hair that cascades down her back. I can't quite see her eye color from this distance, but I do note that she's petite.

She ducks inside an abandoned pharmacy—the building sun-kissed and crumbling with age—and then disappears from sight. Less than an hour later, she returns, standing at the entrance with a bulky backpack slung over her shoulder. She once again checks her surroundings and then races down the cracked asphalt dodging around the detritus left by the flood.

Not a single monster attacks her.

From my position on the balcony of the hotel we've taken over, I have a perfect view of the city, though I doubt anyone is capable of seeing me.

After all, most of the monsters in Ebony Kingdom were wiped out by Uni's flood.

It's only been in the last few weeks that the water has begun to recede, retreating back to the rivers and flowing out to the ocean. Most of the buildings have been damaged, but some—especially the ones on the outskirts of the city—remain.

Perfect for the humans to raid.

A tiny smile touches my lips instinctively.

It's only been a few weeks since the fight at the Empire State Building, yet I feel as if I'm living in an entirely new world. The few times I ventured down to street level, I saw very few monsters, and those I did see stayed out of my way. I've actually seen more *humans* than monsters.

For the first time in forever, they have a fighting chance.

A clearing throat behind me pulls my attention off of the street and towards the tall, lean male beside me.

Tennious.

Behind him, his green eyes intent on me, is Chase. And I can only tell it's Chase by the way he stands. Em would be leaning against the door by now, too lazy to remain upright.

Tennious clears his throat again, seemingly just as uncomfortable as I am, and then says, "Your mates let me in."

Which probably explains why Chase is hovering.

I haven't really had a chance to talk to Tennious since everything went down. Yes, he's been around, but conversation between the two of us has been strained. He hasn't brought up this elusive "Illy," and I haven't asked him. A part of me doesn't want to know what he has to say.

"They seem a little overbearing, do they not?" Tennious continues in his cold, monotone voice.

He flicks his gaze towards first Chase and then the window beside the balcony door. I turn as well—just in time to see Tesq, Dev, and Creep all duck down.

I snort.

Overprotective fools.

And *that's* another reason why I haven't been able to have alone time with my so-called bio father. All of my mates have been extremely needy since my apparent death. I'm barely able to leave the bed, let alone the room.

Well, all of my mates except for the Empty Man and Chase. Those two have been abnormally quiet lately. During the day, they travel into the city to find the Bell Witch who placed the spell on them, trapping Em in Chase's body. At night, they retreat to their own room with only a mumbled word or two to me.

I thought when I woke up and Chase held me in his arms that all of our problems would magically melt away. But then, an off-handed, arrogant comment from Chase set me off. I got angry…and neither he nor I is the best at apologizing.

I hate the distance between us, but I know it's not just their fault. At some point, I need to put on my big-girl panties and talk to them face-to-face. We can't keep tiptoeing around each other.

But later.

Right now, I have a bio dad to deal with.

Tennious moves to join me at the railing. The wind stirs his white-blond hair, so much like the streaks in my own. We don't speak for a long moment, but surprisingly, the silence

isn't uncomfortable nor fraught with tension. It's almost…
companionable.

Tennious breaks the silence at last. "You probably have
questions."

"You mentioned someone named Illy… Who is that?" I shift
slightly so I'm able to see him fully.

The setting sun paints his white hair in swatches of red and
orange.

"Illy…" A sad smile touches his lips, and I think it may be the
first time I've seen an emotion on him that isn't confusion or
anger. "Illy was my mate. My *human* mate."

"Mate?"

Tennious…has a mate? No, he said "was." So he had a mate?
What happened to her?

I try to picture this stone-cold monster loving anyone, but
the image evades me. I'm not even sure if he loves *me*, and
I'm apparently his daughter.

"Illy… Is that my mom?" I venture tentatively, unsure if I
want to hear the answer.

"We met when she was nineteen. I tried to kill her." He says
this all the same way he says everything else—utterly expres-
sionless.

I can't help but smile, remembering all of the times I tried to
murder my own mates.

"Must run in the family," I murmur.

"I remember she stabbed me in the arm and then ran away
with a backpack full of supplies she stole from my home." He
absently scratches at a spot on his bicep, and I wonder if

that's where she injured him. "We met a few more times after that, but it was only during the fifth meeting that we actually talked for more than a minute. I knew immediately she was my mate, but she remained oblivious. Humans, apparently, don't sense mate bonds the way monsters do.

"She didn't care that I was different from most monsters and humans, that I didn't feel emotions the same way she did. I believe I loved her." His eyes glaze, as if he's trapped in a memory invisible to the naked eye. "And she loved me too.

"When she became pregnant with you, she was worried. The resistance camp she was a part of didn't know about her relationship with me.

"She gave birth to you and immediately fell in love. However, shortly after you came into the world, she fell sick with a disease the humans call cancer." Another emotion flashes across his face, quick as lightning.

Grief.

My stomach turns painfully at the thought of this mother who loved me…one I never got to know. What would my life have been like if Illy raised me? Would I have had a relationship with Tennious? Would I have met my mates? I don't dare ponder the "what ifs." I'll go insane if I do.

"We discussed you at length before she passed, but we both agreed that I wasn't fit to take care of a child. Illy decided she would give you to her sister to raise." Tennious absently scratches at the nape of his neck.

It's such a human gesture that I almost forget he's a monster. Almost. I think it'd be impossible to forget completely.

"After Illy died, I kept an eye on you for a while, but your resistance camp constantly moved around. It didn't take long before I lost track of you." A muscle in his throat bobs as he swallows. "When Barnabas talked about a white-haired girl mated to four monsters, I knew in my soul that he was talking about you. I couldn't allow him to kill you."

He shakes his head slowly from side to side. "I may not feel things the way others do, but I know you're my daughter, and I don't want you dead.

"I'm not sure if Barnabas trusted me or simply feared me. Either way, he kept me at his side, so I was able to hear all of his plans. When I heard he wanted to kill you, I knew I needed to stop him. I'd actually planned on killing him that day." A cold smile curls up his lips. "But you and your mates beat me to it."

I don't know how to respond to the bombshell he just tossed at me. In a span of minutes, I learned the people who raised me were actually my aunt and uncle, my mother died of cancer, and I have a sociopathic monster as a father.

Clearing my throat, I glance at Tennious sheepishly through my fringe of lashes. "Can you…?" I break off and have to start again. "Can you tell me about her? Illy, I mean?"

"Of course."

And he does.

We stand on the balcony for over three hours talking. I'm not sure that Tennious will ever be the father to teach me how to ride a bike or braid my hair or throw a baseball…but he seems to care for me in his own monstrous way.

What more could I ask for?

WHEN TENNIOUS RETREATS TO HIS OWN HOTEL ROOM LATER that night, I'm exhausted.

Through it all, my mates have remained nearby, granting me privacy but also prepared to fight at a moment's notice if Tennious decides to hurt me.

But I know that he won't. He's a lot of things, most of them horrible, but he seems to care for me in his own twisted way.

Talking to him has reaffirmed one thing for me, though—life is too short to push away the people you love. Death is everywhere, and there's no escaping it. No running away.

Which means you need to live life to the fullest and have no regrets.

At some point during my conversation with Tennious, Chase moved to sit on the patio chair. His eyes remain fixed on the horizon, where the sun has disappeared behind mutilated skyscrapers. He doesn't look in my direction as I step closer, but I know he can sense me. His shoulder muscles tighten beneath his sea-blue shirt.

"You've been avoiding me." There's no point in beating around the bush.

"We believe the Bell Witch is dead," Chase says, and there's a slight hitch to his voice I've never heard before. "It'll be impossible for Em to leave my body now."

My brows furrow. "Chase, I'm sorry—"

"Don't." He turns his head away as if it pains him to stare directly at me. "Just…don't. I should be the one apologizing to you."

Out of everything I expected him to say, it wasn't *that*.

361

"What do you mean?" I take a single step closer until I'm between his spread legs.

His hands twitch by his sides as if he wants to place them on my hips but is restraining himself. His chest heaves with shallow breaths.

"You'll always be stuck with me," he whispers. "I can't just... I can't just fade away."

"Fade away?" My voice rises in pitch.

"You'll never just have your mate, Aliana." Chase's voice is uncharacteristically gentle, even as his green eyes glimmer with unshed tears. "It'll always be him and me. Em thinks that I won't even age—that I'll be stuck like this forever, with him inside of me." He laughs, but the noise is dry and humorless, the scratching of fingernails against a chalkboard. "I'm sorry, Aliana. If I could fade away, I would—"

"You stop this nonsense right the fuck now!" I'm suddenly angry. Furious, even.

I knew I should've had this conversation earlier, but I thought I was being a stubborn ass, when actually I was being a coward. Now, my fear is coming back to bite me in the ass.

How could Chase think this about himself?

How could he believe that I'd want him to fade away?

"I want you to listen to me closely, Chase. And Em, you too. I want you to listen too." I take a deep breath to gather my courage, drawing lungfuls of air. "I love you. Both of you. I don't know when it happened or how, but I don't want you to *fade away*, Chase. And I don't want you to fade either, Em. I love you both. This may be fucked up, but I'm *happy* Em's trapped in your body. Because that means you won't die on me, and I won't have to lose you. I love you both and—"

Chase grabs hold of my hips and stands as he yanks my lips to his.

And. I. See. Fireworks.

ALIANA

Chase unexpectedly breaks off our kiss, staring down at me. Though his tongue doesn't move, his gaze speaks volumes, and I understand each and every word. I lean in and brush my lips over the smooth cut of his jaw.

"Yes," I whisper along his skin, answering the question he didn't ask.

His arms sweep around me then and scoop me up into a bridal carry as if I weigh nothing. Our grins are a matching set full of eager anticipation and giddiness as he carries me sideways through the open balcony door.

I can't help but reach up and run a hand through his moonlit blond hair, sighing at how beautiful he looks. Chase has always been a gorgeous specimen of a man. But now that he's mine? Now that I know he and Em are aware of how I truly feel, under the layers of everyday agitation and the monotony of quibbling?

I've spoken aloud about the tenderness throbbing inside of me, that tug to be with them, and it's as if I've freed up some part of myself that was tight and twisted by holding back.

I'm done holding back.

Upon entering the living room of the presidential suite my monsters have commandeered, I spot the rest of my mates scattered around the room. My father's gone, but Creep lounges sideways across an armchair, an old book clutched in his hands.

Tesq is lighting candles in the numerous candelabras he's scouted out and set around the room, from old silver pieces that are blackened by age and new crystal contraptions that are abstract shapes. He's created an eclectic collection to light our evenings, and he wears a soft smile in the flickering glow of the newest candle.

Dev has set up a wooden panel in the corner of the room and is halfway through an abstract painting. He's not quite relaxed, but his posture is full of intense concentration as he leans forward and adds a tiny splotch of color.

They're totally pretending they weren't spying on me during my talk with Tennious. Idiots.

But *my* idiots.

"Clear out. Aliana and I need some alone time," Em declares.

Immediately, Dev stiffens and turns. Tesq freezes, candles flickering in his hand due to the breeze brought in by the open door behind us.

Creep closes his book and glances over at me. "Shouldn't you take her in a bed the first time?"

"So you can be jerking off under it?" Em rolls his eyes.

"What happened to sharing?" Dev calls out, having done a complete one-eighty on the sharing front. He's now an enthusiastic proponent of it.

"It's my first time. Not happening. Get out!" Em commands, and with a wave of his hand, Fluffy, who was just stalking into the room, slides back into the dining room.

The door bangs shut in her whiskered face.

A red silk sheet drifts into the space from the bedroom, undulating like a kite. It wraps around Em and me like a cocoon, shielding us from view.

"Someone's been practicing," I tease him as I lean in for a quick kiss.

"That's nothing," he breathes.

And then our feet lift off the floor, and we float up toward the high ceiling. Em levitates the two of us until we're next to the chandelier full of dangling crystals.

I can't help but glance down, noting the disapproving looks the rest of my mates are giving us.

Em hums happily, seemingly unconcerned by them as he waves a hand and commands the red sheet to tie to either side of the brass chandelier arms, creating a soft swing. Floating through the air, he gently sets me into it, carefully wrapping my hands around either side.

"I'm impressed," I tell him as he presses his body between my thighs.

His smile only widens as he snaps his fingers.

All of the candles that Tesq has lit float up and bob in the air around us like tiny man-made stars.

Em floats in closer, and I wrap my legs around his torso, leaning up to kiss him. Our lips brush, and our souls begin to mingle. I swear it almost feels as if Empty extends himself beyond Chase's skin and enters mine, sending a shiver running across my entire body at once.

I'm hot and cold and delighted but filled with nervous butterflies. It's so many things to feel at once, and I may just burst out of my skin.

I take my feelings out on Em, twisting a rough hand into his hair and yanking as I nip on his lower lip. I stop kissing and start devouring, leaning dangerously forward in my perch as I rake my nails down the back of his neck.

Pulling back, a bit breathless, utterly insatiable at this point, I order, "Undress."

Em rips at his shirt, throwing it carelessly down. His shoes and socks drop off without his touch, his telekinesis at work. After he yanks off his pants and boxers in a single move, I expect him to throw them with the same disregard he showed his shirt, but he balls them up and pitches them right at Dev.

"Something for you to sniff, pup, while I fuck our mate."

Dev growls beneath us and takes a threatening step forward, but Em just laughs and spins in midair as he strokes his cock, already long and thick, the deep-pink color of it several shades darker than his stomach.

I reach for it, but he glides backward, floating beyond my reach as he says, "Your clothes now, mistress."

I take one hand from the swing and reach for the hem of my shirt, but the black material bunches up on its own, wrinkling until the bottom of my stomach is exposed.

"Allow me," Em says.

And so, I simply lift both hands over my head and let Em drag my shirt off. He unclasps my bra, and it floats away, though neither of my items of clothing fall to the floor. Em leaves them hovering past the candles, out of our immediate view but also out of the reach of my other mates.

He's taunting them.

I'm about to tell him to play nice when the seams of my pants rip, all the way up and down. The material on top of my thighs floats off, while the underside yanks at me, making me swing in midair until I lean to one side and let the fabric fly off.

"These I want to do by hand," Em murmurs as he comes forward and drags his hand up my inner thigh before laying his palm directly over my panties.

His fingers are so warm that a spiral of need begins to spin inside my belly, circling until it makes me dizzy with lust.

His fingers stroke up and down along my slit as he leans in and kisses me gently. So gently that my eyes pop open and my head tilts.

I grab his shoulder, leaning back and studying his expression. "Chase?"

He nods, a soft and pleased expression on his face. "I can't stay long… We'll fall. But I had to kiss you."

With a luminous, extravagant emotion blooming inside my chest, I lean forward and kiss him back—harder than before. He leans over me, and I end up halfway reclined in my silky hammock swing as his body hovers just above mine. The skin of our shins brushes together. Our thighs press against

369

one another. His chest with its light smattering of hair grazes against mine.

And then, as if a gust of wind blew him away, the tone of the kiss changes. Chase is gone, and Em has returned. Slow, seductive kisses ply my lips apart, and the hand stroking over my panties increases its speed.

My legs stretch and my toes curl, and I grab the sides of my swing tighter as Em's touch enhances the swell of my senses and turns my thoughts into a hazy mist.

He starts to trace the infinity symbol along my slit, circling my clit, and I can't help but moan in delight.

Floating a bit higher, Em uses his free hand to slide my panties down my thighs. Once they hit my knees, I all but fling them off with a kick, desperate for him to come back down to me, to feel that thick cock of his hot and heavy against me.

He quickly obliges, sliding between my thighs and pressing against me, his hand resuming that leisurely infinity sign while the length of him drags temptingly over my slit.

I lean back, hair tumbling off my shoulders as I buck up into his body and the swing starts to sway. The crystals on the chandelier clink lightly, a pleasant sound raining down on us as Em leans down and captures one of my nipples with his mouth.

"Holy fuck, can you paint this shit?" Creep asks, most likely to Dev.

The steady thwack of someone jerking off is the only sound in reply, but I lose focus after that. It feels too good, the steady rub of his fingers, his warm dick sliding over me and showcasing just how wet I am, the flick of his tongue against the underside of my nipple.

My fingers and stomach clench. And then my pussy does the same, tightening on nothing as I buck and moan and beg him to fill me.

He sucks my nipple harder and presses his finger down on my clit, the direct stimulation shooting me even farther out into space. I can't think. Can't breathe. There's no oxygen and no gravity. I'm just floating.

Panting and limp, my hands barely clinging to the sides of the swing, I fear I may melt right off of it into a puddle on the floor.

That's when Em plunges into me in one fell swoop, bottoming out.

I have to bite down on a yelp because the stretch, the heat of him sliding into me, the smack of his balls against me—it's all so intense. When a crystal from the chandelier detaches, its golden ring floating off so that only a dangling cut teardrop is left behind, my lips part in confusion.

But then…Em grins at me. And the crystal starts to shake.

Not shake. Vibrate in midair.

Jittering through the atmosphere, the little crystal glides between our bodies and slides across the wetness seeping from me, lubing up. Then it settles right over my clit. My hands reflexively clench down on the swing, and I buck up into Em with all my might, writhing, mindless, howling.

"Fucking SHARE!" Dev growls up at us, and some piece of furniture smashes into the far wall.

The candelabras floating around me shiver, as if Em's maxing out his abilities, but he doesn't stop. He rails me so hard that the chandelier swings with us, pumping in and out quickly.

Because he's floating, he hits an angle I've never experienced before, and it makes my eyes threaten to roll back in my head and wave the white flag. I'm on the verge of surrender to another orgasm in less than two minutes. My arms are aching, my thighs have never clenched around another man this hard, but my core is steaming out bright sensations that blind me.

Em's grip on my hips tightens as he rams into me one last time and holds himself in place, head tipped back, a bead of sweat trailing deliciously down his pec.

When both our bodies have settled from the high, I untangle my legs from around him with a rueful grin. "That was…"

"Everything."

"Did you let Chase feel any of it?" I wonder.

His expression changes, and I can see Chase emerge for a moment. "I felt it all, Aliana. I was right there with you."

I bite my lip as I grin. "Good. But next time when we fuck on the ground, I want to have you two alternate. Feel what it's like to fuck two of you at once."

"Get down here and you can fuck two of us at once," Dev calls out impatiently.

Em slides out of me, the crystal floats off, and we both watch as his cum begins to leak out onto my curls. For some reason, staring at the evidence of what we just did gets me riled up all over again.

"What do you want, mistress?" Em whispers, eyes twinkling with mischief. "Do you want me to let you down so your other mates can ravage your body? Or do you want to stay up here in your sex swing, taunting them with the sight of that freshly fucked pussy as it leaks my cum?"

My thighs rub together at his naughty words before I pull them wide and deliberately look down to find my other three mates staring hungrily up at me.

A surge of sexual power vaults through me, buzzing with the knowledge that they're all absolutely feral right now.

Dev and Creep are both naked with their dicks out, and Tesq is standing with his hands fig-leafing over his crotch, trying to hide the erection I know is there. Their gazes feel like heat rays darting across my skin, and I revel in it for a moment, widening my thighs and being just a bit more salacious.

But when the teasing has worked me into a frenzy, I glance over at Em. "Let me down, please."

Gently, he unties each side of the swing, though he doesn't allow me to fall. He keeps me aloft, the candlesticks bobbing all around us, and then makes the red sheet curl and twist around my body like it's a living thing, hiding bits of me and revealing others, circling me as I descend toward my other mates.

My feet have hardly touched down before Dev and Creep are on me, ripping the red sheet away and tossing it aside, their hands roughly palming my breasts, sliding over my hips.

"Fuck, you smell so good like this," Dev admits as the cande-labras clink down on the floor around us and light us from beneath with dancing bits of color.

"You'll smell even better when our cum is leaking out too." Creep uses his claws on my hips to lift me, and without preamble, slides me right onto his swollen dick.

Slowly, slowly, because the head of his member is bulging, and it's a tight fit. But I'm plenty wet, and the stretch is delicious, particularly when Dev reaches around and helps pull me open, his palm grazing over my clit.

"That's it, kitten, stretch for him. Stretch for him, and then I'm going to fuck that pretty ass. We're going to bounce this body between us until you're screaming."

His promises alone nearly send me off into another orgasm. I teeter on the brink, pinned between the two of them as they stand in the middle of the room, holding me as if I weigh nothing.

But I want all of my mates to join in this moment—this raunchy, debauched fucking—so I hold my hand out to Tesq.

"Naked. Hand job. Now." I can't get out any other words, and the ones I speak are a bit gruff, hampered by Creep sliding farther into me inch by inch.

But my gargoyle doesn't complain. He simply does what I've ordered. And when he's standing at my side, that thick, twisted dick of his standing at attention, already lubricated in precum, I can't help but lick my lips at the sight.

"I'm going to use your cum to lube Dev up," I tell him, my gaze steadily on his to make sure that's all right.

He gives a single nod.

Putting a hand on Creep's chest, I ask him to pause and hold me in place, my thighs perhaps an inch from being fully seated on his cock.

He gives a groan of impatience, but his hands shift, and he does what I ask, the bulge of his biceps delicious and enticing as my hand goes to work.

I glide it steadily up and down Tesq's cock, ensuring I pay attention to both sensitive heads. Though my gargoyle stays completely silent, I'm rewarded with additional precum.

"Dev," I call out, and he quickly steps farther into me, tweaking my nipples as his hard cock slides against the outside of my thigh as he presents it for lubing up.

Such an eager participant in group activities now, when he was such a selfish bastard before. I grin as I reach down and spread the wet, purple cum across his dick, slathering it on in a thick layer.

He sucks in a breath through his teeth.

"Don't you dare come early, Dev. Or I won't let you tap my ass again."

"I won't fucking come early," he snarls, quickly stepping back from my grip.

He releases my breasts before roughly yanking my ass cheeks apart. Meanwhile, Creep pulls me down and fully seats himself inside. The rough sensations and the attention of both of them at once send up a shower of sparks inside my stomach.

The tip of Dev's dick glides against my opening, teasing me until I moan and swivel my hips, grinding against Creep's cock.

"You'll give me that ass whenever I want," my wolf-like monster asserts.

"Fuck. Put it in me already," I beg, past the point of angry banter.

"Say you need it." Dev's whisper washes over my shoulder.

"I need it."

"You need my. Big. Fucking. Dick." He starts to press against me, and I reach out, grabbing Tesq's cock again, squeezing down tightly whenever the pressure inside me starts to overwhelm me.

My gargoyle takes it all in stride, stepping closer and reaching up to tweak my nipples with his magma-laced fingers. Heat shoots straight down through me, and I moan again, wrapping my legs around Creep's waist and clinging to him as Dev pushes in farther, molding himself against my spine.

A gust of wind blows into the room and makes my skin prickle as my mates start to fuck me in earnest, and I'm caught up between them, lust overtaking every other sense.

Em slowly floats down after me, his gaze pensive as if he's trying to memorize this moment. I make eye contact with him just as Dev's motions make my chest smash up against Creep. And even though I'm already overwhelmed, it's not quite enough. I need more.

"Chase. I want Chase," I demand breathily.

And then he's there, on my left side, his hand gliding over my shoulder, adding soft touches to the rough fucking from my other mates. His teasing fingertips slide across my skin, and he slowly drags them down my side, over my hip, across my belly, and toward my clit. It's a tight fit, but me manages to wedge his palm in there and brush against me as Dev pummels me from behind.

Panting. Moaning. Crying out. I shatter into a million tiny pieces as my fist tightens around Tesq's cock.

"YESSS," Dev roars when my entire body clenches down.

With two more pumps, he spills warmly into me. Tesq spurts next, cum splattering against my stomach. Creep's grip on my hips intensifies, his fingers digging in as he bounces me up and down until his own release pulses inside of me.

And as I slump against my mates, utterly spent and sated, I can't help but think how the worst nightmare I could ever imagine—being caught and sold to monsters—turned into this perfect dream.

Sometimes, life's twisted path has more in store for us than we can ever imagine and a happier ending than we ever could have conceived.

EPILOGUE - ALIANA

"Do you want to play a game?" Creep's silky voice precedes the man himself wrapping his arms around me from behind.

As always when I'm with one of my mates, goose bumps pebble on my arms, and heat explodes in my stomach.

"What kind of game are we talking about?" I ask coyly, turning to stare at him over my shoulder and forgetting I'm supposed to be setting the table for dinner. "Because if it's a sexy game, I'm afraid I'm gonna have to decline." I make a face and place a hand on my protruding belly. "I'm way too big for that."

Creep scoffs and plants a slobbery kiss against my cheek, making me laugh. "Don't be ridiculous. You're gorgeous."

Gentle, blue fingers caress my chin as he turns my head to face him completely. His lips touch my own, and colors explode behind my closed eyelids. A flurry of butterflies unleashes in my stomach.

"Ewwww. Momma's kissing Daddy Creep!"

Creep and I immediately pull away to see our oldest daughter, Maddi, gaping at us in disgust.

Maddi's white-blonde hair has been artfully styled into two French braids, courtesy of Tesq, with tiny bows at the end. She wears a frilly pink skirt and matching shirt, both of them the exact same shade as the horns protruding from her head.

None of us know who Maddi's bio father is, but we don't care. It could be Dev or Em or Chase or Tesq or Creep. All of my mates love her as if she were their own.

"Oh, am I?" Creep lifts an arrogant eyebrow and then begins to plant open-mounted, slobbering kisses across my face.

"Ew!" Maddi and I both exclaim in unison.

I attempt to swat my playful mate away, but he simply laughs, the noise reverberating through the room like wind chimes.

Years ago, we chose to move out of the city and into a home in the woods. The mansion we found had been abandoned for years but was in good enough shape to be repaired to its former glory. It also has a guest house that my father uses when he comes to visit me and my children.

He doesn't live with us—I don't think anyone could get Tennious to stay in one place longer than a few weeks—but he does appear often enough for my children to eagerly await the appearance of Grandpa.

Movement in the kitchen behind Maddi causes the little girl to let out a squeak and race behind us. She grabs my legs and attempts to hide herself behind me.

"What are you doing, you crazy girl?" I ask, shifting slightly so I can see her.

She places a single finger to her lips and shushes me exaggeratedly.

A second later, Dev appears in the doorway on all fours. Our second child, Brett, sits on his back.

Unlike Maddi, whose parentage is ambiguous, Brett very clearly takes after Creep with bark-like blue skin, curled antlers, and glimmering eyes. But just like with Maddi, all of my mates treat him like their biological son. It doesn't matter who actually provided the sperm.

Dev playfully rocks back on his hind legs and swats at the air with a roar. My wolf mate is half shifted, most of his body covered in dark fur.

Brett, on his back, giggles and holds a plastic sword in the air.

"For-ard, Daddy!" He grabs at my mate's long hair and gives it a tug.

I laugh softly at my son's attempt to say "forward."

Dev stalks forward with a smile, and Maddi squeals, racing from her hiding place towards the living room.

"Yaw! Horsey! Yaw!" Brett tugs at Dev's hair yet again, and with another roar, Dev takes off after our giggling daughter.

"Dinner will be ready in an hour!" I call after them, but of course, no one responds. "Just what game are they playing this time around?" I ask no one in particular.

But it's Em who answers, exiting the kitchen with a red welt on his cheek. He touches his skin tentatively with a grimace.

"Knights and princesses. Maddi is an escaped princess, and Brett is the knight in charge of bringing her home. Dev is the steed, obviously."

I pull away from Creep to walk towards Em. I touch his reddened skin gingerly. "And what were you supposed to be?"

"I was the dragon," he confesses with a cocky smile. "They killed me, but I put up one hell of a fight."

"I can see that."

He'll definitely have a bruise on his cheek, but it'll heal in time.

Turning to face the room at large, I ask, "Shouldn't we be teaching our children *not* to hit people?"

Warm arms wrap around me, and I know immediately this touch is from Chase. Don't ask me how I can tell the difference between him and Em. I won't be able to tell you. A part of me can differentiate between the two men as if they're separate beings, not one body with two souls.

"They're monsters, my love," Chase whispers, biting down on my earlobe. "Let them be."

My stomach begins to flutter like mad. Even after all of this time, my mates are still able to elicit a visceral reaction from me.

They all look exactly the same as they did when I first met them. Even Chase hasn't aged, a feat I'm immensely grateful for. Em was right. As long as he's in Chase's body, my cocky human will never age, never die.

I'll be able to have him forever, along with my other mates.

It's every dream I never hoped to have wrapped up into one immaculate package.

"Enough about the children!" Creep throws his arms up in the air dramatically. "We have a crisis here!"

"Crisis?" Tesq asks, leaning against the doorframe.

In his arms is our youngest child, Illy—named after the grandma she never got to know. Illy has her thumb in her mouth as she sleeps peacefully, her long lashes sooty twigs against her chubby cheeks. She's the world's most adorable two-year-old.

I desperately want to take my baby from Tesq and give her all the snuggles, but she looks so peaceful that I don't want to disturb her.

Illy's black hair curls around her angelic face and nearly hides her ivory horns from view. We can't tell yet who she'll take after, but if I had to hazard a guess, I would say she's Tesq's biological daughter.

"Aliana here doesn't think she's desirable enough for sexy times with her pregnant belly!" Creep declares dramatically.

I roll my eyes. "I did *not* say that."

"It was implied," Creep counters.

"Don't go putting words in my mouth."

"So you're okay with some pregnant sexy times?" Em's fingers brush across the back of my neck, and I shiver, goose bumps peppering both of my arms.

"I didn't say that either." I purse my lips. "I'm so freaking big that I can't even bend. All I do is lie there like a beach ball—"

"A sexy beach ball," Creep interrupts.

"—while you guys do all the work." I throw my hands up in the air. "It can't be enjoyable for you."

"Oh, trust me." Em kisses my cheek and then allows his lips to linger there. "Any time I'm inside of you is *definitely* enjoyable for me. I love the feel of your pussy squeezing my cock."

My body flushes with heat.

"She's probably just… What's that term we read about in the pregnancy book?" Tesq cocks his head to the side.

"Hormonal?" Creep suggests.

Tesq nods seriously. "Yes. She's probably just hormonal. Hormonal females often think they're not desirable to their lovers."

"Tesq, if you weren't holding our daughter right now, I would castrate your dick," I tell him seriously.

My gargoyle mate stares at me in surprise.

"What did I say?" he asks, confused.

Creep leans in on my opposite side to lick up my cheek. When he reaches my ear, he pauses there to whisper, "You like his dick too much to castrate it."

"Maybe," I grumble.

Dammit. He's right. These monsters dick-notized me.

"I think we need to show our mate how desirable she truly is," Creep declares with a wicked, lurid grin. "Pregnant or not. Illy's asleep, right?"

Tesq's answering smile makes heat build in my core. "I'll put her in her crib and be right back."

He hurries out of the room before I can reply.

"And Dev is distracting the kids, yes?" Creep continues.

Em grins wickedly. "He's going to be so pissed he missed this."

"Eh. He can go next time." Creep twists my face to his as one of his hands roams my body. "Now, let us remind our mate how much we adore and love her…"

And I allow myself to be worshipped by my monsters.

Want More by Katie May & Ann Denton?
Read the Darkest Flames Series Now!

Katrina tries a love spell on the hottest guy at school. But whoops, it's a summoning spell. Now, five smoking hot demons are determined to make her wildest dreams come true.

ACKNOWLEDGMENTS

Special thanks to Tami, Lysanne, Rachel, and Ashley for helping us tweak things.

A huge shoutout to Lindsey Loucks of Midnight Editing for making us appear more perfect than we are.

And massive gratitude to the talented Sanja Balan at Covers by Sanja for this drool-worthy cover.

ABOUT THE AUTHORS

Katie and Ann have written a bazillion and a half books together and are now quite adept at literally finishing one another's sentences. One of them is young and hip while the other is a crusty old poltergeist like the Empty Man and merely posing as human. Both happen to think dogs are typically better than people and that book boyfriends should be utterly obsessive. Thanks for reading!

20596134R00236